THE
MARSH
PEOPLE

The Marsh People
Second edition published 2018
by Victorina Press
Adderley Lodge Farm,
Adderley Road,
Market Drayton, TF9 3ST, England.

First edition published 2012 by Immanion Press

Cover Art and Design: © Fiona Zechmeister
Interior Design and Layout: Jack Williams
Inside artwork: @Jack Williams

British Library Cataloguing in Publication Data
A catalogue record for this book is available from the British Library.
ISBN: 978-0-9957547-4-4 (pbk)

Printed and bound in Great Britain by Charlesworth Press

THE
MARSH
PEOPLE

M. Valentine Williams

◆ ◆

www.valentinewilliams.co.uk

Victorina Press
www.victorinapress.com

Other books published by M. Valentine Williams

A Far Cry (2017), Mantle Lane Press.

The Poison Garden of Dorelia Jones (2010) Immanion Press.

Unconfirmed Reports from Out There (2014) Self-published.

Make Up or Break Up? (2003) Sheldon(SPCK).

Overcoming Impotence (2004) Sheldon (SPCK).

Acknowledgements

Thanks to my general editor Consuelo Rivera-Fuentes and to my copy editor Katherine Trail. Also, to members of Drayton Writers, family members and friends, who kept me on course and gave me encouragement.

Dedicated to library staff everywhere

Chapter 1

Scummo curled up tighter under his dirty blankets. His hair itched, and the sour smell of stale damp bedding made his nostrils widen. It was barely light but already the dog warden was doing its rounds. He heard the rattle of the creature's nails on the gritty concrete outside as it sniffed at his door. He threw a shoe at the door, recklessly. There was a loud growling from the other side and then a frantic scrabbling as the animal tried to get in. Scummo had nailed a piece of tin over the lower part of the door. The dog retreated, and he could hear its paws padding away down the landing.

A child screamed loudly. Minna's daughter, Kelpin, Scummo guessed. Well, she shouldn't be out on the landing at this hour. He heard more barking and the sound of doors slamming, then it was quiet again. Scummo reluctantly pushed the blanket to one side, sat up, swinging his pale legs over the end of the mattress, and scratched his dry wiry hair. The apartment was cold, and Scummo lost no time in pulling on his second pair of felt overtrousers before making some brew. The large dried leaves wilted under the water from the hot kettle and the rust-coloured liquid began seeping into the drink. Scummo drank it slowly; it had enough caffeine in it to wake him up, but there was no nourishment in it. He investigated his cupboard, searching for the remains of his biscuit ration. There were several broken pieces at the back

1

of the shelf. They were soft and stale, but better than nothing. His ankle tag chafed his skin as it always did. He ignored it.

He listened to make sure the dog warden wasn't waiting for him, then opened the door cautiously. The early fog hung like a blanket over the dingy City. Opposite him across the rubble-strewn courtyard someone was beating a mat on the balcony wall, and a woman was pegging out faded washing on a line strung along the narrow walkway. He gazed down.

This building, with its tiers of walkways and identical doors, was like an amphitheatre. The remote-controlled truck that collected the night's accumulation of dirt and debris was doing its rounds, and there were sharp beeps as it changed direction at different points, reversing rapidly as it navigated sharp corners.

There was often cleaning up to do on Firstday morning after the trials in the arena below. There were bits of clothing and hair, stuff that had been thrown from the balconies, dried splashes of blood to be mopped up, teeth to be swept. His eye picked out the discarded bits of metal or wood that had served as weapons. These would find their way back by some mysterious process, into the Apartments. Only the bodies of the dead and wounded had already been dragged away. Disputes in the blocks were sorted out in trials in the arena every week. Nobody questioned it. Once the aggrieved parties had their names put on the board with the challenge,

2

the fight was on, and the whole population became spectators at this bloody and lethal duel. The Masters had got the idea from somewhere called Rome, Scummo had heard, and adapted it for their own use.

Warkin, who had been one of Scummo's neighbours, died only last Sevenday in a duel with Beeza, who had the apartment above. Scummo had wanted to ask him some questions; it seemed as though Warkin knew the answers. Now he was gone.

Scummo saw that the food wagon hadn't arrived yet. The mobile cook-house that came every morning and evening to Broilerhouse Four always parked in the centre of the arena. Every resident had a rations tin, a metal container with a compartment for dry food that slotted in under the lid. Scummo's tin dangled from his fingers as he waited. Lining up in order of apartment number, residents often swung their tins from their handles, removing the tops and covers when they got to the front of the line. The sticky field-bean stew, turnips or porridge allowed that day was ladled into the bottom. The tray fitted in above it neatly, with a metal clunk, and some dry biscuits or a portion of dried gabbo leaves were placed above it before the lid was put down. The dogs saw to it that no one had more than their fair share. Dropping the inner tray or its contents meant being badly bitten trying to retrieve it. The food wagon came in now as he watched, gliding silently into the arena, and he hurried down to take his place in the queue.

The dogs, heavy unintelligent mastiff cross-breeds, herded the residents as they might sheep and were only directed by whistles inaudible to the human ear. The Master in charge of the food wagon ladled each portion out with precise movements. The featureless oval of the face registered only what it needed to: the number of the resident. *Numbers,* thought Scummo. *That's all we are, numbers.* His own number was above the door: SCUM04. He took his ration into his flat, noticing that the woman next door had not been behind him in the dinner queue. Her door was shut. He didn't have time to worry about it. Rinsing out his ration tin, he heard the sound of the transit vehicle approaching and ran down the concrete stairs before he missed it.

Scummo waited by the transit area for the float to come by, a large conveyor platform on which workers had to jump as it passed on its way to the factory. Several others from his block jumped aboard. Scummo fished his identity tag out of his felt trousers and slipped it into the transit machine. A click told him it had been accepted. The conveyor platform bobbed its way along between the Apartments, picking up workers as it went. Scummo knew his allocation. It was in the clothing plant, feeding discarded rags into the shredder to be processed to make the coarse material he was now wearing.

4

Nothing could be wasted. His trousers, made of coarse and scratchy felt, had been recycled several times already. The work wasn't hard but it was physically tiring. Scummo had extra rations once a week to help keep his strength up. Last week it had been a carton of mashed turnip, and he'd been glad of it in the chill of his room, but this week it would probably be boiled potatoes, or if he was really lucky, field beans. These were usually cooked to a mush, and gave him indigestion, but he welcomed the small amount of extra protein they gave him. Kelpin, his neighbour's daughter, had a ration of dried milk and water handed to her every day from the dispenser on the landing. The Masters used electronic surveillance to ensure only those entitled to the milk received it, and the few children who were eligible on each balcony lined up and drank their quota every morning under their watchful electronic eye.

Kelpin must have been hungry and come out onto the landing earlier than she should to collect her ration, Scummo thought. The conveyor platform slowed and stopped. He jumped off and went into the factory.

The noise was terrible – whirring, ripping, clacking and a high electronic whine all formed part of the sound background of the factory. A bitter smell hung in the air, the smell of synthetic fabric being shredded, and it never failed to make Scummo sneeze with an explosive effort to expel the dust that threatened to choke him.

He noticed that Posa from Broilerhouse Five was missing. Posa usually acted as maintenance man for the machines and positioned his plump body next to the door so that he could report any problems with machines to the workers as they came in. In his place sat a skinny lad Scummo had never seen before, shifting his feet back and forth in the dusty debris with bored resignation.

'Where's old Posa got to then?' Scummo wanted to know.

The skinny lad shrugged. 'Probably a cull,' he offered. 'I was just told to report here this morning. By the way, there's a problem with your machine. One of the blades has snapped. But I think I fixed it okay. Any problems, give me a call.' He began to sweep the factory floor, thin rope-muscled arms wielding the scooper-pan like a weapon as he swept round Scummo's feet. Scummo knew he wouldn't be seeing Posa again. A cull was serious. Certain individuals' names were drawn in a lottery every six months, and the list was pinned to the noticeboard in every block entrance two days before the cull. Scummo could picture it. The notice would have been very upbeat:

'The following members of Broilerhouse Five have been chosen, by reason of their hard work, effort and punctuality, to go on an extended vacation to Jamarama. All those chosen for this trip of a lifetime should wait with their belongings at the entrance to Broilerhouse Five at 11 a.m. on Secondday. Happy holidays!'

There followed a list of names in alphabetical order. The chosen ones waited on the appointed day with their bags all packed by the Apartments entrance for the special wagons, brightly painted with *Holiday to Jamarama* in loud splashy colours on the side.

No one saw or heard from them again. The idea that this was, in fact, a cull was slow to emerge. It was Warkin who had first expressed the thought, in the food queue one cold morning. Scummo had been standing behind him, arms folded across his chest to keep out the cold, and in front of both of them was Randis, a Geld, whose plump body shook a little as he held out his food tin. Scummo noticed that he was served double portions of something that wasn't the normal ration of beans and mashed turnip. Randis held his tin carefully as he turned back towards them, smiling all over his face.

'Special rations,' he confided. 'They've awarded me a holiday; I've just had the notification.'

Warkin turned to Scummo and whispered out of the side of his mouth. 'Special rations my arse. It's another cull; they always take the fat ones. Poor bugger thinks he's going on holiday.'

Scummo was shocked. 'A cull?'

Warkin nodded sagely.

'You mean? They pick some of us out to . . .' His lips could not utter the words his mind was thinking. 'To get rid of?'

'Well, have you ever seen any of them again? No, because wherever they go after they get on that bus, none of them ever come back.'

'They might hear you,' Scummo hissed urgently. 'Keep your voice down.'

It was true. Scummo knew it. How had he never noticed it before? The routines that held their lives in place were fixed by fear: fear of the dogs, fear of not getting enough food, fear of the invisible threat that constantly hung over them all. Their lives had become so controlled that they no longer dreamed of escape. Unspoken rules and edicts from the

Masters governed their lives from the moment they rose in the morning until the time they went to bed. Nobody flouted the rules. Having total control, the Masters could put in place any number of cruelties, knowing that dependence breeds apathy and the need to survive ensured the maintenance of the status quo.

Scummo brooded on his existence after this. What if Warkin was right, as Scummo was sure he was? Did that mean they had no free will at all? What would he do if his name were chosen for one of these 'holidays'? He felt acute despair gnaw at his heart. Later, the idea of a cull slipped into the collective vocabulary as though it had always been there, with some people arguing that it was for the best, that some people needed to be taken out of the system so that others could have a turn. Others merely expressed indifference. Close relationships that grew despite the Masters' efforts to put a stop to them often ended with one of the pair, usually the fatter one, being sent on an enforced holiday, from which he or she did not return. There were stories about these people. They had been chosen for a better life elsewhere. They had been seen elsewhere outside the Apartments. They had escaped, been carried up into the sky by the Masters, been forced to donate eggs and sperm, been rewarded in some unspecified way, or been boiled up to use as soap. This last suggestion came from Arisa, a busybody of thirty-one who lived below Scummo. Maybe she was right.

Scummo remembered with distress the recent fight to the death between Warkin and Beeza from Kincaidy Building. Warkin was tired of Beeza leaving his tap running and flooding his bedroom, and Beeza was incensed that Warkin should bang on his ceiling with a broom to stop him. Before they had time to sort it out any other way, Beeza and Warkin had their names put down on the challenge post and a bloody fight ensued. Beeza, who was not noted for being rational at the best of times, favoured a knife, while Warkin, who was short, armed himself with a homemade spear. Fending off Beeza seemed easy enough to do, and the crowd loved it. But then Beeza threw his knife, missed, and in the ensuing confusion grabbed hold of the spear and snapped it in two over his knee. Warkin aimed a kick at Beeza's head; Beeza clobbered him with the dropped spear-end, missed and staggered.

Finally, Beeza sagged to the ground like a sack of cabbages, holding his head, and blood trickled in a dark line from his ear. Warkin was victorious. It was then the crowd took over and hurled whatever they had picked up from the streets – most had no possessions to throw – at the victor, who fell to his knees as a stone smacked him in the centre of his forehead. Scummo had seen the stone-thrower and marvelled at the precision of the aim. It was his neighbour, Andalou. As soon as the fight was over, the dog wardens came out and tugged away the bodies and the big cleaning machines swept up anything that remained the next morning. Newcomers, driven in by the Masters in small trucks from the clearing-houses where they had been waiting, took over the flats occupied by the unfortunate tenants immediately. At lunchtime, Scummo sat in the yard in the shadow of these flats and allowed his mind to wander.

***

He could just remember a time when life had been a little better. He seemed to remember trees, real trees, and eating some stew his mother had cooked for him on a trestle table somewhere in the sunshine. That was before the Masters had extended their activities to the countryside.

First there were disappearances. His father, whom he could just recall, left the house one evening to attend a meeting. He heard angry shouts in the street and saw how his mother clung to his father's arm, not wanting to let him go. His father had gently removed her arm, kissed her on the cheek and picked up his tattered coat.

'I won't be long, Ruga,' he told her. 'Stop worrying.' And he was gone. It was after his disappearance that the dogs started prowling after dark and nobody dared to leave their houses. Then the orders began to come from loudspeakers on high platforms erected overnight at the four corners of the village. The orders were strange, as they gave people permission to do things they had already been doing for years.

'You may now leave your houses,' boomed the loudspeaker. 'You are permitted to tend to your animals between the hours of 7 a.m. and 7 p.m.' At first, the people ignored these messages. Then came more directives.

'Meetings held for any purposes must take place in the designated meeting house. Repeat. All meetings held for any purposes must take place in the designated meeting house. No other venue is permitted at this time. Failure to comply will result in severe penalties.'

The people found out what these were when the store shut and the food distribution point failed to open for two days. The Masters had started supplying them with free food during one hard winter, and now they were dependent on it.

Protest was useless; there was no one to protest against. The people who used the meeting house for group activities were angered at the actions of the few who wanted to hold secret meetings away from the venue that they were sure was bugged.

'Why are we being punished for things you lot are doing?' asked one man. 'We've already had to manage without food for two days; who knows what else might happen? Just do what they say and we'll all be all right. Why do you always have to make trouble?'

The Masters had never interfered with their lives before, though officious messages had frequently appeared on the noticeboard by the food distribution point. They had got on with their lives, tending their hens and cattle, growing their vegetables, mending their houses. Social life was based around the meetinghouse the Masters had built. The village people wanted to help in the building of their meetinghouse, but were not allowed. There were rumours that the Masters had cameras and surveillance equipment hidden in the walls. Scummo's father, rebellious by nature, organised meetings for the people in the open air, at the back of the barn where winter fodder was stored, then later organised the building of a shed where meetings could take place, although the space was limited. They searched it thoroughly for hidden cameras or microphones but discovered nothing.

When his father had not returned home, his mother went out looking for him, despite the danger. He had gone, and with him had also gone many of the younger men from the village. The shed had a notice on the door: *Premises now closed until further notice.* The faceless, unreachable Masters – how could you ask them what had happened? Who was accountable?

The pressure on them grew. Scummo's mother was not the same after his father left, though she did her best to see he was cared for. Life became harder and his mother more worn down by the relentless quest for extra food and her allocated work in the fields.

He watched her grow thinner, until her ankle tag drooped over her foot and rubbed a raw spot on her heel. He hardly noticed his own.

Following the Herdings, he saw no more of his mother after they were shepherded along the narrow lanes leading from his village. The last he had seen of her was her arm, waving goodbye to him before they were separated forever by the tide of people surging around them. The dog wardens were snapping at their heels all the way to the City, as the Masters in their spy posts watched and gave orders. People no longer talked about the Herdings, but they remembered them all too vividly. Some still had the bite marks on their calves as a permanent reminder. Every day was a struggle to get through. Get up, collect a food ration, go to the allotted workplace, return to the buildings, collect a ration of food, prepare for the visit of the dog wardens by being safely indoors at eight thirty, sleep. Every day was the same except for Sevenday. He never heard anyone complain openly. Minna down the landing managed to conceive Kelpin despite the social restrictions, but Scummo didn't know how she'd done it. The Masters did not encourage procreation, and the children who were born were given only slightly better treatment than their parents.

Scummo returned from work that evening tired and hungry, clutching his food ration to his chest. His feet automatically trudged up the stairs to his landing. Then he stopped. The door to Minna's apartment was open and a small shadowy person was in the doorway, crying. Kelpin. Cautiously, Scummo moved forwards. He squatted down to the same level as Kelpin, by instinct.

'What's the matter?'

The little girl turned a tear-stained face towards him. 'She's ill.' Kelpin pointed inside. Scummo stood up and took her hand, feeling embarrassed as he did so. Together, they went into the flat. Minna lay on the grey blankets of her mattress, and it was clear to Scummo, even with his limited knowledge, that she was dying. He suddenly realised he hardly knew her. Yet she had been his neighbour for seven years. She had appeared one morning, her grey felt jacket and trousers flapping around her thin body, scurrying along the landing towards her new flat with the dog in hot pursuit. Where had she come from? He didn't know. People were pushed into the Apartments to be processed. The flat she was allocated had been inhabited by a large, pale man with a consumptive cough who never spoke to Scummo but spat vigorously over the balcony as he entered or left his apartment.

Over the months, as his health declined, the phlegm had turned the side of the balcony a sickly green where he had missed. One day he was there, a sickly, consumptive presence; the next he had gone. Scummo presumed that something had happened while he was at work; the Masters usually made sure that people coming and going and any other major changes happened at times when the Apartments were empty of workers. Possibly there had been another cull. He had ceased to be surprised by any changes. Nevertheless, he registered Minna's arrival, while ducking indoors quickly to avoid the snarling beast barking and nipping at her heels. He looked down at her, helplessly. Her pale, cold hands seemed devoid of any life when Scummo felt them and her breathing was shallow. She was unconscious. He ushered Kelpin from the room. She put a finger in her mouth and looked at him with solemn eyes. The dog wardens would take care of the body.

Back in his own flat, he made Kelpin sit down while he thought what to do. As he sat there, head in his hands, Kelpin edged along the mattress until she was within reach of him and laid her head on his arm. The soft black curls were limp, and Scummo could see the thinness of her shoulder blades under her shirt. Something inside him was moved, and without thinking, he placed his calloused, work-stained hand on her back. This act surprised him. Every day was a struggle to survive – only just enough food, only just enough heating, only just enough of anything. There was nothing to spare. Yet something in him remembered his mother's love and responded to this little girl, so young, so vulnerable. Almost at once he felt angry with himself. It was hopeless. She'd be taken away; of course she would ... yet for an instant a notion had flicked across his mind to care for her. He knew that young children without parents were put into the compound, where they quickly succumbed to illness and lack of care. He had only just survived himself. He had seen pinched little faces and bony fingers of very young children through the railings when he first arrived in the compound near the hover-platform. Although this compound was now shut, the memory still haunted him. He himself had narrowly escaped being taken there by being bigger than the other children of his age. He had never seen his smaller classmates again after the Herdings. Allocated a flat and made to work, he had accepted his fate, seeing no way to escape from this new and dreadful life.

Officially, he was now supposed to report to the buildings office to tell them what had happened and ask what should be done with Kelpin. She had curled up, leaning against him, her legs snugly tucked under his blankets, half asleep. He knew he had to make a decision. He thought about the way his life was. It had no purpose, no love and no beauty. The excitement of the savage battles in the arena on Sevenday were the only opportunity anyone had to show excitement, cheer, clap and throw stones. A ritual bloodletting, it was the only safety valve on offer. Even sex, that most urgent and primitive of drives, was dormant in them. He never worked out whether there was some chemical in the rations they were given that dulled their appetites, or whether the senseless, ceaseless grind with no opportunity to socialise simply left them with no energy to spare for it. Across on the other side of the central arena were the Apartments of the plump, sexless men that lived all together in one block and had special rations, the Gelds. Scummo could only guess what had happened to them. Sex was not on the menu for any of them. All the more surprising then that Minna had conceived Kelpin, no doubt by accident. Poor little Kelpin. His thoughts returned to the predicament he was in and he looked down at her trusting little face and knew he couldn't let her go into the compound. At the next cull, if not before, she would surely perish.

He could hide her, but the dog wardens would be sure to smell her. He had an idea. In three hours' time, the wardens would be out doing their rounds. He could take Kelpin back to her own flat, take Minna's body out and leave it on the landing for them to find and hide with Kelpin in her flat until they had gone. Minna's body should prove enough of a distraction for them. He hoped they wouldn't realise he was in the flat with Kelpin or they'd start howling and scratching the door. He went back to Minna's flat. Kelpin was asleep on his bed and he left her there. He'd carry her round in a minute or so.

Minna's body was cold. He put a sheet around her and lifted her lightly off the mattress and out onto the landing, then he put her down at the top of the stairs where the wardens always came in. He went back to his own flat and lifted Kelpin, who opened one eye sleepily and put her arms around his neck.

'Close your eyes,' he instructed her, whisking her past her mother's body and into her flat. She obeyed him.

They packed up some of her pathetic clothing in a bag, found a few rations Minna had hoarded and ate those, then waited for the dog wardens. Scummo put chairs and a table in front of the door, jamming them tightly. The door to his own flat was locked securely. Soon there was the rattle of nails on concrete and a growl as the body was discovered, followed by excited barking and the feet of many large animals pounding along the landings. Then there was growling, snarls, whines, snapping teeth and the sound of paws scrabbling to get purchase on the blood-slippery floor. He could picture the bared teeth and bristled fur.

He held his hands over Kelpin's ears and wished he didn't have to hear it. They had all heard these sounds before, many times. Too often, he thought. Suddenly he was overwhelmingly sickened by his life, their lives, the lives they all had to lead now that the Masters were in charge.

He wondered what had happened to the land he grew up in, all the fields and rivers. Who was in charge of it now? The future held nothing for him or for Kelpin, except work. If Kelpin were put in the compound, she would die, he was sure about that. With him, with the two of them together, they might stand a chance.

Who was he kidding?

Suddenly, he made up his mind. Yesterday, this morning, he had been alone. Now he had a child to look after. She had clung to him; she had slept in his arms. He could not abandon her. He waited until it was nearly midnight, wrapped Kelpin in as many sweaters as he could find and, holding her hand, tiptoed out of the door. Putting his hand over her eyes, he turned her away from the inky stickiness of the blood still spreading over the landing. At least there was nothing else. The wardens did this job efficiently. Turning their backs to it, they slipped down the back stairs and out into the night. Gorged to capacity, the resident dog warden slumbered happily as Scummo and Kelpin moved quickly and silently away from the buildings and vanished into the Old Quarter.

M. Valentine Williams

Chapter 2

In the early September dawn, two figures, one tall, the other little, struggled towards the outskirts of the town. Behind them, they could hear the barking and growls of the dog wardens in the buildings. Danger was approaching. Ahead of them lay the barbed wire and concrete buttresses of the city wall, watchtowers and kennels, and beyond those lay a land he could barely remember and which Kelpin had never seen. They had to find cover soon and think how they were going to slip out through the gateway up ahead. Scummo searched the land, looking for something.

At last he found it: a dirty manhole cover in the midst of some ruins. He had to hurry. The sound of dogs grew louder. He tugged at the cover and it came loose. Another heave and it was pushed to one side.

'What are you doing?' asked Kelpin, big eyes exploring the darkness inside the hole.

'We've got to go down there,' he said, putting one foot on the rusted steel ladder. 'It's not deep. I'll go first.' He was hoping that there was dry land at the bottom. If there was, he could leave Kelpin and climb back up to re-fasten the manhole cover; if there wasn't – well, he didn't like to think about that. He went down a few steps, made Kelpin turn around and guided her feet down the rungs. She was nimble and light and seemed to be finding it all rather exciting. They went down about forty rungs before Scummo put his foot on something solid. Rubble, he guessed, stopping. Kelpin, still descending, trod on his fingers. He yelped.

'Wait a minute, I think we're at the bottom.' He stepped gingerly onto the rubble beneath his feet and it held firm. He lifted Kelpin down.

'Can you hold the ladder and stay still while I go back up and pull the cover over?'

She nodded in the darkness, holding the rungs tightly. 'Don't leave me, Scummo.'

'Don't worry about that, kiddo, it's you and me together against the world.' And he climbed back up the clammy rungs, his hands sore and his arms aching, and pulled over them the heavy metal cover that would seal them in here, under the ground for the next few hours in the total darkness of a tomb. Below, he could hear Kelpin whimper.

'I'm coming down – don't worry, it'll all be all right. Kelpin?'

'Yes?'

'Tell me when you can hear my feet close to you, okay?'

'Okay.'

In the pitch darkness, he reached the bottom, taking care not to step on her, and found her little hand on his ankle. She guided him down the rest of the way. He held her to him, feeling comfort in the beating of her small heart. Soon above them they could hear sounds of workers being driven out to work on the fields and the barking of dogs. They sat down on the damp stones and rested. He felt the urge to piss, and did so, the warm steam rising around them.

'Are you having a wee?'

'Yes,' he answered, embarrassed. 'There's no toilet out here, so we have to wee on the ground.' She sighed, and Scummo could hear her moving cautiously in the dark next to him. He reached out and guided her next to him.

'We don't want to sit in the pee, do we? Go here.'

She obeyed, giggling. 'Stinky old pee,' she said, pulling up her felt trousers. She almost lost her balance getting up but he steadied her with his hand. They sat in silence together, then slept. On waking, she was restless and frightened and clutched at his arm.

They would have to leave this place soon, he reflected. When would it be safe? Once everyone was at work there was usually a lull as the dogs rested, but they would stand out if anyone spotted them. Eventually he could put it off no longer. He had to make a difficult decision: to climb up the ladder, open the hatch and go down again, letting Kelpin climb up ahead of him into the daylight. He prayed no one would be waiting for them, but he couldn't risk her falling as she followed him up. He climbed up the ladder, banging his head on the metal cover as he reached it. He held on to the ladder tightly with one hand while he pushed, hard, with other. Sweat shone on his forehead. The cover was heavy, but it moved a fraction and slid sideways with a metallic thud. He poked his head out and looked round. There was no one about. Quickly, he descended again and lifted Kelpin onto the ladder.

'Climb. I'll be right behind you. Good girl.' She swarmed up like a monkey and he had a job to keep up with her. At the top she had jumped out and was looking at his face with amused eyes as it emerged.

'You're all sooty,' she said. 'What a mucky face!' Before he could stop her, she spat on a corner of her pullover and wiped his face. He was suddenly touched and put his arm round her in a quick hug. They were very hungry by now, but all he had left was a little dried milk. He gave it to her and she licked it off the paper wrapper thoughtfully.

'We need a drink,' he observed. Moving slowly and quietly along the ruined streets of the old town, they came across a standpipe and some containers. Drinking water for the dogs, he thought. He turned the tap on and a slow trickle of water slid into his cupped hands. He cleaned them and drank, letting Kelpin do the same. He picked up one of the containers and filled it with water. It would be hard to carry it any distance without a lid on it. He untied the piece of plastic sheeting that was holding the bundle of Kelpin's clothes together and wrapped it around the container. It would have to do. He tied her clothes together again as well as he could and fastened them around his waist. At the end of the road, they came across something they had not been expecting: a footpath leading through the wall into the countryside beyond. A camera was mounted on the wall to observe all who passed. Scummo kept well back. He explained to Kelpin that he was going to throw one of her pullovers over the camera, and she pulled a face.

Carefully, she selected one and gave it to him. He dared not miss. He approached the camera from the side and swung the pullover at it. It stayed, draped like some strange flag, and Kelpin and Scummo passed through the entry way and left the City behind.

***

The two High Masters of the City, playing chess in their watchtower, watched them go with slight interest. This was another battery chicken falling off the back of the lorry on the way to the chicken factory. As far as they were concerned, Scummo had saved them the trouble of fetching the little girl and placing her in a compound. They only died there anyway, deprived of their mothers. They would, of course, die here too, deprived of food and shelter. It would take slightly longer, perhaps, but die they would, and the dogs would have their bodies.

***

Scummo and Kelpin, holding hands, walked through a green sea of tall grass towards the distant line where land and sky met. Were there trees somewhere? Flowers? Kelpin knew nothing about such things, but Scummo had a distant memory somewhere about them. They were surrounded by green now. He realised what a soothing colour it is, how refreshing to the eyes. Kelpin was frightened and enchanted. He wondered when she would start really missing her mother and howl, and wondered if he would be able to handle her rage with him when she did so. She had no one else. His hair was dirty and itched; his feet ached. Kelpin was weary too. Perhaps they should sit down in this green space and rest. He stopped and threw down the pullover he was carrying.

'We need to stop and have a rest.' She nodded in

complete agreement and sank to the ground. It was evening, and they had eaten nothing except the dried milk all day. Could they eat the grass? Scummo thought not. The grass, when he investigated it, was perfect and clean and he could not find a single weed or insect in it. He looked around him at ground level. He could not be certain, but it did look as though there might be a small animal runway in the grass near where Kelpin was sitting. He bent his narrow body in her direction and looked more closely. Kelpin's gaze followed his. He rolled onto his stomach and put his face to the round gap in the grass stems. The grass tunnel went for some way, then turned out of sight.

They slept then for a while, in the green circle, while the fronds of tall grasses nodded over their heads. The sun was warm. Scummo's lips were parched. Wakening, he sat up, wondering where he was. Kelpin was curled up at his side, her fluffy curls glossy on the sweater she was using for a pillow. He undid the water container he had carried so carefully and had a drink.

He looked around him. There was something in the circle that had not been there when he went to sleep. Three complete ears of maize, their golden succulent seeds hidden by a covering of corn-husk, lay in a row at his feet. Someone was helping them, but whom?

Something rustled in the grass behind him. He turned quickly and whatever it was vanished into the grass tunnel. Another ear of maize.

Scummo called down the grassy tunnel. 'Please come back. We need your help.' But there was only silence.

Kelpin had woken, frightened, and Scummo reassured her as best he could. 'A little animal has paid us a visit and left us some food. Look.' He picked up the corn and stripped it of its husk. 'Sweetcorn. We must eat this slowly and chew it well. You okay to eat this?' Kelpin nodded wordlessly, her eyes huge and shining. Scummo remembered sweetcorn, from his early days, but Kelpin had never seen such a thing before. She gazed at it, not knowing how to tackle it, and watched as Scummo took a large bite and chewed. The taste was as he remembered, sweet and juicy. Kelpin followed suit. They both drank from the water container. There were two cups left.

They ate one corncob each, Kelpin managing with difficulty as one front tooth was missing. Scummo put the remaining husks into his bundle. They would do for later. Standing, Kelpin staggered sideways and upset the remaining water. It was all Scummo could do not to shout at her. She sobbed at his anger, then sat down again, getting to her feet only when he coaxed her.

'It's okay, Kelpin. It wasn't your fault.'

They trudged on towards the horizon, through the long lines of high grass. The far sky was pewter-coloured, with menacing thunderclouds massing up ahead.

The scenery changed after a while. It appeared that they had reached some field boundary, and the crop ahead of them was some sort of wheat, still greenish in its ear. Scummo picked an ear, as he had done as a child, and picked off the green grains. He chewed one. It was soft and milky inside, with a slight nutty flavour. He passed it over to Kelpin.

'This might be easier for you to eat.' She put it in her pocket, thoughtfully.

Good kid, he thought. *She never moans or grumbles.*

She looked up at him. 'I want my mummy.'

Oh hell. What do I do now? 'Let's sit down,' he suggested, trampling the long grass a little to make a space. They sat side by side, the green shoots of the grasses surrounding them like an enclosing wall. Kelpin was looking at him, her face crumpled, her little girl's mouth quivering. He didn't know what to do, so he put his arm round her protectively.

'Mummy's gone.' She said the words sadly. It was both a statement and a question.

'Yes, she has. I'm sorry.' He pulled her closer to him. 'My mother's gone as well. We have to manage by ourselves. I'll look after you, Kelpin. Will you look after me?'

She turned to face him thoughtfully. 'Only if I can have a drink of water.'

He smiled at her. His mouth felt paper dry; hers must feel the same. He had an idea. 'Let's ask the sky to drop some rain. Shall we?'

She smiled and stood up, flinging her arms up into the sky. 'We want rain! We want water! We want rain! Rainy old rain!' She chanted this refrain as he sat and watched, amazed at the life that burned so brightly in her. 'You say it too,' she ordered him. So he did.

They trudged forwards together into the storm and soon the big raindrops burst on their faces and ran down their foreheads, washing the salty grime from their skin, and their eager tongues stuck out to lick off the water that was running down their bodies in bigger and bigger streams. There was no shelter. Scummo took the square of plastic sheeting that had been wrapped around Kelpin's clothes and held it out to catch the rain. Her clothes were already saturated. His felt trousers were soggy and heavy with the wet. At least they had enough to drink, and Scummo tipped the plastic over to let the raindrops trickle down into Kelpin's mouth, and then his own. The rain tasted flat and different from the water in his old apartment, though he couldn't identify the difference.

'Your rain-dance worked,' he said. 'Drink as much as you want, because I don't know when we'll have another chance.'

She pulled a face but continued to drink, then stood back, wiping her mouth with a wet and ragged sleeve. 'That's better. Scummo?'

He looked at her.

'We'll be all right, won't we?'

'Of course we will, kiddo.' But he didn't feel optimistic, at all. His uncertainty showed on his face, and Kelpin took him by the hand and swung their arms back and forth as they walked. Scummo was touched.

If they could reach shelter of some sort they could dry off their clothes before night, he thought, and he stuffed his pockets with the green ears of corn. Kelpin, watching him, did the same. Scanning the horizon, Scummo became aware of something that looked like trees in the distance, a dense dark rounded mass. He remembered trees from his childhood. He whooped excitedly.

'I can see trees!'

Kelpin looked sideways at him. 'What are trees?'

'Very big plants, so big you can climb up them, or shelter under them. Some of them have fruit on.'

'What's fruit?'

He remembered that she wouldn't know what fruit was. In fact, he hardly remembered himself. 'Like beans and turnips, only sweet and juicy,' he said at last. Her eyes grew rounded at the thought. What if there was nothing to eat when they got there? What if the trees were elm or ash or conifers with nothing edible on them at all? Scummo knew he had to be brave and optimistic for the two of them. At least they were alive, out here on this empty plain, full of waving green corn. Back in the Apartments life had been grey and routine, lived within two sets of tramlines that represented the extremes of emotion. All expression of anger had been kept to the Sevenday afternoon and the tournaments; aside from this, there was little else. He remembered it had been different in his village. In the City, funerals did not take place; nobody got married, nobody became bleakly depressed, or joyous, or rebellious, or filled with mystic wonder, or passionate, or fell in love. None of these emotional highs and lows were allowed, it seemed. Instead, there was a blanket of grey and fuzzy fog that blurred the details of their lives; survival was what counted, the daily grind, the monotonous acceptance of their lives. They had been half living, all the real feeling suppressed by conditioning and whatever was added to their food or water. Out here one could breathe. It was tougher, more challenging, but it felt like living.

The clump of trees grew larger and they could begin to make out individual shapes and spaces. At last, Scummo, squinting through half-closed eyes, thought he spotted a building. He couldn't be quite sure, but as they drew nearer, he could see that what he had been looking at was in fact a ruined building. He took Kelpin's hand and they walked faster. He picked some corn as they went, filling his pockets. Finally, they were on the outskirts of the wood, and there before them lay the ruined building, half hidden by tangled vines and low tree branches. He found a place where the corn stopped and the grass began. Here there were patches of green that were short and littered with small pellets. A memory came back to him. Rabbits! He sat Kelpin down and told her to wait for him.

'Where are you going?' she demanded, though clearly welcoming a rest.

'To have a look in the building there.' He pointed. 'Sit still and wait for me to come back.'

'I want to come,' she protested, her mouth turning down at the corners.

'I'll be back soon, and then we'll both go and have a

look,' he replied. She pulled a face but did not object again. He went forwards to see what was there.

The building had once been painted white, but this had flaked off and ivy and dead leaves covered its roof. He couldn't see inside. The door had fallen off its hinges long ago and lay diagonally, partially obscuring the doorway. Scummo moved it aside. A bird, startled, flew out of the eaves. He had to bend to go inside. It was a while before his eyes became used to the light. Inside, there was a wooden bench and a stone slab, with a piece of dusty dried-up rag on one end. He looked up. Cobwebs and a disused bird's nest were visible in one corner. Then he saw something shining up behind the bird's nest, a glint of reflected light that caught his eye. He moved closer and put his hand up. Suddenly the thing shot backwards, retracted with a slight whirring noise and a click and then was no longer visible. He moved the bench across and climbed onto it. His eyes were now used to the darkness, but he had to squint to see it. The object no longer reflected any light. He put his hand up and moved it forwards towards the object, gingerly. His fingers closed around it and pulled it towards him. A tiny spy camera. He cupped his other hand around it. He hadn't seen one before close up, but he guessed what it was. He thought for a while. Then he put the camera back inside the hole in the roof corner but facing the other way, into the darkness of the roof timbers. He'd like to see the pictures they got back from that.

He searched to see if there were any more hidden surprises in the hut, but could find nothing. Outside, he searched for a pump or a standpipe. He found one eventually, Kelpin following his movements with her head.

'Did you find water?'

He nodded. 'Would you like a proper drink now, Kelpin?'

She stuck out her lower lip. 'My name's Kiddo. Don't like Kelpin.'

'Okay, Kiddo. Help me get a drink then.'

There was a rubbish pile covered by grass outside the hut, containing some half-rotten plastic bottles and one glass bottle, filled with green algae. Scummo pulled off the ancient metal cap and filled it with water.

Kelpin pulled a face. 'Not going to drink that!'

No, he wasn't. 'Wait,' he told her. He went back to the edge of the field and carefully pulled two or three ears of corn on their stalks. He inserted these into the neck of the bottle and swirled them around, rinsing out the green water. It was cleaner than when he first started and he held it up to her. 'Clean enough?' She shook her head vigorously. He'd have to do better. He tried again, marvelling at the tyranny of this determined little girl. Finally, it was acceptable, and he filled it and passed it to her. She pulled a face but drank it. He filled a leaky plastic bottle for himself, having evicted the spider. He turned his attention to their clothes. Some of their garments had dried stuck to them. He decided to leave it up to her. They had a few of her clothes still in the bundle. She went behind the hut and changed into some dry things. Scummo had to sit in his wet ones.

It was getting dark. He decided that they should stay there for the night. There was nowhere else to go. He found a stone and washed it, then took the remaining corncobs into the hut and mashed them to a paste, scraping it off the slab as he went. They ate the mush outside, silently.

Scummo was wondering whether it would be safer to sleep in the hut, which was at least dry, or to go outside and try to find a dry spot under the trees. The shadows lengthened. Kelpin yawned.

'We'll sleep in the hut tonight,' he told her. 'You can have the slab to sleep on and I'll keep guard near the door.'

She got up wearily and moved as if in a trance towards the hut door. 'Promise no spiders?' she asked, sleepily.

'Promise.' He looked at her. She was filthy dirty but her hair, with its wild black ringlets, twisted and shone around her little face. Her grubby fingers waved towards the hut roof where the spiders, if there were any, might be. Time to wash in the morning. Scummo didn't know about what small children needed, especially little girls. He'd have to tackle this at some point. Now was not the right time. He fetched two stones and placed them a little way away from the door, outside, and balanced a thin stick across them. If anyone came near the hut, the stick would fall or be moved. It was deathly quiet now that it was dark. Already he could hear Kelpin breathing in her sleep. He sat down with his back to the wall just inside the hut, with his feet across the entrance. He didn't attempt to close the door. Soon he had nodded off, waking with a start as his head tipped forwards onto his chest, jerking his neck. He gave up then and lay down on the dusty floor of the hut and slept.

High in the watchtower, the Masters were placing bets. One glanced up at the screen and noted the slumbering shapes of Kelpin and Scummo.

'Subject A has deactivated the second camera. A point to you, I think?'

'He learns quite quickly. How many years did he have at the time of the Herdings?'

'Twelve. But he has remembered more than we thought.'

'Interesting. I notice he looks after her.'

'Learned behaviour. Most of them wouldn't have done what he's done, though.'

'Perhaps we should review the mix? It would be inconvenient if more of them got out, surely?'

'It will be dealt with.'

Chapter 3

S cummo woke with a start, his neck aching and stiff. He shouldn't have slept. He gazed anxiously at the small dark shape still sleeping on the bench. Kelpin's hands opened and shut. She muttered something in her sleep. Scummo rose stiffly and stretched, yawning. After a moment, he went to the standpipe and washed his hands, then rubbed them over his face. Better than nothing, he supposed. He drank long and deeply. His clothes smelled damp and unpleasant, but the sun was nearly up and he was cheered by the growing warmth and light. As he turned around, a rabbit hopped away into the bushes. *Other life forms*, thought Scummo. *I remember rabbits. We are not alone.* He found this thought comforting and remembered the corn in the field, placed there for his benefit. He scanned the horizon, looking for he knew not what. The fields stretched into the distance in front of him; behind him was the shadowy apparition of the city they had left, rising up out of the fields like some ghostly submarine. He explored further around the copse. The trees were old, but he didn't remember what species they were. Two had yellow bobbles on them; he supposed they were flowers. There was nothing edible, anyway. He began to climb one of the trees, hoping he might see further. Kelpin called to him from the hut.

'I'm up the tree,' he called back. 'Give yourself a wash and I'll be down in a minute.' He watched the newly awakened child emerge from the hut, clothing trailing around her as she went behind the hut to pee and then tried to clean herself by the standpipe. His eyes strained to make out the dim shapes in the distance. He didn't know what he was looking at. 'Good girl. I'm coming down now.'

The fields around them stretched way in to the distance. What could they find to eat in such a place? He was hungry and his growling stomach would not be pacified. He tried to remember from his childhood the things he had eaten then – things he had found outdoors with his mother. He searched the patch of land around the hut, looking in every crevice, investigating every tree. After twenty minutes of close searching, he returned to where Kelpin was sitting and put his collection on the slab: five large snails, a pile of hoarded beech mast, a bracket fungus, and six pig-nuts he had unearthed from the edge of the field, remembering how as a child these were treats he once enjoyed, digging up the delicate white plant with a teaspoon. Here, he had had to use his fingers and a stick, but the pig-nuts were whole and now sat neatly in his hand. He added them to the pile.

Kelpin watched him curiously. 'What's them?'

'Sort of like small potatoes,' he answered. But did she know what potatoes were? He thought not. Food was one thing that was predictable at the Broilerhouse, and he had eaten potatoes only twice since his arrival. He hadn't liked the food, but it had kept him alive at least. His mother had found it hard to get enough to feed them, at the end, and when the Herdings started, the dogs had killed and eaten their three chickens within seconds of bounding up to the cottage gate, while his mother stood there with tears in her eyes, ordering him to be still. She had grown their food, what there was of it, and he was thankful now that she had shown him where to hunt for food. *It's a poor chick that cannot scratch for itself*, his mother had said, watching their own three hens scratching up the dirt with their supple yellow feet. He had remembered that.

Scummo looked at the pathetic handful of items on the bench. One of the snails was already on its way back to the grassy patch where he had found it. He picked it off the ground and put it back with its brothers. Could he cook them somehow? Would they be edible if he did? He had nothing to cook them with and no means of starting a fire. Instead, he used a rose thorn to spear each snail and twist it, winkle-like, out of its shell. Then he placed the slimy remains in the bottom of a smashed glass bottle and let the sun dry them out. He showed Kelpin how to peel and eat the beech mast, and her little fingers were dexterous at removing the sweet nut from its triangle of brown shell. As she peeled them she fed him, then herself, and the tiny morsels she popped into his mouth with her dirty fingers tasted good, with the slight dryness in the aftertaste in his mouth that he remembered from his childhood.

They would have to push on and hope to find something more substantial. He washed the pig-nuts and gave her four, eating the remainder himself. She crunched them thoughtfully, unsure whether she liked them.

He climbed the tree again to look once more at the distant view. Kelpin followed him up the tree before he could stop her. Her eyes were keener than his, but she lacked the experience to know what she was seeing.

'What can you see, Kelpin?'

She was quiet for a moment, wondering how to explain it. 'It looks like it ends.'

'What ends?'

'Where we are. The ground. It's all shiny and bright, with something moving.' She turned and looked at him intently, but he was lost in thought. 'What is it, Scummo?'

'I'm not sure, Kiddo. But it could be water.'

'It's rather a lot of water.'

'Want to go and find out?'

She hung her head. 'Do we have to? I like this little house.' She gestured towards the hut and pulled a face.

'We can come back here again,' he lied, hoping they would never need to. Who could say what cameras had watched them here, what dangers lurked in this woodland grove? They collected their belongings and set off once more across the endless fields. This time it was kale they were walking through, and the smell of the bruised leaves as they passed was strong and unpleasant.

'Ugh! Nasty smell,' Kelpin complained as the tall plants brushed her sides. Neither of them could identify this plant. The kale gave way to swedes with scarcely a pause. Scummo recognised these and smashed one with his foot. They picked up the orange fragments and chewed them. The juice was both sweet and bitter, but it stopped the hunger pangs for a while. Far off in the distance to the left of them they could see the outline of a large machine trundling along the skyline. They hurried on, unsure whether they could be seen.

A fly landed on Kelpin's head as she bobbed along and annoyingly buzzed around her ears. Another tried to settle on Scummo. He brushed it off, then realised that these were the first real insects they'd seen in a long while. More flies flew round them, settling on their necks and arms. Kelpin began yelling. Scummo pulled some swede leaves off and gave them to her.

'Wave them away with these,' he instructed her. He did the same. A little further on they found what was attracting the flies. Something large and white and hairy was lying among the swedes, on its side, dead.

At first, Scummo thought it was a dog, though the mastiff cross-breeds were usually black or dark brown. He trawled his memory for clues. The thing was large and had a rubbery-looking nose and a long jaw, in which Scummo could see sharp white teeth. Flies had settled on its blank, unseeing eyes and were clustered around a wound in the creature's side. Kelpin stared at it, then gave it a kick. The flies scattered then re-grouped, a live seething mass.

'Don't do that,' Scummo ordered her.

She looked defiant. 'What is it?'

'I think it's what they called a pig. I remember my mother talking about them. It's dead.'

'Like Mummy,' Kelpin replied, without a trace of self-pity.

He took her hand and looked at it again. Under the seething mass of flies was a large wound in the side of the pig, and from it protruded a metal pole, with a shiny sphere on the end. As he bent to look at it, it rotated and withdrew itself until all he could see was a small metal disc inside the wound, quickly obscured by flies. Scummo shuddered. He knew that they had been watched and monitored in the buildings because things happened without warning at times and the dog wardens were sent out to silence anyone who seemed about to disobey the rules. The pig must have posed some kind of a threat, maybe to the crops they were growing, but Scummo did not understand the purpose or function of the metal pole he had seen. Was it a weapon with eyes? Another camera? It was too late to do anything to it now.

Silently, they walked away from it towards the horizon, which grew brighter as they got closer. They came to a ditch and he had to help Kelpin across. He noted that there were marks on the muddy banks – footprints of some description, but of what he didn't know. He decided to follow the course of the ditch, as it seemed to curve towards the horizon. What would he see there? Would there be water? And if so, what sort of water would it be? All he could remember was the stream by his house before the Herdings happened, and the puddles that formed in the arena of the Apartments when it rained heavily. The change in the light told him that this would be different, bigger, wider than any water he had seen before. The plants were changing as they walked, too. The crop of swedes had changed into rough grass, broken up by patches of dried muddy areas where reeds were growing, and some plant with yellow starry flowers. Kelpin was tiring, and they sat down on a grassy mound and rested. At their feet were the tidal trails of debris – twigs, grass and crab shells left by the last high tide. They must be near the water now. Kelpin took her shoes off and put her feet in a puddle. He noticed that the shoes she had on were worn and her little feet were dirty between the toes. He'd have to remind her about washing. When he stood up after they had rested, he felt light-headed with hunger. The light was much brighter now, and there was water – yes there was water, coming towards them, flowing smoothly and steadily across the muddy reaches ahead of them.

He held Kelpin up to look. 'There's the water. It's coming to meet us. See it?'

'Why is it? Will it stop?' she asked him, watching the brown froth spreading lacy patterns as it approached. He looked at the spot they had rested in. It was green and dry. There were rocks under it, and he guessed the water would not rise over it.

Kelpin sniffed the air experimentally. 'Smells funny,' she informed him. His mother had told him about the sea; he had once had a storybook about a sea creature, with pictures. Kelpin was right; it did smell funny, but not nasty funny. He breathed it in deeply and inhaled the salt weed smell of it. Something else tickled the back of his nose. Wood smoke.

He stood up and jumped from the grassy mound they were on to another drier patch, then realised how sensible Kelpin had been in taking off her shoes. He sat down next to her again and removed his boots. The rubber under-soles were worn, and his feet, when they emerged into the light, looked grey and unhealthy.

'You took your shoes off too,' exclaimed Kelpin delightedly. 'Ugh! What dirty feet!'

'Can you smell smoke, Kelpin?'

She sniffed the air, black tangled curls shiny round her head. Before he could stop her, she had darted off, nimbly leaping from tussock to tussock as the fingers of brown water felt their way over the sand and mud around them.

'It's here,' she told him, peering down at something. 'Something long and fat with smoke coming out of one end.' He joined her, slipping on the muddy sea grass.

A creek had been carved out of the land by the water and in it was floating a long barge with a hooped cover. Smoke curled gracefully into the sky from a bent stove-pipe at the far end. The barge shook in the water slightly and Scummo realised that the inhabitant was moving about inside. Scummo had never seen a boat before, but he guessed it was some sort of dwelling place on the water. Was there an advantage to living this way? Perhaps. He stood and watched.

His ankle tag, sandy with grit, irritated his foot. He scratched at it. He wasn't certain what its function was, except as identification, but suddenly he wanted to be rid of it.

He called out, 'Anyone at home?' The barge rocked a little and someone emerged from the interior. The figure stood up slowly on the deck space. It was a youth of around sixteen, dressed in a ragged coat under which a pair of shorts was just visible. He was wielding a sharp stick in one hand and looked as if he might be about to threaten them with it. His long hair was tied behind his neck with a rag, and he was barefoot. He eyed them suspiciously.

Kelpin called out, 'We don't want to hurt you. What's your name?'

Scummo was taken back by her brashness. He stood still. The boy lowered his stick so that it rested on the ground, but he continued to hold the end tightly. His fingernails were long and ragged. He eyed them slowly, his face expressionless save for a nervous blink.

'What you want to know for?' The words came hesitantly.

Scummo thought before responding. 'I'm known as Scummo. This is Kelpin.' He gestured to where she stood, dirty hands twisting the hem of her ragged sweater.

She spoke up. 'We runned away. My mummy's dead. Scummo looks after me.'

'Where you run from?' He was still suspicious.

Scummo spoke, aware of an urge to say too much, tell all the facts, in order to get things clear in his own head. 'The City. I was in the Herdings when I was twelve; Kelpin was born there in the Apartments. I knew they'd take her to the nursery after her mother died and you know – poor kid – what happens to kids who are sent there. I knew her mother and I just couldn't let them do it. So we ran away. It wasn't as hard as everyone says. What about you?'

The youth sighed and jabbed his stick in the mud. His eyelids flickered with agitation. 'They tried to take my parents in the Herdings. I was just a baby.'

Scummo waited for more. 'How come you escaped?'

'They hid in the woods but the Masters found them eventually. I don't know what happened to them.'

'What happened then? To you?' It was like getting blood out of a stone. The young man was finding it difficult to talk about himself.

'The Masters put me in the nursery and somehow I survived. I escaped when I was nine, after there was a fire in the City. I think they thought I'd died in the fire, because they didn't come looking for me. I hate them. I'd rather die than go back there.' A look of intense hatred came over his face. 'I've only seen three other people since, until you came.'

'Who were they?' Scummo really wanted to know.

'People like you. The Masters always find you eventually; that is, if they want to.'

'But they haven't found you yet?'

The boy shrugged. 'It's only a matter of time. But there are others out here.'

Scummo was excited to hear that. 'How do you know?'

'I see lights out there.' He pointed to the sea opening out ahead of them. 'They are moving at night. I hear voices from across the water.' So they were not alone. The boy gestured towards the inside of the barge. 'Come down and have a look?'

Kelpin's eyes shone at this invitation and she hopped aboard, leaving Scummo to step across uncertainly as the barge shifted under their weight.

The barge interior was simplicity itself. There were hay bundles at the far end forming a primitive mattress and, on the deck, an old enamel bowl stood to catch rain, while a tar-speckled wood stove burned inside, the chimney of which rose through a hole in the corrugated iron roof. Some dirty-looking clothing was piled next to the hay piles. The only other item in this space appeared to be a rickety wooden locker where the boy presumably kept anything else he didn't want to carry with him. Scummo realised that because the boat was low and in a creek, it was difficult for others to find, but it had been the smell of wood smoke that gave his presence away. The boy beckoned them inside and sat down, cross-legged, on the floor.

Scummo said, 'I've told you our names. What's yours?'

'Darfi. That's what they called me. Funny, I've almost forgotten I had a name.' Again, the eyes blinked, nervously. 'What's that on your ankle? A tag?'

Scummo looked at the metal hoop that encircled his ankle. 'You haven't got one?' he enquired.

'I never had one,' Darfi admitted. 'They were going to tag me but I ran away. They usually wait until you're half grown. The others who came here said the tags were to let the Masters know where you are, and who you are if you get killed. Can you take yours off?'

'Don't think so.' Scummo sat down heavily and drew his left foot towards him. The ragged nails and calloused heel were thick with dirt. He was unaccustomed to seeing his feet at such close quarters and pulled a face. The ring that encircled his ankle was metal, and except for one small area where it was studded with holes in a random pattern, appeared to be featureless. Under it he could just see tender, pale skin. 'There seems to be some holes in it here. Could be a lock or something.' He tugged at it but nothing happened. Darfi came closer and inspected it. Kelpin squatted down next to him.

'I haven't got one,' she said, rubbing her own ankle. Darfi smiled. He found a fish-hook and tried to pierce the holes in the metal. There was a brief buzzing sound. He tried again, but nothing happened.

'Tamper-proof. Let's see if it likes water.' Scummo stayed seated, contemplating his foot. Darfi fetched a bucket of seawater. 'Stand up and put your foot in this.' Scummo moved from under the covered area of the barge to a place where he could stand upright at the back of the boat and put his foot into the bucket. The electric shock threw him across the barge.

'Yow! That hurt!' He picked himself up slowly and limped to where he could sit. 'Hey, the tag's come off!' His ankle was red and a bright red burn mark ran around it. The metal ring lay on the deck. Darfi got a stick and pushed it overboard.

Silently, Darfi refilled the bucket with seawater and Scummo put his foot into it, feeling the relief of cool water on the burn as he did so. Although badly shaken, he recovered enough to reassure Kelpin, who had been watching with a mixture of horror, concern and fascination.

'I'll be okay, Kiddo.'

'Does it hurt very, very much?'

He looked at her, her black curls soft against her cheeks, her expression serious. 'Yes,' he admitted truthfully. 'But it'll get better.' After a while he was able to take his foot out of the water. A diversion would be helpful, he thought. 'Okay, Darfi. What do we do now? Any ideas?'

Darfi thought for a moment. 'Catch fish; that is, if you want to eat tonight. Give me a hand.' As he spoke, he pulled out some lengths of fishing line from the locker and handed them to Scummo. 'Got anything on you that would make a hook? A safety pin, anything like that?'

Scummo shook his head. Kelpin listened carefully, then reached inside her clothes and after a moment held out to them a rusty white enamel badge with the letters B8 on it.

'It's my milk powder badge,' she explained, offering it to them.

Darfi took it from her and took out the sprung metal pin. 'Perfect,' he said. 'Thanks, Kelpin.' She beamed at him. Scummo watched as Darfi lashed the nylon line around the end of the hook. He gave it to Scummo to hold and without a word, jumped onto the bank and spent several minutes looking for something before returning with a rusty tin can. This he tipped out on the deck and several large worm-like creatures tried to make their way to the dark corners of the boat. Deftly, Darfi captured them and impaled them on Scummo's pin before baiting his own hook.

Kelpin's lower lip stuck out and a fierce expression came over her face. 'I want one,' she said with force. 'It was my pin Scummo's got anyway.'

Scummo turned to her with surprise. 'Sorry, Kelpin. I didn't think you'd want to go fishing.' He handed the line over to her. 'Be careful of your fingers.'

She held the line gingerly, the baited end dangling as the worms twisted in death agony on the end. Darfi went on to the deck and threw his line in and Kelpin followed him. Darfi held the end for her while she threw her bait at the water, catching it on the deck and the grass of the banks. Scummo watched her carefully. This activity was new to him, and he couldn't help her. He felt oddly useless. Darfi was patient and guided her hand so that the baited end fell with a plop into the water. She watched, disappointed, as nothing happened for several minutes. Then, suddenly, the water began to seethe and boil around the lines. Scummo came across to watch as Darfi tugged quickly and suddenly on the line. Scummo held Kelpin's line as they did the same. The first fish appeared above the surface as Darfi pulled it in, and it wasn't long before Scummo and Kelpin also had a catch. The fish they hauled up the side of the barge was greenish grey, with bright challenging eyes and spiky, wicked teeth. Darfi hit it on the head with a stick and did the same to Kelpin's fish. Both fish ceased to struggle and lay still, their gills moving a fraction as they died. Kelpin investigated the fish closely. The largest fish, Darfi's, had something unusual about its tail. The backbone seemed to be forked so that the fish had two tail fins. Darfi saw them looking.

'It's a changeling,' he said. 'Someone's tried to clone it and failed. The man who was here before told me.' Darfi slit the fish belly with a tin lid and hooked the innards out with his finger. He stuck a stick through it and put in on the stove to cook. The smell of hot cooked fish soon filled the little cabin and their mouths watered. Meanwhile, Darfi caught several more fish and there were others that had strange abnormalities among them. 'I used not to eat them if they looked strange,' he confided, 'but when you're hungry and there's nothing else . . .' His voice trailed off. They understood only too well.

'Is this what you live on?' enquired Scummo, eagerly sucking all the meat he could off the bony fish as Kelpin carefully investigated it with her fingers first, picking out the bones. 'I don't think I've eaten proper fish before. Fish-meal soup was something we used to have when we first arrived. They used to give it to us in powder form and pour boiling water on it. This is good.' He licked his fingers appreciatively.

'The others said it was okay to eat the crabs and something they called kelp. Before they came I tried everything and got really sick. I found out that the best food was the golden stuff that grows high in the fields, but if I only ate that my stomach swelled up so much it really hurt. I was a mess when they found me. They brought me here and showed me how to fish. They went off on a fishing trip in the end but they never came back. I don't know what happened to them. That was two years ago.' The effort of saying so much had exhausted Darfi. He sighed and jabbed his stick at the bank. The tide was going out now and the barge was dropping down the bank with the receding water. There were holes in the bank and Darfi prodded them with his stick.

'Crabs,' he said.

'What are crabs?' asked Kelpin.

By way of an answer, Darfi took a fish head, speared it with the stick and held it close to the entrance to the hole. A

58

grey pincer appeared at the entrance, then another, and a pair of eyes on stalks weighed up the fish head. Darfi waggled it temptingly across the hole. One pincer shot out and gripped the fish head. With lightning speed, Darfi twisted the stick and flipped the crab into the boat, where it lay upside down, eyes waving wildly in outrage, legs scrabbling for purchase.

'That was lucky,' Darfi mused. 'Sometimes I can stand here for hours and not catch one.'

Kelpin was mesmerised. 'What a funny thing!' she said, taking care not to go too near it.

Darfi went to it and slid a finger and thumb around its tail end and picked it up. Its legs waved violently but couldn't reach him. 'I boil these,' he said, reaching out for the empty tin can with his free hand. Scummo dipped it in the rainwater bowl and passed it to him. Darfi put the can on the fire and waited. When it was hot, he popped the crab into the water and the escaping steam hissed loudly. A smell of fresh crab, salty and strong, filled the little cabin. 'There's bits of it you can't eat. I'll show you when it cools down.'

He put the cooked crab on a wooden plank and when it was cool enough, he banged the underside of the shell with his stick and twisted out the legs and body sac. Kelpin got very close, fascinated by this unknown creature. Scummo, too, watched, knowing their survival might depend on whatever they could find. Darfi showed them the grey gill fronds on the crab. 'Dead men's fingers,' he explained. 'Pull them off like this.' He tugged at the fronds with his stained fingers until they came away. He put them on one side. 'Tomorrow's bait. I take the stomach out too – it's full of rubbish.' He poked with a sharp twig at the crab's insides and levered it out. Scummo held the square parchment-like organ in his hand, seeing inside it the debris Darfi had talked about. 'Throw it away,' ordered Darfi. Scummo did as he was told.

Darfi picked up the shell and scooped the meat out with his stick. He gave them each a mouthful to try. He offered them each a leg and showed them how to crack them with their teeth and extract the white, sweet flesh. Then he smacked the pincers with a stone until they cracked and the flesh could be extracted.

'It's a lot of bother for a very little meat,' said Scummo, grudgingly. 'But it *is* delicious.'

Kelpin agreed. Again, Scummo marvelled at how quickly she learned anything that might help her own survival. Her cheeks and hands were filthy but her eyes shone. He felt a surge of affection for her, followed almost at once by anxiety. He had a rival now. Darfi.

Chapter 4

They spent their third cold night aboard the barge as fog came down and muffled the slap, slap of the water on the banks. Rousing a little from his sleep, Scummo's ears received a different noise. Voices. He put an arm out and poked Darfi.

'Shh. I can hear voices.' Scummo put his fingers to his lips. Alert now, they listened, but the words were muffled and hushed. Then the silence returned, filling up the creek and the sky as the damp rolls of mist unravelled around the barge. Darfi waited a little, then crept to the stern, parted the hanging curtain and cautiously poked his nose through. Nothing. He turned his head.

'They've gone,' he hissed. Around him, the fog lifted a little as the dawn and a light breeze crept in from the sea.

'Who were they?' Scummo was shivering with cold and anxiety. His ankle, now he was awake, began to throb. Kelpin snuffled and turned over on her pile of hay and slept on.

'Don't know. We'll look for tracks at daybreak.'

'Is it safe?'

Darfi was scornful. 'Nothing's safe,' he said. 'It could have been other travellers, or someone *they* sent. No one's come here before, except the ones I told you about. But they wouldn't come at night.'

'This place isn't safe,' Scummo repeated, feeling forlorn. 'Nowhere is. All the time there are things watching us. I know it. In the City you knew they watched you, but there were so many of us that they couldn't watch everyone all the time. Here it's different.' He was thoughtful. 'Will you stay here?'

Before Darfi could answer, Scummo caught a flicker of movement in the corner of his eye. Something just inside the hooped roof of the barge had glinted. He followed his line of vision, never taking his eye off the place. A tiny round tube protruded from the roof, and as he approached, it withdrew quickly and silently until it was flush with the roof lining. Darfi saw what he was looking at.

'Spy-tube?' he asked. Scummo nodded. Darfi fetched his stick and cautiously went outside. All was quiet. He gouged some mud from the bank with the end of his stick and withdrew it. Carefully, he removed the mud with his fingers and spread it over the small hole around the spy-tube, then used his stick to push more mud into the hole, blocking the spy-tube completely. He grinned and wiped his fingers on his ragged trousers,

'What you doing?' asked Kelpin, now awake and sitting up, eyes wide with interest.

'You know that shiny metal thing we saw sticking out of the pig?' Kelpin nodded. 'Well, there's one here. Darfi has just put mud in its eye.'

Kelpin giggled. 'What is it?' she asked again, all curiosity.

'A spy-tube,' said Darfi. 'It's so other people can watch what we're doing.'

'Even when I have a wee?'

Darfi smiled. 'Probably. If you see any more, will you tell us?' Kelpin nodded.

Scummo turned to Darfi. 'We have to talk seriously about what we do now,' he said. 'They must have followed us here somehow. I'm sorry if we've brought you this, Darfi. Now they know where we are, they'll probably be back. Kelpin and I have to move on.'

Darfi's lean sallow face, with its wispy beard, looked concerned. 'Where to?'

'I don't know. As far away as we can, I suppose. Does this barge move? I mean, could we travel along the coast on it?'

Darfi thought about it. 'It's moored to a stake in the bank. I've never tried to move it. We'd have to pull it out of the creek ourselves. There's no other way it'd move. Unless we wait for the tide to come up and then undo the rope and hope the tide will carry it out. We'd need something to push against the banks with to stop it getting caught, and once we got out onto the sea there'd be no way of getting back.'

Scummo thought it over. 'Which direction did the others go in when they left here?'

Darfi pointed up the coast. 'But they didn't come back.' He returned to the prow of the boat and threw the curtain over the top of the iron roof. The grey dawn light was strong now and the fog had cleared. Darfi stood and, with agility, threw the plank across and jumped onto the bank. Scummo watched him. Darfi searched the bank carefully for footprints or any signs of their visitors and returned after an interval.

'Find anything?' Scummo asked eagerly.

'Two sets of footprints, leading back the way you came. They spent time on the bank here, then retraced their steps. One was heavy, the other light. Probably both male, though I can't be certain of that.'

Scummo was impressed. 'How can you tell all that?'

'The prints of one show they wore shoes with thick soles. The Masters only employ males, or at least they *did*, to do their work for them. The prints of the other are lighter, less distinct. But he could be a technician or something and not entitled to the same shoes.'

'Any dog prints?'

'No. That was my main worry, too. Maybe they don't let the dogs out of the City without their Masters.'

'How far have you been along the coast in the other direction? The way the others went?'

Darfi thought for a minute. 'I once went on a fishing trip with them and we walked for six hours, until we reached a headland. That was where they wanted to fish from. We caught some big fish there because the water was deep. That's the furthest I've been. The coast continues after that in a series of bays and creeks, a bit like this one but with more sand. There are some trees further along, too.'

'Will you come with us if we walk?'

Darfi considered it. 'No,' he answered finally. Kelpin looked very disappointed. 'It's not me they're looking for. I like it here. I've sort of got used to it, and this is my home.'

'And if we cut the barge loose and let it drift out to sea?'

Darfi thought. 'Well – okay, I'd agree to that. But we have no idea if we can do it, or even if we could ever get back on shore. It's pretty risky. But like you said, I think they'll be back. Yes – let's do it. All right with you, Kelpin? If we wait till high tide and push the barge out to sea?'

Kelpin considered this. 'We can't get off the boat then,' she observed.

'That's right.'

'We'll need to take some food and water,' she said thoughtfully, and before they could stop her she was on the bank and searching the sea grass and mud for anything that might be useful. The tide was out and there were the marks of molluscs and sea creatures in the mud, tracking across the soft hollows between the grassy tussocks. Kelpin jumped with agile strength along the grassy mounds until she reached a point where the soft mud changed to pebbles and the ground was firm to walk on. Some kelp grew among the stones at low tide. This she picked, and then overturned the stones as she had seen Darfi do. Black crabs with green eyes scurried away, but Kelpin grabbed them and stuffed them into the square of cloth she was holding, along with the kelp. In the shallows, transparent shrimps darted backwards out of reach when she approached, and tiny fish flicked silver lines as the sun caught them before they, too, shot away into the deeper water. Kelpin was enchanted. The two men watched her with fond amusement. They called her back to the barge and she returned, clutching her trophies to her waist in the cloth square. She boarded the barge and sat down cross-legged, waiting for their full attention before she revealed the contents. With a magician's flourish, she undid the cloth and eight small crabs fell out and sidestepped in different directions towards the water. Darfi and Scummo caught them with difficulty and put them in the tin Darfi had used for the bait. Some live shellfish and the kelp were added to the crabs.

'Well done, Kelpin!' Darfi was quick to praise, and Kelpin glowed. Their drinking water had begun to run low and it was this more than the absence of food that worried Scummo. The enamel bowl Darfi kept for rainwater now contained only an inch or so of water, and although Scummo had filled up some bottles at the hut, they were now empty. He discounted going back to the hut, feeling that it would take too long. With or without water, they would let loose the anchor at high tide and hope that the ebb and flow would carry the barge out beyond reach of the land. Before that happened, Scummo knew there was one thing he must do. He found Darfi's stick and went to the muddy opening in the roof where the spy-tube had been. He aimed the pointed end of the stick at the hole and jabbed it with all his might. There was a jolt and Scummo flew backwards onto the deck as something fell off the roof into the water with a fizz, and a shower of sparks buzzed on the surface of the sea.

'What happened?' Darfi was beside him in an instant.

'Got rid of the spy-tube,' said Scummo, winded. 'I'm okay. They don't want you to meddle with those things, do they?'

'Are you sure you're all right?'

Scummo rubbed his arm ruefully. Kelpin came over and massaged it for him solicitously. His ankle, healing now, still troubled him if he knocked it. The stick had prevented another electric shock. He thought himself lucky.

'Thanks, Kiddo. Let's pack up and get moving, shall we?' It was almost high tide. Darfi untied the rope and the slop slop of the water changed as the barge inched back into the deeper water, so slowly that Kelpin, watching from the prow, was silent as the grey bank slowly retreated in front of them.

Carried out on the tide, the old barge had to be fended off from the banks of the creek with the pole. It was slow going and hard work, but by low tide they were just off the coast, in the estuary mouth. Darfi searched the skyline with narrowed eyes. Water, sand or mud, salt flats, and away in the far distance, trees and higher land. Beyond that, he couldn't see. Seawards, the horizon was empty, the swell on the calm sea rocking the barge a little as it lay. The sun was warm. Kelpin leaned over the side of the barge and trailed her hands through the water. Bubbles came up to meet her waving fingertips. There was a current moving through the water, and the barge started to turn on its axis. Scummo crossed over and sat beside her. He examined the seething water below them, then, acting on curiosity, dipped the can into the water, rinsed and filled it, then put it to his lips. The water was very slightly salty. He tried again. This time, he reached into the centre of the up-swelling current, almost falling out of the barge, and the water was pure and sweet.

'Quick, Darfi! Fetch the bowl! Kelpin, see if there's anything else that will hold water.' They ran to do his bidding. Soon, they had filled the bowl to the brim and all the bottles and cans they could find. Kelpin tasted the water all around the boat and every time she pulled a face.

'It's all salty water,' she said, with disgust. 'That bit we found is the only bit of the sea that's not salty.'

'We found fresh water,' replied Darfi. 'I don't know how it got there, but there are some springs of water on the land the fishing people showed me when they came. They were a long way from the barge, or we could have gone there.'

'It must have come up from under the sea,' said Scummo. 'We had a spring in our garden when I was a child, before the Herdings. My mother used to fetch water from there sometimes, when it was dangerous to use the pump in the street.' His face grew wistful. Kelpin went across and put her hand in his. There was silence.

'Do you think there are any more of those spy-tubes on here?' asked Darfi after a while.

'I suppose we'd better search.' They all examined every inch of the barge but found nothing. Satisfied, they sat down and thought about the future. Darfi fished while Scummo scanned the shoreline and the horizon out to sea. Kelpin curled up on the hay and sucked her thumb, twisting the tight black curls around her face with her index finger. Scummo watched her out of the corner of his eye. *Poor kid*, he thought. *At last she can relax.* He wished he could.

The tide was now on the turn again and the bobbing barge was drifting towards the shore again, slightly further up than before. They couldn't continue this indefinitely, he thought. A terrible weariness came over him too, and he lay down next to Kelpin and shut his eyes. Darfi, watchful and awake, continued to fish.

It was evening when they awoke, and the fish Darfi had caught were cooking on the little stove. A soft lilac dusk enveloped them. The Apartments seemed a long way away now, along with all the ugliness and squalor, the oppressive sense of confinement, the mad and hungry dogs. Here there was peace, a time to reflect. They ate in near silence. Darfi was comfortable with this, Scummo less so. Kelpin was too busy picking the sharp bones out of the fish to talk, but she seemed rested.

It was Darfi who spotted the tiny speck of light, like a distant star, on the horizon, out to sea. The barge was in darkness, with only a glow from the stove to see by.

'There's a light out there. See?' He pointed. Scummo and Kelpin peered through the gloom and could just make out a bobbing speck of light.

'What is it?' asked Kelpin. Scummo, next to her, peered long and hard through the gloom, willing his eyes to focus more exactly.

Darfi spoke. 'They can't see us from where they are. We don't know if they're friendly, anyhow. But if we decide to make contact, then now's the time. This is the first light I've seen for months.'

Scummo was anxious. 'It could be a trap.'

Darfi considered this. 'We have to take a chance. What are we going to do, anyhow? Drift around here forever?' He went under the hooped roof and emerged with a bundle of hay, his stick and his tinderbox. He pushed the pointed end of the stick through an old felt sock, filled it with hay and poked it in the fire. After a minute it began to smoulder and then burst into flames. Darfi waved it back and forth, slowly. It sent out a shower of sparks and he waved it again.

'I could throw it high into the air,' offered Scummo.

'We'd lose the stick,' replied Darfi sensibly.

'What about calling across the water? Would they hear us?'

'The wind's not blowing the right way, but we could try – if you're sure you want to take the chance?'

'Wait! Look, the light's moving!' The light over the water seemed a little closer to them now, and it was being swung in an arc. Three times it swung from side to side, then stopped. Scummo took the burning stick and copied the movement he had seen. Three times, up, over and down. The light over the water appeared again, repeating the pattern. They followed suit. They called, then, across the sea, hoping to maintain contact when the hay stopped burning. Kelpin put her ear close to the water and could hear the far-off sound of voices as the other boat came towards them.

The tension on the barge was unbearable. They all realised the gamble they had taken. They also knew that they had no real choice. Scummo called again across the water and this time he was answered, but the words were indistinct. As the boat came towards them they could just make out a sail, the mast inky dark against the sky.

Neither Scummo nor Darfi had seen a sailing boat before, though Scummo had seen pictures of one when he was a child. More and more he recognised that he was raiding this precious storehouse of memories to help him survive now. He hoped there would be enough. Darfi had learned what he could from the people he'd seen since he ran away, and he was quick to take in information, but Scummo realised how inept they both were at surviving in the world outside the Apartments. Kelpin, with her curiosity and natural instinct for survival, was more adept at making herself at home.

The dark shape of the other boat loomed through the darkness.

'We're coming alongside.' They drew close. How many people were in the boat? Darfi and Scummo peered but could not be certain whether the dark mounds they could make out were people or objects. The speaker, now struggling to close with the barge without colliding with it, was a tall middle-aged man with thin blond hair framing his high cheekbones.

'Grab the stick.' It was Darfi, trying to draw them alongside. They did so and the man made the two vessels fast.

'Can we come on board?'

Darfi looked at Scummo, who nodded his agreement. Darfi extended his hand and the man jumped across. The dark mounds began to stir. Two figures unwound themselves from the tarpaulin that covered them and stiffly and awkwardly stretched their limbs.

'I don't know how many people the barge can take,' said Scummo, anxiously.

'This is an old barge,' Darfi reassured him. 'Used to be used for carrying animal feed around. It can take us. The sea's calm tonight. If it wasn't, it would be a different story.'

The visitors prepared to board. Kelpin piped up. 'My name's Kelpin but Scummo calls me Kiddo. What's your name?'

'Jankin. Pleased to meet you, Kelpin.' He sat down stiffly under the covered area of the barge. Scummo helped the other two figures aboard. They appeared to be very weak, and it took some time before they were settled on the deck.

'This is Fanna, and this is Rondi.' Jankin pointed at the two figures. Fanna pushed some material back from her face. Her long black hair escaped in thin wisps around her neck. She tried to say something but failed. Rondi, between Darfi and Kelpin in age, had close-cropped hair and patches of baldness showing through, so his head had an odd tufted look. Both were very thin and looked unwell. Kelpin wormed her way between them and gazed at them as if searching for something. Fanna put her hand out and lightly touched Kelpin's arm.

'Are you my mother?' asked Kelpin. Scummo's heart gave a lurch. She shouldn't be asking those questions.

Fanna's voice was weak. 'Would you like me to be your mother, Kelpin? I'm not very well, I'm afraid. When I'm stronger, ask me again.' Her tone was gentle. Kelpin looked thoughtful.

They shared out some of their water and the three newcomers gulped it down eagerly. Jankin and the others settled down and the serious talking began. Darfi put out a night line as they were talking and at intervals got up to inspect it, impaling the fish on a stick through their gills as they were caught. Jankin watched Darfi's graceful movements with interest as he talked.

Scummo explained that he and Kelpin had left the City after her mother died. He watched for Kelpin's reaction at this point, but she stared at the ground. Darfi said little about himself, except that he, like them, had chosen to stay outside the City.

Jankin, in his calm reflective way, told how he and the other two had been living in a small coastal settlement on an island several miles away. They had escaped the first Herdings because the Masters had been interrupted by rocket attacks on their vessel from the other side of the headland. Jankin did not know who was responsible. A number of villagers had been herded onto the vessel by the dogs when the rocket was launched, and the vessel was able to leave, although damaged. When the Masters had returned with their dogs, the three of them ran to the beach and swam to one of the fishing boats moored in the bay. The water was cold, but they clung to the seaward side of the boat, not daring to speak or move. They hid until the dogs and their handlers had gone, climbed aboard, very cold now, and rested on the deck. Far away, they could see lines of villagers who had not got on the boat ascending the cliffs, dogs snapping at their heels. They watched in horror as the line of people faltered at the clifftop, paused, then were forced over the edge by the advancing dogs. From where they were hiding, they could hear the screams as figure after figure toppled off the clifftop and fell to their death. Trying not to listen, the three of them huddled together for warmth and wrapped themselves in the old clothes the fishermen had stowed in the cabin. That night, Jankin took stock of their situation. Fanna was still cold but willing to help him, while Rondi seemed to be in shock. Jankin and Fanna, who had sailed before, took charge of the boat, a thirty-foot bawley, and managed to navigate their way out of the harbour and around the headland. By morning they were exhausted but well away from land. There was a light swell. They dropped anchor and tried to fish, with some success, and the fine nets stowed under the seats allowed them to catch smaller fish and shrimps. There was a little water on board, and they would have to rely on rainwater for more. They had sailed along the coast for nearly two weeks before finding the barge, and they were now all weak with hunger and thirst.

Scummo and Darfi told their stories. Then Fanna spoke. The shadows under her eyes gave her pale face a sombre look, and she gestured with her long beautiful hands as she related their story. Her tired smile lit up her face when she became aware that Kelpin was snuggled up next to her.

'Our experience out here has been different from yours. For years, we have watched the Masters at work and heard reports of the Herdings you speak about. We lived in the fear that it could happen to us, but the resistance group we told you about, who fired on the boats as the Herdings were about to commence, they held them off. We all lost our families. I'll never forget the sight of people falling from that clifftop.' She shuddered. 'I still can't believe it's happened.'

Jankin looked at her and then down at his long bony hands. He knew she'd cry if he touched her, but he wanted to all the same. He took up the tale.

'We kept seeing the bodies in the water as they floated past us.' The others were quiet, waiting for him to continue. 'Then we saw things in the water, coming up from the deep.' He tailed off. 'Horrible things, like eels but with two heads, and big, big as a log. Ugh! They went after the floating bodies in the water. Then we didn't see as many.'

'They ate the bodies?' Darfi wanted to know.

Jankin nodded.

'Where are they now, these creatures?'

Jankin shrugged. 'Gone back down into wherever they came from, presumably.' They were silent, each thinking their own thoughts.

Kelpin broke the silence. 'I'm going to smack one on the nose if it comes near our boat,' she said. The others smiled ruefully at her.

'What do we do now? That's the point,' said Scummo. 'If we stay here, we'll run out of water or starve. Tying the boats together has given us a bit more space and makes them a bit more stable too, but the sail on the bawley won't shift all of us.'

Dawn was breaking over the estuary now. Rondi, still huddled in a frightened heap, began to take heart from Kelpin's nonchalant attitude and announced he was hungry. Darfi handed him the remains of a fish cooked earlier. He brightened and began to look around him. Fanna rubbed his shoulder protectively, causing Kelpin to shift further up the seat towards her.

'Looks like I'm going to be Mother,' said Fanna, smiling tiredly at them.

Scummo chuckled. 'Any ideas about what we do now?'

'Where's the nearest land?' Darfi asked.

Jankin looked at the dawning light in the east. 'I'd say it was in that direction. In fact, I can just make out something on the horizon. See where I mean?'

Darfi and Scummo peered over the quiet water. A long low shape was just visible.

'Are you sure that's not cloud?'

'Don't think so. We're being taken that way by the current at present, so we'll know for sure in a short while.'

Scummo was thinking. 'We have to get back on land again. If we can find the people who are attacking the Masters, we might have a chance – what do you think?'

'It depends who they are. They could want us for their own purposes. Suppose we can't find them?'

'Do you have a better plan?'

There wasn't one. They decided to drift with the current as near to the distant shore as they could, then take the bawley and sail her to the coast. Jankin was uncertain whether the boat could handle six people but decided against saying anything for the moment. With a calm sea, he thought they might have a chance.

They became livelier after that. The sips of water and mouthfuls of fish had begun to revive them, and Rondi in particular began to look more cheerful. Slowly, the land they were drifting towards came closer. They could see trees and rocky cliffs. The three men talked about their lives before the Herdings, while Fanna listened, too tired to join in. When it was clear that they had almost reached the shore and the current had started to carry them along the coast, they untied the boats and climbed carefully across into the bawley, while Darfi carried across anything that might be of use to them. While he was carrying the basin of water across, Scummo let go of the barge for an instant and Darfi wobbled and fell between the boats, his arms still clutching the bowl, which floated above him until his thrashing arms submerged it. Scummo and Jankin both reached into the water, trying desperately to reach Darfi, who, panic-stricken, was about to go under again.

'Kick with your legs,' ordered Jankin. 'That will keep you on top of the water and we can reach you.'

Darfi, eyes wide with fear, thrashed about but managed to kick his legs just enough to prevent him sinking. Scummo looked at Jankin with respect. Kelpin, watching it all with terror in her eyes as she held Fanna's hand tightly, noticed it first. Something was moving fast through the water towards them. She pointed wildly at the furrows in the water opened up by some creature bigger than a fish. Darfi, with a supreme effort, flung his arms up and grabbed the sides of the bawley as Scummo and Jankin, taking an arm each, managed to haul him on board.

When his feet were only just clear of the water, the others looked down where Kelpin was pointing as a log-sized, smooth olive body slid under the boat and out the other side, rocking it slightly.

'Saint Emilia!' Jankin invoked the old saint's name. It stirred something in Scummo's brain. It had been many years since he had heard this exclamation. Suddenly, a wave of self-pity washed over him. He refocused quickly and paid attention. Hauling Darfi over the side of the boat, he followed the pointing hand of Jankin. The furrow in the water became fainter as the creature took a diagonal course to the bottom again. The barge drifted away behind them.

Darfi was shivering with cold and fear, and he was badly bruised where they had hauled him over the side, but he was safe. He took off his wet clothes, untroubled by the curious eyes of Kelpin and the bashful eyes of Fanna, and the others donated whatever garments they could spare while they hung his wet clothes on the bawley's side to dry. The barge drifted away from them now, and they watched it go with regret. Land was closer now, but they would need to get the sail up and steer if they were going to make it.

'Look for a promontory,' ordered Jankin, once they were under way. 'We need deep water to take her in, if we can find it. Don't want to risk that thing coming back if we try to wade in.'

Darfi shuddered. Scummo was new to all of this but learning fast. He had taken over the tiller and Jankin explained briefly how it worked. Fanna trimmed the sail, and soon the bawley was tacking across the bay towards the nearest point of land. It was almost night by the time they managed to steer close enough to the land for Scummo to scramble ashore. The rocks cut his feet, but despite this, he managed to make the bawley fast to a rock so that they could all come ashore.

They brought with them anything they felt might be useful. Jankin and Fanna had a fish-gutting knife from the boat and some nets. Scummo still had Kelpin's badge fishing hook and various containers and plastic bottles, two filled with fresh water from the spring. At last, they had reached a destination.

Chapter 5

The climb over the rocks in the dusk onto the low cliff was tiring, but Kelpin found kelp and crabs and made them stop and help her pick them. Slowly, they made their way up to the clifftop. The bawley bobbed on the water as she lay. Jankin wished the boat were less visible. But if things turned ugly here on land, at least they had some means of escape.

The land at the top of the cliffs was uneven grassland, closely grazed. As they paused after the scramble up the rocks, a large number of rabbit-sized furry animals with long bushy tails hopped away into the burrows that covered the slopes. Kelpin was enchanted. Only Jankin and Fanna knew what they were.

'Rossells,' said Jankin. 'We used to have things that lived in the trees, I forget what they were called, and things called rabbits that lived on the ground and in burrows. Then about five years ago they died off and these things appeared. We called them rossells because they seem to be a mixture of both animals. The Masters bred them for fur and food. That was one of the reasons the Masters came back to our village. People had begun to kill the rossells and eat them because the fishing was no longer much good and no one wanted to eat the fish with two heads or tails.' It was very quiet. There were no birds and no animals visible, now that the rossells had gone.

'There are some rabbits left,' Scummo informed them. 'Kelpin and I saw one on our way to the coast.'

'Well there are none here,' Jankin said.

It was almost dark now, and the party stopped to rest under a dune. Darfi was still cold and wet. They had nothing to burn to keep them warm and very little food or water. First, they needed to rest. Darfi stood up and began to jump up and down, trying to warm himself up. After a while, Scummo stood in the darkness and announced he was going to go a little way from the group to see if he could spot any lights over the dunes. The land was uneven and full of the holes of rossells, so it was slow going and Scummo was anxious not to get lost. After he had fallen for the third time, his foot caught in a rossell hole, he stood ruefully rubbing his twisted ankle. It was then that he saw it: a bobbing light only a hundred yards away. The light was very feeble, no more than a candle flicker, but it was there, being carried by someone. Did he dare to call out? Had he been seen? Scummo didn't know the answers.

He called out softly. 'Hello-oh.' The light stopped bobbing. Scummo called again. A slender figure was just visible, half-lit by the flickering lantern. The figure was still, then came towards him slowly. It stopped, and again Scummo called out. 'Over here.'

The figure picked its way through the rossell holes towards him. 'Who are you?' The voice was female, cautious.

'We are people like you.'

'Where did you come from?'

'We came here in a boat, yesterday.'

'How many are there of you?'

'Six. We have not been together long. You?'

'There are eight or so. I cannot say exactly because two weeks ago some of us left the group and we have not seen them since that time. We were aware of your arrival. Where did you come from?'

'The City. I was in the Apartments since the Herdings, when I was about twelve. I left with my neighbour's daughter, Kelpin. Her mother died and they would have taken her to the nursery.' His voice cracked a little. He went on quickly, lest his emotion overtake him. 'I just couldn't let that happen, so we left. She's with the others.'

There was silence as the girl digested this information. 'I will meet them.' It was said forcefully, with emphasis. She was used to making decisions.

'I'll show you where we are – if I can find them again myself. This land is tricky to walk over in the dark, with all the holes.' He turned back the way he had come and headed towards the sea.

A voice greeted him. It was Kelpin. 'Scummo!' It was a small, lost, imploring voice.

'Here, Kiddo. I've brought someone back to see us.' He saw dark shapes sitting up at this. 'We've got company.' The girl squatted down on the grassy dune and put her lantern in the middle of them. Darfi's eyes were sunk in their sockets and he was still shivering. Fanna lay next to him, watchful. Jankin and Rondi, recovered now that he was no longer on the boat, sat side by side next to her. Kelpin was on her feet, eager to meet this stranger.

Jankin spoke first. 'It seems we're not alone after all. I'm Jankin.' He pointed to those next to him and introduced them. 'And you are?'

'Sita. You'll understand I can't give you the names of the others. Sita is the name the group gave me, not the one the Masters knew me by.'

As they talked, the history of the group unfolded. These people had been among the last of the groups to be herded, and they had witnessed other groups being rounded up and taken away. Some had decided to make plans to resist the Masters, and they had been brutally killed, or forced to kill themselves. Others, seeing them fail, decided instead to make a run for it and left before the Masters could return. They had access to an old ammunition store, forgotten about by the Masters, and they had led raiding parties from time to time, trying to prevent the herding of other groups along the estuary. They themselves kept moving, unsure what they might achieve, only knowing, as Scummo did, that life under the Masters was no longer an option.

Sita satisfied herself that the group were who they said they were. She would report back to *her* group and they would make contact when it was light. They had to be satisfied with this. Scummo settled down again for what was left of the night and slept, knowing that Sita and her group meant they were no longer alone. He could, temporarily anyway, allow himself to relax.

They spent a cold but hopeful night under the stars and in the morning were relieved to see Sita approaching the hollow where they sat. They stood stiffly and followed her from the clifftop down a shallow verdant valley to a wooded area. The camp here was an arrangement of logs around a hearth and some simple shelters made from saplings and hurdles and roofed with turf and dried grass. The leader, Bethyl, an older woman with a direct gaze and strong, capable hands, invited them to sit and introduced the other group members. There they rested and exchanged stories, and tried to remember all the names, but their tired brains finally begged for sleep, and they were invited to rest on the hay and bracken piles in the shelter. Kelpin felt an instant trust in Bethyl, who had taken on the leader's role and, she understood, had actively fought the Masters and escaped the Herdings. There were several others in the group she did not automatically trust, and she stayed close to Scummo until she felt more at ease. When Scummo wasn't available, she went to Fanna, who sensed her need for affection and gave it unstintingly. Time passed.

Chapter 6

Darfi and Fanna were fishing with Kelpin off the beach with Anga, a plump dark girl of about Darfi's age, and Kelpin was hauling in fish after fish. Those that were malformed in some way she threw back, but the sharpened stick held almost twenty small sardines, pierced through the gills and strung in a line like flags on a pole. It was quiet. The two adults finally called a halt and added their catches to hers.

Darfi called to her. 'Got enough now, Kelpin.' It was a statement.

She pulled a face but gave in gracefully enough. 'Scummo should have seen me,' she said, lower lip quivering a bit. 'When will he come back?' The others looked at one another and Fanna squatted down to be on a level with the little girl.

'We hope he'll come back very soon. But what he is doing is dangerous, so we're all worried about him.'

'Even Darfi?'

'Especially Darfi. You've got us to look after you, as well as the others, until Scummo gets back.'

Darfi came over and patted her head. He was thinner and had grown a little. His hair was now almost to his waist.

'Let's take our fish back to show the others, shall we? Who caught most?'

'I did! Let me carry them.' But she couldn't manage to carry all the fish, which kept slipping off the stick until Darfi took the other end. Together, they walked back along the headland and turned inland along a narrow cleft in the cliffs where a stream ran down to the sea. Continuing into a wooded area, they went down into the hollow where the group was camped.

Sita was on lookout. 'The fishermen are back,' she called to the others.

They handed the fish over to Rondi, who cleaned them and put them on the fire to cook. 'You caught a lot,' he observed, smiling at Kelpin, who was far and away the youngest of the group. He quite enjoyed being a big brother to Kelpin, who was jealous of him for his relationship with Fanna, but who nonetheless was hungry for praise wherever she could find it, even from Rondi. She beamed with pride and wiped her fishy fingers on her felt trousers.

'You'll stink of fish,' he warned her.

'Don't care.'

Rondi sighed. 'Go and ask Fanna for some water to wash in.'

The group settled down to eat, using clam shells as plates, or the large smooth leaves from the plant that grew in clusters at the edge of the stream. Someone had been out collecting nuts, another field mushrooms. These were shared round. It was monotonous fare.

Jankin, the senior male in the group, looked around him at the other members. He was still strong and had his wits about him, but with winter fast approaching, he could feel his bones aching in a way that was new to him and was a portent of things to come. Scummo had gone; whether he would ever return was something none of them knew. With him had gone the group's leader, Bethyl. She would oversee the trip and ensure, if it were possible, that Scummo get back out. She was clever at disguise, knew the City intimately and had her own personal reasons for hating everything the Masters stood for. Jankin had wondered whether he should take on the role of leader in her absence, but he found himself secretly relieved that this had not been expected of him. They were such a precious group of people, faced with such implacable, inhuman adversaries, that each group member had to be valued for whatever unique talents they had. Scummo had found this hard to get used to as the newest arrival, while, for Jankin, it was more or less how the village had operated before the Masters came, except that there the older males had always been in charge of things. Besides Sita and Bethyl, the group they had joined comprised Magrab, who had a stutter and a nervous way of bobbing his head, Anga, Shaful, whom Kelpin took an instant dislike to, Doran, a quiet, solid balding man of twenty-eight, and three young males, Pasto, Arkis and Seton.

There was going to be a meeting once everyone had eaten. He wondered who would lead it. It was often Fanna. Her quiet unassuming style allowed the quieter members of the group to have their say, and they found that the contributions of Darfi, Rondi, Sita and Kelpin, all younger members, were often valuable in looking at the problems they faced with fresh eyes. Jankin had learned something by watching her.

They drew close around the fire and sat down on whatever they could find. Some had clothing or skins taken from abandoned houses during raiding parties; others had made mattresses from sacks stuffed with moss or hay and rested on these. Jankin was uncertain where to sit. Sita gestured to him to share her hay pillow and he sat down, aching a little in the joints as he did so. The firelight flickered on the faces of the group members as they held their hands out towards the flames, trying to wrest the warmth from the fire into their bony fingers.

Darfi asked the question. His long, thick hair, though it was still tied back and fell down his back almost to his waist, also looped in heavy dreadlocks around the side of his face so that it was difficult to see his features clearly from the side. He looked round as he spoke. 'Who will lead the meeting?'

Several hands pointed to Fanna, some to other members. Fanna spoke. 'I would like Jankin to be the leader of this meeting. He is an older member of our group and it is right that he is represented now. Jankin?'

There was a murmur of assent and several members said. 'Aye. Jankin.'

Doran, younger than Jankin, , looked away and said nothing.

'Thank you for your trust, Fanna. As you know, Fanna and I have known one another for a while, as we came from the same village and escaped during the Herdings at the same time.' The members were interested in this. 'Bethyl and Scummo are in the City. Their mission has been to deactivate the food orderly and to take out and destroy the activation device and to find a means of making the dogs helpless. Most of you have not had to live in the City – it's a dreadful place, as I understand it, and I have heard enough about it from Darfi and Scummo to make me realise that we are better off here.

'Scummo went back because he knows the City and he knows how things operate there. Bethyl the same. You or I wouldn't know what to do. Our mission is to survive here, and tomorrow we are going to move this camp to a safer, and we hope warmer, place around the headland, where there are some caves Rondi discovered yesterday. The younger members of this group have once more shown their talents. Rondi, will you tell us about what you found?'

Rondi's hair was still sticking up in tufts where it was regrowing, but his voice was strong, though poised uncertainly between child and adult. 'I found these caves, right? Long way from here – you'd never know they were there. I had to climb over rocks to find them and then the bushes were in the way.'

'How many caves are there?' Fanna asked, gently guiding him.

'There's two big ones, enough to hold all of us, and a little one. Well, not really a cave, more of a hole under the cliff. The stream comes out there.' He paused. He had the attention of the group, and there was a thoughtful silence for a while. Sita spoke first. Her dark curly hair bobbed up and down as she spoke. Though light in build, she had a strong, calm presence.

'We haven't talked about our long-term plans since Bethyl and Scummo left. It's my understanding that when' – she avoided saying *if* – 'they return, we are going to look at ways of setting the occupants of the City free and forcing the

Masters to go back to wherever they came from.'

Kelpin was open-eyed at this. 'My mum was ill and no one looked after her, in the 'partments,' she said.

Fanna and Scummo had formed a team to look after Kelpin, and Kelpin was sharp enough to see the benefits of being cared for in a family group. 'Is it different here, Kelpin?' Fanna asked.

'Yes. It's much gooder,' she answered, making them smile. 'Darfi goes fishing with me and Fanna tells me stories. If I hurt myself, someone makes it better.'

'And that doesn't happen in the City?'

'No.' Kelpin was very emphatic.

Darfi spoke then. 'I was there for a while, in the compound where they keep children, but I ran away when there was a fire. We just used to fight each other. There was nothing else to do. There was more food than there is here, but I wouldn't go back there.'

Jankin asked another question. 'How can so many people be kept in such conditions like prisoners by these Masters? Surely there are enough of them to rebel?'

Fanna spoke for all of them. 'Did you rebel? I didn't, not until I saw what they were capable of. By then it was too late.

Once you let people like that have charge over your food, your housing, work, travel – everything – you come to rely on it. Why would you rebel when you have all you need? Here, all we have is ourselves.'

'But is that better?' Shaful, a man of around twenty-five, with missing teeth, said. 'You're saying we're hungry, cold and poor now that the Masters have destroyed our villages. But is our freedom better than life in the City? We would at least be warm and fed there.'

Others in the group murmured assent.

Jankin realised that he needed to pull them back together, quickly. 'It's more uncomfortable for us being here, that's true, because we don't yet know how to fend for ourselves now we can no longer hunt or farm or fish as we used to. But becoming dependent on the people who drove our neighbours and friends to kill themselves . . . That's not an option for me, anyway. You remember watching your family driven off the cliff, Fanna?'

She nodded.

'Who could allow themselves to trust such people now? And are they even people? They're not like us, remember? They sit up in the sky on those platforms and let the dogs do the work. Did you actually ever see one of them close up?'

None of them had.

'So they don't care about us – we're being used, like we once used our cattle, for their own purposes. We have to stay free. We have to develop a new way of doing things. Above all, we have to look after one another.' Jankin finished speaking and there was a silence in the group.

After a moment, Darfi said, 'Do we know what they might be using us for? We don't have hide or wool, we don't lay eggs, so what are the cities for? Scummo told me about culls, when people are told they're going on a holiday, but no one ever sees them again. But the thing is, they are fattened up before they disappear.'

A dawning look of horror came over the faces of the people round the fire. 'So they're for consumption, you mean? They're being eaten? What a horrible idea!' It was Sita who spoke.

'But maybe a true one,' replied Fanna, holding her hair back with her hands. Her face was grave and thoughtful. 'They must have other uses too. What about the things we saw in the water? What were they eating?' There was silence. Kelpin began to cry, and Fanna squeezed her shoulder.

Sita took up the theme. 'They don't just need us as foodstuff. Scummo said everyone has to work there. What

I don't understand is what their main purpose is. I mean, what are *they'* – she gestured upwards – 'getting out of it? Scummo worked in a mill that recycled fabric into some sort of clothing that they had to wear.'

Kelpin patted her battered felt trousers. The listeners nodded. Fanna shrugged. 'All we know is that we are here because we escaped the Herdings or we escaped from the City. Something in us refused to be rounded up like sheep and made to live in some sort of dreadful compound. We are free, but there are many restrictions on that freedom. We will go hungry, we may be cold, we may lack shelter, but we are not slaves. When the others return we will understand more fully what our choices are and if we submit to the Masters, as certain members here might wish' – here there were some averted eyes – 'then that too will be a decision freely taken.'

Shaful shook his head vehemently. 'I for one reserve the right to return to the City. My life in the village was hard enough, God knows. It will be doubly hard living like this. In three months it will be winter. How in heaven's name will we survive that?'

'Tomorrow we are going to the caves. We will leave a sign for the others to follow when they return. Once they're back, we will know better what to do next.'

During the night, the boat was taken and Shaful and the three young men had gone.

***

The next day the remaining members of the group discovered the loss. But there was nothing to be done. Sita took it badly, for she had tried to befriend Shaful. Forlornly, they assembled the items they would carry with them and began the journey to the caves.

Rondi led the way, full of self-importance, jumping from rock to rock and urging them on with impatience when they lagged behind. It was evening when they arrived, and the sun's low rays were flooding across the sea towards them as they toiled towards their destination.

'It's just round this bend,' he announced finally as they came to the last stretch of rocky headland. The other party members were pleased to hear that, having trailed with their bundles over woodland trails, long grass and finally along the rocky shoreline. Around the bend were trees growing from the cliff face and a stream spreading out over the beach. Sita examined the ground carefully as they went. There were no tracks of anything except rossells, and these ceased when they reached the beach. The caves were hidden under the rocky overhang. A tree partly obscured one entrance, which was halfway up the cliff. Rondi was very excited, but nervous.

Fanna tried to calm him. 'Which cave have you been in, Rondi?'

He pointed eagerly ahead to the lower one. 'There's room for some of us in there.' The others were already investigating. 'And the other one's big,' he went on.

'But you haven't been inside?'

Rondi shook his head. He had been frightened to go in. Fanna understood. She called up to Darfi, who was about to go up there. 'Careful, Darfi. We don't know what might be in there.' Darfi looked at her, paused, then, crouching, entered the uppermost cave. A rossell shot out of it, nearly bringing Darfi out with it.

'Shh,' ordered Fanna as Darfi's yell echoed round the rocks. Jankin followed him up while Kelpin and the others rested, their feet in a pool of seawater, warming their bodies in the sun's last rays.

Suddenly, Kelpin gave a yell. 'Aaaargh! There!' They looked in horror as a large, glistening eel-like shape approached the rock pools from the sea, heading towards them, winding its wicked head along the wet brown sand pools between the rocks. It pushed itself, wet unblinking yellow eyes gleaming, barbed teeth exposed, from the sea to the rock pool they were resting by, but by then they had fled to dry ground and the safety of the cliffs as the creature snaked along, searching for them, then gave up as the ground became dry and retreated back into the sea again.

They stood in a line, watching, clutching their few possessions and shocked by what they had just seen.

Darfi, who hadn't seen the creature, came out of the cave entrance a little way. 'What's up? Come on up here. It's safe.' He ducked inside again.

Fanna's hands were shaking. 'One of the eel things that we saw before came up the beach just now. Was that the same as the creatures we've seen before? Jankin?'

'Maybe. The ones you mentioned had two heads, this had only one.'

Darfi peered anxiously out to sea, but the creature had disappeared; only the setting sun glinted on the calm water as the sea ebbed out bit by bit, exposing the rocks and the sand pools. The others were struggling with tiredness and a sense of having arrived somewhere only to be met with further dangers. A sombre mood settled on the party.

They all went up the rocky path to the higher cave and after examining it, sat down one by one. There was Fanna, serious and gentle, and Darfi with his long hair, who squatted next to Kelpin, her small face determined as always. Jankin, older, reflective, careful, was next to Sita, her rounded, neat features silhouetted against the light slanting into the cave entrance. Rondi was looking anxiously to see what they made of the cave he had led them to. Doran grunted his approval, while Anga, a plump beauty just older than Sita, looked around the cave with interest, though wherever she looked her eyes came back to rest on Darfi. Last to enter was Magrab, whose eyelids nervously twitched as he, too, found his place.

They arranged themselves somehow around the floor of the cave. The floor was level, at least, and filled with pebbles and sand. There were some rossell holes in the corners and an inconvenient root or two from the trees above broke up the sides a little. But the cave was roomy and dry, and the floor could be hollowed out a little to allow for seating. They put their belongings down. There were ten of them, and the cave was crowded.

'What's wrong with the lower cave? We'll be on top of one another in here,' said Darfi.

'We may need to use the lower cave,' Jankin replied, 'but for now we stay here together. The eel thing we saw may not be able to reach the lower cave, but at high tide – well, who knows? We need to be safe for now, all of us. Tomorrow we can see how far the water comes up and if there are tracks in the sand. Here, we can take it in turns to keep watch.'

'What about a fire? That should keep anything away.'

Fanna shook her head. 'Maybe tomorrow night. We don't know who might spot us. We can have a fire before it gets dark – that'll give us just enough time to cook the fish we brought.' The fish, impaled on their sticks, were stiff and beginning to smell. Darfi and Kelpin had caught them forty-eight hours ago.

'What do we do for water?' Darfi asked. Jankin and Fanna were silent.

Rondi, quick-witted, realised that this was not a simple question. 'We can fetch water from the stream,' he observed, 'but one will have to stand guard in case the eel thing comes up the stream.'

'Why don't we trap it?' Kelpin suggested.

Fanna looked at her. 'How would you do that?'

'Make it go into a hole and then block up the hole?'

Rondi was scornful. 'Where is this "hole"? And how could we make it go into it if we had one?'

Kelpin was thoughtful. 'You could make a house for it out of very heavy rocks. Or you could make it come up the stream to the pool then batter it with rocks. Or stab it through the eye. Yow!' She jabbed the air with her finger.

Fanna was astonished. The child had a vivid and practical imagination. 'Kelpin, these are good ideas,' she said. 'Let's eat now, then sleep and talk about this tomorrow. Okay?' The others agreed, and Fanna, looking at Kelpin, realised she would have come up with more answers by dawn. She needed distracting. 'Can I leave you in charge of the fish, Kelpin?'

She was eager to help and soon squatted by the fire Anga and Sita had made from driftwood, holding the fish over the flames. The oil in the fish spat and spluttered a little and the aroma filled the cave. Soon, they had eaten enough. Water was fetched from the stream, and there was no sign of the eel thing. Darfi, fetching the water, with Jankin as lookout, noted that the water came out of the cliff base and entered a pool before trickling its way down the beach. They would need to enlarge the stream bed, make it deeper and wider, if they were to entice the eel thing up into the pool. It was almost dark. He shivered as he pulled up the water container and climbed back up the cliff to the cave.

Fanna kept first watch. They had no means of keeping the time, so she watched until she could keep her eyelids open no longer and woke Darfi, who jumped, forgetting he had been chosen to take the second watch. Apart from the sigh of the sea, all was still and silent.

Anga had just been woken by Darfi for her turn when she felt something brush past her leg. She stifled a scream as a large rossell shot out of the cave, and she clung to Darfi, her heart thumping. Darfi held her warm body close to him and found himself reluctant to let her go. Anga was in no hurry to resume the watch. Something had started between them, and the others noticed in the morning that the two of them were sitting very close together.

As soon as they were awake and had drunk their water, their stomachs still rumbling with hunger despite many days without breakfast, Jankin and Fanna called for the attention of the group. Sleepily, they yawned and stretched and sat up.

'We need to rest and collect food. Those are the first priorities. We have to keep safe from the eel creatures while we do this, so we'll need to keep guard if anyone goes down to the beach. Agreed?' They did. Though the beach looked as clean and unsullied as when they had first set foot there, the tide having washed away all evidence of their arrival, somewhere out there was the eel creature they had seen the day before. How many more might there be? Darfi, cuddled next to Anga, remembered that Kelpin had voiced some ideas about catching the eel. He prodded her. She looked at him sleepily. 'What?'

'Tell us your ideas about catching the eel thing.'

She pulled a face. 'Well, you can catch him in a pond or make a house for him out of big rocks and tempt him to come in. Then when he comes in, batter him.'

Fanna gave this some thought. 'The eel thing is very long, Kelpin. How would we get all of it into a pond or a house trap? And how would we kill it if we did?'

'With all of us there to throw rocks at its head, it shouldn't be too much of a problem.' It was Jankin. 'Attack the head. If you damage that, the rest of the body will die, believe me.' The others looked sceptical.

Rondi said, ''Course we know that. I'm thinking that there may be hundreds of them things – and the ones with two heads – that'll have us whatever we do.'

'If we kill one, we can eat it.' Kelpin, practical as always, spoke up. 'We can't do nothing 'bout the others. But if we learn to kill them, p'raps they'll leave us alone.'

Fanna patted Kelpin on the shoulder. 'Anyone got a better plan?' They hadn't. 'Now, the question is: how?'

After much discussion, they decided to lure the eel thing into the pool and then cut off its escape while they attacked it. Darfi and Rondi would make the pool exit narrower by damming it, which would also make the pool deeper. The water would flow out again through a narrower opening, which they would attempt to close off once the creature was in the pool. They discussed the idea of someone acting as bait. Surprisingly, it was Magrab who volunteered.

'I could do with a good wash,' he told them. 'I shall sit in the pool and wash myself and rely on you lot to keep lookout.'

'Magrab, that's very noble of you,' said Fanna, trying to keep the surprise out of her voice. 'Thank you. Do we all accept Magrab's offer?' There was a general cautious acceptance. They set to work to deepen the pool, taking rocks from the base to build a dam, leaving an outlet just large enough, they hoped, for the eel thing to slip through. It took them most of the morning, and they worked silently and intently. Just after midday, when they were all tired and resting on the rocks near the cave entrances, Kelpin spotted movement in the sea. Several hundred yards away, a dark winding shape was wending its way towards them on the advancing tide.

'Quick! It's coming!' Magrab, shivering with fear, got into the pool, hastily stripping off his overgarments as he did so. The others armed themselves with sharpened sticks and stones and waited behind the rocks where the stream trickled down into the pool.

Magrab splashed himself noisily and called out, 'Where is it?'

'Still coming up the beach. Looks the same one as before.'

The eel thing snaked along through the wet sand pools and rocks, pausing now and then to investigate patches of weed. Reaching the drier sand, it slithered towards the channel made by the stream and began the ascent to the pool. The tide washed along behind it. They watched it approach, filled with terror and fascination. Magrab was shivering uncontrollably, his eyes watching the narrow gap through which the eel thing would come. It paused, tasting the water, before slithering upstream until it reached the entrance to the pool. Here it paused again, moving its snake-like head back and forth to see what lay beyond the gap in the rocks. Magrab saw its eyes sizing him up through the gap as the head waved back and forth. It was then that Magrab panicked and leapt up, slithering over the rocks at the back of the pool while Darfi and Jankin grabbed his arms. The eel thing, far from being frightened, slithered through the hole, desperate to catch this prey that was suddenly evading it. Magrab's leg was inches from its mouth.

But one person had not lost their nerve. Kelpin, watching from the cliff, hurled down a large stone that missed the three men and landed on the eel's back, splashing up water all around. Sita and Darfi, who had moved to the pool entrance, blocked up the hole while the others, taking their cue from Kelpin, attacked the creature with whatever they could find. Still, the snake-head of the thing rose from the water, weaving back and forth in an effort to locate its prey. Then a mighty blow from a rock thrown by Jankin seemed to stun it, and it sank to the bottom of the pool. Fanna, using her stick as a spear, gave the fatal blow, stabbing it through the eye as it writhed furiously on the muddy rocks at the bottom of the pool. Then it was still.

They were all covered with sand, mud, and eel-slime. Magrab's legs were bruised and cut where they had been pulled over the rocks. Anga was weeping on Darfi's shoulder. Kelpin sought Fanna and wrapped her arms around her legs. Jankin prodded the eel again, carefully, but it didn't move. 'Looks like supper's taken care of. Who's got the knife?'

Darfi produced it and, deftly, Jankin cut the head of the eel off and dragged the rest of the body onto the beach. He left the head where it was in the pool, the undamaged eye now clouding over, the wicked little teeth bared in a deathly grin.

All the while they were working, Rondi kept lookout. They were all frightened in case there might be creatures that, scenting blood, might decide to join them. Remembering the practices in the village before the Masters came, they cut the eel into strips and with difficulty, for the eel-skin was tough, strung them on sharpened sticks.

Fanna had a suggestion. 'We can use a small cave as a smoke hole and smoke the meat in there – then it would keep for ages. My grandfather used to do that; he told me about it. There was a smoke room in our village, but it was gone before I was born.'

Jankin took up the theme. 'I remember where it was. The roof was all black and sticky. They had it knocked down – I never saw it working. We could try it?'

Sita was sceptical. 'And waste the precious meat if it doesn't work?'

'We don't have many alternatives. Personally, I'd be happy to give it a try. Dry some in the open air, smoke some and eat some today – that's best.'

'Meanwhile, the flies are going to have a feast.' It was true; the flies were beginning to arrive. They would have to do something. The eel head lay in its pool of cloudy, bloody water, teeth tipping the surface, where they had thrown it further down the beach. Flies obscured it.

There was debate about whether to light a fire then or wait until night.

No one was sure about the Masters. Just because they had been no sign of them didn't mean they were not being watched, eavesdropped on and spied upon.

Hunger took over. They lit a fire in the entrance to the large cave and toasted the eel then ate it. It was tough and stringy, but they were no longer hungry. Kelpin was thoughtful as she looked at the sharp bones of the eel's vertebra littering the cave. 'P'raps we could use these for something.'

'What?' Sita asked.

'They're very sharp. Like pins. They can make holes in things.'

Darfi stopped munching and picked up a white, sharp segment. 'We should make use of everything we have.' He held the segment up. It was sticky and beginning to smell. 'If we bury the bones they won't smell, and the insects will eat the meat, so they'll be clean. Nothing to lose anyway.'

'Will you do it?'

Darfi sighed. 'Yes – maybe here.' He used a stick to dig out a shallow hole in the dirt on the cliff side, piled the bones in and covered them over, marking the place with a stick. 'There.'

'All of you listen a minute,' Jankin said. 'Since the Masters arrived, our way of life has changed so much most of us, especially the young ones, won't remember what life was like before they came. We've forgotten so much – all the things that we depended on for our survival. Do you remember that there was a time when we grew our own crops, kept our own animals, made what we needed and traded with the other villages to get things we didn't have? When the Masters arrived, we became dependent on them and we lost our skills. Now we have to find them again. Use your memories. It's all you have to guide you. Remember what your parents, your grandparents, told you. We have to invent a new way of living now.'

There was silence in the group and finally Fanna spoke. 'We are up against some things we have never come across before. We don't know what other dangers face us. I've never known what it's like to live in a City and be fed and housed by other people – we've always built our own houses, looked after one another, haven't we, Jankin? Sita has never known the City, neither has Magrab, yet it's little Kelpin who seems to be leading the way. The point I'm making is that we all have different experiences and talents and knowledge, and we have to make use of all of them. We have to decide together how we live, where we go, what we do. We're not all going to agree all of the time, but only by sticking together and facing these problems will we survive at all. Do you agree?'

They did.

'We faced a huge danger just a while ago, and we don't know whether the eel things will come back or how many there are, but we did well. We did well.'

There were nodding heads and smiles as she spoke. Darfi, who had been piling up sand on top of the eel mound with Rondi, wanted to know what the plan was. What would they do now?

'I think,' said Darfi, speaking for the first time but warming to the theme, 'that we must keep ourselves safe first of all. While we've been talking, who's been watching to see if any more eel things are coming to get us?'

The group looked guiltily around them, scanning the tide line.

'We've killed one, but that doesn't mean we can relax. I was safe on my barge for a long time, until Scummo and Kelpin arrived, then because it wasn't safe, we had to leave. It's still not safe. But I remember the City. I don't want to go back there. All I want is for us to have some agreement about how we do things now.'

Magrab spoke, his nervous tic accentuated by the attention. 'We have several pressing needs – food, shelter, p-protection from danger. We have to p-protect ourselves first otherwise the other two don't matter. We've got the cave, thanks to Rondi. That makes me think there can't be too many of the eel things along this coast or Rondi wouldn't have been able to explore it so well in the first place.'

They nodded at this.

'But we mustn't be complacent. Just now we have food, shelter and experience of protecting ourselves from one danger at least. I think we've done well. What concerns me, which no one's talked about before, is how Scummo and Bethyl will find us again if they return.'

Kelpin pulled a face and looked about to cry. Fanna put a hand on her arm. 'I left a sign,' she said, 'leading along the coast this way. Bethyl and I talked about it before she left. Unless they cut all the trees down it'll be there when they come back.' She didn't say 'if', but the word hung in the air, unanswered.

Kelpin dreamed about Scummo most nights. He was trying to come back, but something was stopping him. He was locked in a dark smelly hole with no food or water. They were in the hut once more, and the silver spy camera thing came out of the wall this time and twisted around like the eel thing on the beach. She woke from these dreams sweating and clutching at Fanna's garments. She did not dream of Bethyl.

Chapter 7

It was Sevenday afternoon in the Apartments of Broilerhouse Eight, and the Apartment-dwellers were out on their balconies, waiting for the contests to start. On the boards in the entrance were the names of those scheduled to fight. Andalou, the rangy, stringy-muscled neighbour, was leaning over the balcony outside the apartment that had belonged to Scummo. Another woman had been moved into Minna's apartment. Andalou was interested in her, but so far she hadn't responded. He hugged a mug of gabbobrew and watched the crowds collect around him.

He thought of Scummo. What had happened to him? Andalou missed him. There were few friendships in the Apartments. The effort of living day by day left little time for socialising, but Scummo was around the same age as Andalou and each had acknowledged the presence of the other as a young male. Andalou knew Scummo's name had not been on the cull list; neither had he been in a fight. Had he died? Mysterious outbreaks of a flu-like illness killed a number of residents every year, leading to quarantine restrictions for those around them. So far, the virus had been contained by locking the landings of any apartment with a sick member, putting the dogs at the entrance to prevent escape. The sick ones soon died, their bodies dragged away by the dogs and devoured. After twenty-four hours of no new cases, those who were left alive were allowed off their balconies again. Scummo had not been part of any quarantine that Andalou knew of. That left only one alternative. He had left the City, either by being taken or by running away. The fight below began, and it was short and bloody. Andalou felt excited and sickened by the spectacle. The contest ran its grisly course, and as the bodies were cleared away, the chorus of dogs baying reached a crescendo. Feeding time.

He still shuddered, despite having heard it all before. The crowd was disgruntled at the brief contest; they had hoped for a longer, more exciting spectacle. They began to drift away. He looked across to the other side of the arena. A man was making his way down the stairway. He looked oddly familiar. Something about the walk and the way he held himself reminded Andalou of Scummo. He blinked and looked away, then looked back and saw that the figure was looking across at him. As he returned the man's gaze, the other put his finger to his lips in a gesture of secrecy. Andalou silently held his thumb up, not looking at the man. His heart beat fast. Was it? *Could* it be Scummo? And if he were not, why the gesture enjoining him to silence? Andalou went back into his apartment.

In the morning, he looked for the man again in the food queue. He was there, lining up with the rest of his block at the very end of his line. The man had a slight stoop and several days' growth of beard. His hair was longer than Scummo's had been and a darker colour. Yet the resemblance was striking. Andalou held out his tin as he reached the front of the queue and received, from the blank-faced creature in charge of the van, the expected portion of porridge, gabbo leaves and biscuit. As he turned away and began to walk back to his apartment, a scuffle began behind him. He turned and saw that the man had grabbed hold of the clothes of the creature in the van and now had him by the throat. The dogs were barking now in frenzy, but Andalou, frozen to the spot, saw that they were not biting the man, whose grip on the throat of the creature had not weakened. The dogs were staying back, unsure. The remaining residents fled to their Apartments, terror on their faces. Andalou stayed where he was. Then something strange began to take place; the dogs began to run in circles, chasing their own tails. This was something he had never observed them do before, and he watched in astonishment as the dogs ran faster and faster. Round and round they went, like spinning tops. Then at some inaudible signal they stopped, wobbled, fell over, flopped down, staggered upright, shook themselves and gave a pathetic whimper. Then together, as if to a signal, they lay down. Andalou was amazed. The Scummo-like man, his arm still round the neck of the Masters' creature, was busily manipulating something in the back of its head with his other arm. The blank white oval face of the thing began to turn red, then dark. The lights that had flickered under the surface went out. Andalou guessed the thing must have been deactivated. He was impressed. The man let go of the creature he had been holding and it fell to the floor with a noise like a bag of loose bones. Andalou stepped towards the man, now looking him full in the face. It was Scummo. It really was.

Scummo stood up straight. 'Andalou.'

'Scummo. I thought it was you.'

'No time to talk. We have work to do.'

'We? Me? Or are you with someone else?'

'Both. Want to join us? Too late – you're in it now. Over here.' He gestured to the stairwell. 'They can't watch us here.'

Together, they huddled under the stairs. The dogs got up all of a sudden and trotted away. The mobile canteen, which usually left the compound as soon as the rations had been dispensed, was still there. Scummo left the shelter of the stairway and beckoned to Andalou to follow. He approached the canteen from the back and got inside. Orderly canisters of beans, turnips and other rations filled up the space, but under the serving hatch was a closed container with some writing on it. Quickly, Scummo opened it. Special rations. A cull must be planned. Scummo filled his pockets and a plastic bag with the stuff. Andalou, hesitating at first, did the same.

'No time to talk,' Scummo hissed urgently at him. 'We have to get this thing moving again.' They worked out the primitive controls and moved it backwards, out of the arena of Broilerhouse Eight.

'Now what?' Andalou knew the Masters would be watching now, watching and deciding what to do. Scummo wished he could be reassuring. So far, the plan was working, but he hadn't reckoned on having another person with him, though Andalou was the one person he might have chosen, had he had the option.

'Over here. This should do it.' They steered the canteen towards the underpass, out of sight of the buildings. Several workers returning from a shift were coming back through the underpass and gaped in surprise to see the canteen all but blocking their exit. Scummo and Andalou got out and ran through the underpass to the hover-platform stop.

'What happens now?'

'Follow me.' The hover-platform approached. His mouth open in anticipation, Andalou followed Scummo as he jumped on board. The five other passengers watched them with interest but in silence. It was not time for Andalou to go to work. Surely it would be noticed if he was making an unauthorised journey? He clenched his hands, nervously. Scummo did something to the meter, and four blocks along the road, grabbed Andalou's arm.

'Here. Jump.' Andalou did as he was told and the two of them jumped off the moving platform, toppling over as they landed in the dirt at the roadside. Andalou rubbed the grit off his palms ruefully.

'Puts the dogs off our trail,' Scummo explained. 'Over here.' They ran to a building on the edge of the Old Town and Scummo rapped three times on the door. It was opened by a Geld, plump belly jutting out over his felt trousers.

'Come in,' he said, eyebrows arched. 'I'm always happy to welcome visitors.' He gestured to the dimly lit room behind him. 'Make yourselves at home.' Andalou was full of curiosity, full of a million questions that needed to be answered. Scummo's eyes were scanning the room. The Geld came in and closed the door. He stood with hand on hip, appraising them.

'Well. Look at the two of you. Just as well they warned me it was more than one of you. Which one is Scummo?' Scummo raised his arm. 'Lovely name,' he said with heavy sarcasm. 'Whose idea was it?'

'Not mine,' answered Scummo. 'Someone shouted it at me when I arrived and the name stuck. Did you know people had proper names once, before the Herdings? Names their parents gave them?'

'I got my name because of where my father came from,' said Andalou. 'What happens next, Scummo? Because believe me, when they find out what we did to their creature back there and find the trolley, we are going to be in deep shit. Where have you been, anyway?'

Scummo's dark eyes looked far away for a moment. 'Better if I don't tell you too much. Let's just say I'm back here on a mission.'

The Geld was listening, and Scummo stopped.

'A mission? To do what?'

'No time to explain. I'll tell you later. You'll just have to trust me.' Scummo sat on the floor with his legs stretched out in front of him.

'What happened to your ankle tag?' Andalou rubbed his own tag, as if he'd forgotten it was there.

'We cut them off.'

'Who's "we"?'

'The people who are coming.' Scummo twisted his long dirty hair in his fingers. Suddenly there was a knocking coming from the floor below them. The Geld listened intently and then moved aside a mat to reveal a trapdoor with a neatly sunken iron ring. Grabbing this, he pulled up the heavy stone cover and called down.

'Password?'

'Shadowfriend. Who seeks to leave?'

'Greetings, Shadowfriend.' Scummo has with him a person called Andalou, who seeks to leave—'

'Hold on,' interrupted Andalou. 'This means leaving my apartment, my job – everything. Here at least I know where my next meal's coming from and that I'll be safe. Out there, wherever that is, I wouldn't have a clue.'

Scummo's reply was to the point. 'You have to choose. A long slow death by boredom – until they get hold of you for interfering with the canteen – or the chance to hit back, to feel really alive, to do something for once without being programmed to do it. I thought you were sharp and tough – was I wrong?'

Andalou shook his head. 'It's just a very big step to take,' he said, still weighing it up. 'Okay. Count me in.'

Scummo grasped his shoulder in a display of brief affection.

Andalou froze. 'Sorry, Scummo. Just not used to anyone touching me.'

'I was like that myself. It took a small girl to convince me things could be different.' Scummo went carefully down the steps and Andalou followed. The Geld swiftly replaced the stone. The person identified as Shadowfriend beckoned to them to follow, and, stooped over in the dry, narrow passage, they followed the bobbing light of the lantern carried by their guide.

***

The Masters were discussing the problem. 'They appear to have evaded us. The dark one, who has no tag and is identified only as SCUM04, we believe left here for the first time nine months ago with a girl-child. We observed them for a while, then we lost them. The other, BH4A79, known as Andalou, still has his tag. When they come above ground we shall get a signal. Until then, we wait.'

'Inconvenient. The Andalou one was good at working, I think. One of the fitter ones.'

'But no good for reprocessing. Though paste, possibly?'

'One would be inclined to let them go to see what they do next. We learned some useful information from the dark one before his tag was removed. I think we adjusted the feed, did we not, in the light of what we discovered?'

'So we wait for them to reappear, then? And what if the others get ideas?'

'We must discourage independent thought. It's almost bred out of them now anyway, but we don't want any others doing this.'

'Have we sorted out the problem with the dogs now?'

'Yes. But they may have taken the dazer.'

'It can't be helped.'

***

Scummo's head jerked on his scrawny neck. He had been asleep. The gloom around him was much the same whether his eyes were open or shut, but eventually he could make out the details of the space he was in. He was sitting on the stone floor of an underground room, and his back was leaning on a cold, damp wall. He shut his eyes again and leant his head back. Five minutes later, it lolled forwards again and he woke with a jerk.

What had happened to Bethyl? He couldn't tell how long she had been away. Here there was no way to measure time. A draught blew into the room from the far corner. It chilled him but the air was fresh. Someone or something was approaching. He saw a shape move towards him.

'Bethyl?' His voice was a hoarse whisper.

'It's me. I'm sorry it took so long, Scummo.'

'Where's Andalou?'

'Returning. How's the foot?'

'Can't feel it. Don't know if that's good news or not.'

'Could be either. We need to get you out of here so I can have a proper look at it. Can you stand?'

'Not sure. I'll try.' With difficulty, Scummo levered himself upwards with his good leg, holding on to Bethyl. 'I'll try to put some weight on it and see what happens.' He cautiously put some weight on his bad foot. 'I can hobble,' he announced. 'I think I sprained it. I don't think it's broken.'

Andalou met them halfway along the passageway. He was carrying a bundle on his back. In single file, Bethyl leading, they left the cellar and headed along the dank subterranean passages that lay under the old part of the City. Bethyl paused every now and then to check – with her fingers – the stones placed on the corners of each junction. Scummo, hobbling painfully, wondered if it would be like this to have no eyes and to have to rely on touch alone. There were no blind people in the Apartments, no people who couldn't walk. What happened to them? he wondered. He thought he could guess.

They moved on, slowly, carefully, stooping where the ceiling was low. He found this particularly difficult with his painful foot. Sometimes there was no light, sometimes a little, but when it became so dark they couldn't see at all, Bethyl stopped and drew out something from her pocket. It was a penny-sized, luminous dial that gave out a thin green light.

After a while, they came to a storm drain and had to crawl along it to where they could dimly see daylight. The metallic, rusty smell that came from the drain filled their noses as they crawled, knees sliding in the orange sludge, towards the exit. Finally, they were there. It had taken three hours.

The storm drain ended in a broad concrete apron that fed water from the land into the drainage system. They were hidden from view in this apron, but Scummo could see familiar plants waving as they grew at the edges to the fields around the drains. They arranged themselves around the apron and considered the situation. Bethyl sat next to Scummo, reaching towards him with concern in her eyes.

'Let me see the foot.'

Scummo presented his foot for her inspection. The ankle was swollen and discoloured. He winced when she touched it. She prodded it with expert fingers, making him bend and rotate his ankle. His foot was dirty and discoloured with bruising. Bethyl gently wiped it clean, using leaves and some wet, spongy moss growing around the drain opening. The coolness soothed his foot a little.

'A bad sprain. You ought to stay off it for a few hours. Andalou, do you have any ideas for helping Scummo?'

Andalou was gazing at the sky, the green waving tops of the corn above him, the apron of concrete now wet in patches where they had sat, and on his face was a look of awe and astonishment.

'Andalou?'

He turned to look at them, dark eyes full of wonder. 'It's so big. I had no idea all this was out here. So much of it, I mean. I'd forgotten. I want to hide somewhere. Scummo – sorry. I once wrapped some cloth round my arm when I hurt it. I have some clothing you could tear, if you want to try.'

The two men smiled at one another. It was good to have Andalou here, thought Scummo, someone who knew what the City was like. Bethyl had escaped during the Herdings and had never lived there, though she had carried out raiding trips and now knew the layout well. Andalou ripped up his old grey singlet and bound up Scummo's ankle. Bethyl smiled at them. Her strong, weather-beaten face was often very still, a contrast to Fanna's expressive features. Fanna often looked pale and drawn, whereas Bethyl appeared fit and sturdy. Her dark brown eyes scanned the horizon constantly for danger as she stood, brushing the oily slime from the drain on her felt trousers. Her broad, muscular hands could competently mend nets, make snares, shape pots and inflict blows. She used all these skills regularly. Scanning the ground near the apron, she moved with certainty towards a clump of ragwort, a tall yellow weed growing in the uncertain margins of the field. She studied the ground, then leaned forwards and reached for a clump of grass, which she pulled carefully so that a large clod of earth came away. She placed this upside down on the grass. Where the section of grass had been was a hole. Bethyl reached into this and pulled out several bottles and a sturdy plastic bag tied at the top with string. Replacing the clod, she took these to Scummo and Andalou.

'What have you got?'

'Emergency supplies. A previous party left these here. We need something to eat and drink before we can continue, and if we stay here, it will give Scummo's ankle a chance to heal. That is, if it is a sprain and not a break.'

Scummo frowned. 'Better not be a break. But what if it is?'

Bethyl grinned. 'Oh, we just cut your foot off.'

'Thanks – that cheers me up no end.' He gripped the swollen ankle and rubbed it, hard. Then he rotated his foot, carefully, wincing as he did so. 'Hmm. Just have to wait and see.' He stretched out on the grass, changed his mind and turned so that his foot was higher than his head. Bethyl watched him, carefully.

Andalou, quietly resting, took charge of the food. They ate in silence.

Later, they left under the cover of darkness and although Scummo's foot hurt him, the rest had done him good and the ankle was now less swollen. They went up over the field, following the water-course, and over the brow they came to a reservoir, shining like quiet black silk in the darkness.

Here they replenished their water supplies and made their way to the far end, where a dam carried an ancient track across the valley. It became wooded, and the little group kept to the cover of the trees. Andalou found a stick for Scummo to lean on. It was very dark in the wood and Andalou was terrified, but Bethyl, who seemed to have good night vision, led the way unerringly, whispering to them from time to time.

Scummo found the pain in his ankle eased as he exercised it, but he walked cautiously with his stick, aware that any fall or stumble would cause the sharp stabbing pain to shoot up his leg again and make him cry out. Bethyl didn't try to hurry them.

When day broke, they had reached the end of the wood and Bethyl made them stop and rest. They were in a clearing that led to a deserted quarry. The early autumn air was chilly in the dawn light, but they rested in the quarry and Bethyl lit a fire with brushwood to warm them.

'Where now?' Andalou was anxious. He would rather be on the move than holed up in some weird place miles from his familiar world.

Bethyl looked at him with sympathy. 'You're doing well, Andalou. I've known many people who left the City and haven't been able to cope with all the space out here.'

'Where are they now?' Scummo asked. Andalou was silent.

'I wish I knew. We were attacked by a herding party, just as we were reaching the limits of the Masters' territory. I escaped by covering myself with leaves and they would have found me, but the dogs were distracted by a rossell and went after that instead. The others were rounded up and taken back to the City. But they were so afraid of being free I don't think they'd have made it anyway.'

'Why did they come with you to start with?'

Bethyl grinned. 'I didn't give them much choice. They were a little work unit and I was being followed, so I hid with them and then had to take them with me when they discovered where I was. Let's say I talked them into it.'

'But how did you all get out?'

Bethyl smiled her mysterious smile. 'I don't talk about survival secrets because the Masters are very good at interrogating people and the less you know the better. But in answer to your first question – "Where now?" – we are heading for the coast. We should reach it at around midnight tonight. Then we should find the boat we came in waiting to take us round the coast. Does that answer your question?'

They set off again and travelled downhill through a long, wooded valley until at last they could hear the sea gently hissing through the trees. A small sailing boat was waiting for them as Bethyl had predicted, and the skipper introduced himself as Sarnon. They stowed the light bundles they carried in the back of the boat and allowed themselves to sleep while Sarnon expertly moved around them, checking the sails. There was a fresh breeze, and before morning they had reached the rocky headland that signalled the camp they had left. Scummo, awake, saw the dark line of the shore silhouetted on the indigo dark of the water in the faint dawn light. How would Sarnon guide the boat in? He beckoned to Scummo, and they woke the others, Sarnon meantime taking down the sail. They drifted in with the tide as Sarnon and Andalou rowed slowly and steadily towards the shore.

Chapter 8

Time passed. Back in the City, the Apartments were beginning to wake up. The inhabitants of Broilerhouse Eight were still indoors, waiting for the dog wardens to finish their rounds. The claws scratching the walkways, the barking, growls and sniffing at doorways, all these things were part of morning life. In the Apartments, the cell clocks in their clumsy wooden cases all read the same: Twoday, year – 891, time – 6.70. By 7.00, most of the inhabitants would have left their shelf beds, shaken out their bedding and washed in cold water, unless they could be bothered to boil some on the inadequate gas supply. Dressed, they waited for the food wagon to come round, armed with their tins. Once they'd eaten, either standing up or back inside the Apartments, they would head to the conveyor platform stops to await transport to their place of work. Having received their powdered milk ration from the dispenser, children would then go to a collecting point in the yard where the dogs guarded them until the crèche opened on the ground floor. Every day, barring Sevenday, was the same.

The Apartments themselves were very compact. Each door on the landing opened into a narrow room with a shelf bed, a tiny cupboard and a chair. Such personal belongings as there were were stowed under the bed, which could be pushed up and fastened against the wall when extra space was needed. In practice, this rarely happened. The cell-like room gave way to a galley with a cold-water sink, a bucket and a single gas burner. A shelf held the dinner tin, gabbobrew, a mug or two and whatever eating implements there might be. At the end of the galley was a tiny room with a toilet hole set in concrete, covered by a metal lid. Residents were given rations of cleaning tablets once a week, which they were supposed to mix with water in their buckets to clean the concrete hole. Every morning, as the residents rose, the clang of metal lids reverberated on the concrete as each resident used the facility, followed by a sloshing of water from the buckets. Each apartment block had its own laundry and shower room, but these were seldom used, being too cold in the winter or broken.

Hardy women who wanted to make full use of their time did their washing by hand at night and hung the wet laundry out to dry first thing in the morning. No one could move outside in the morning until the dog wardens had finished their rounds, but as soon as their barks and scrabbling paws had died away, the whole building came alive, and workers with breakfast tins descended the stairways and queued for their food.

There were endless fights and squabbles between neighbours about boundaries, party walls and noise. The few hours after work in which it might have been possible to socialise were often taken up in this way, with petty quarrels and shouting matches. People guarded their own space with a jealous fury, and it was rare for one person to enter another's apartment and unknown for anyone to help his neighbour.

In this respect, Scummo was exceptional. Kelpin's direct appeal brought to life something he had almost forgotten: simple, uncomplicated exchange between two people. People mostly lived alone in the Apartments. Being alone, they forgot how to be normal with others in the fight to survive and defend their own space. That this space might not be worth fighting for, they could not even consider. It was all they had.

When another epidemic of sickness came to the Apartments, the first to succumb were the very young and the people who worked in the meat paste factory. As soon as the first workers had staggered out of the factory clutching their sides and moaning, the Masters sent the dogs in and rounded all the workers up and herded them outside the city walls. They placed a cordon around the factory and sent machines in to fumigate it. The workers outside the city walls shivered in the dark as the dogs ran up and down, growling at them. The Masters ordered them to board the buses in groups of twenty, where the signs on the sides saying Jamarama were still just visible. In batches, they were taken away, no one knew where, and other workers were brought in to fill their places. It was as though they had never existed. The empty Apartments were soon filled with new workers, brought in from the clearing-houses they had been processed in. Not all the new workers were as compliant as the older ones had been, despite the processing. The sickness returned, in a lesser form. People collapsed on walkways, passed out on hover-platforms, could not go to work. Those found sick were rounded up and taken to the vans that waited for them outside the City. Then large segments of the City were divided up, and the food rations were increased slightly. Fences were erected around some of the closed sections and the people there did not go to work. Along with the food rations each morning, residents were handed a beaker containing a bitter green liquid and told to drink it. Most did so. Still more people became sick, and the Masters segregated them, removing them group by group in the vans marked Jamarama under the thin white paint. Slowly, the sickness passed.

Of the three that had returned to the City with Shaful, thinking it might be better than life in the open, only Shaful himself was left. The journey had taken many days as they skirted the estuary and headed inland towards the City. One young man had slept too close to the water's edge and been attacked by an eel creature; two had died of the terrible fever after their arrival. The trio had been rounded up as soon as they entered, taken to a central depot and tagged, then allocated Apartments in the same block Scummo and Andalou had inhabited. They were sent to work in a warehouse to work on the conveyor belts, picking stones and leaves out of the steady rows of dark brown beans that flowed past them in an unceasing stream. With aching backs and unfocused eyes, they left this labour at night exhausted and hungry and were transported back to their Apartments, where they could pick up their ration of cooked beans and protein biscuits before going to their living quarters. They became sick in the weeks that followed, and one morning, Shaful looked for them in the food line and they had gone. Truly alone now, Shaful took to talking to himself, profanities that exploded with bitterness from his flapping lips.

He was shunned by the other residents and found himself wondering from time to time if his return had been a mistake. He remembered his past life in the village before the Masters came to dominate their days with their senseless edicts and rules. Chickens had run about there freely before the Masters started interfering in their lives. Afterwards, they were instructed to keep them in closed cages. Some had escaped the cages to lay their eggs in a more private place and sit on them until they hatched. The eggs, being unfertilised, never did hatch, and the hens risked all the terrors of the rapacious wildlife that visited the villages. Would they have gone back into the cages voluntarily? Shaful thought not. Why, he wondered, had he needed to see so badly what life was like in the City? Was it just because it was different? He didn't know. He looked despairingly at the hard shelf bed, the four grey walls of his apartment, his meagre food rations, and felt a loss so acute that his gut ached with the pain of it. He screamed obscenities until his throat hurt. No one appeared to notice.

The first apartment on B Landing belonged to Beggis, a red-haired woman of twenty-one. Beggis and her apartment were slightly different from the others. She had managed to decorate her apartment during the long lonely evenings with an astonishing array of murals. For paint she had used soot, gabbobrew dregs, blood taken from her own hand and colours obtained from boiled-up weeds and whatever else she could find in her work as a rag-sorter. The effect was mainly monochrome, but that didn't diminish the impact. On the wall above the shelf bed was written: *The place is the prisoner: It can't change. We can.* Below was a mural of the scene across the courtyard: stark blocks with walkways and stairs, washing, drainpipes, balcony rails. Beggis wore her felt overtrousers and jacket with pride, twisting her bright hair into corkscrews on top of her head and tying them with string.

She was late for the hover-platform. She tucked a bundle of papers under her jacket as she ran out of the door. The feeding station was about to leave. She had missed her turn, but today she did not mind. She would go hungry until nightfall. She jumped onto the bus, keeping her arms to her sides to avoid losing the bundles of papers under each arm. Clocking in at the factory, she went to her workstation, then, when unobserved, slipped down the side corridor to the ladies' washrooms. Fishing out the bundles of papers, she extracted about twenty and left them neatly in a pile by the door, with a small handwritten note: *Please take one.* Satisfied, she returned to her workstation.

Other women began to come into the factory. The guard dogs at the factory entrance went off duty and the workplace settled into its usual routine. Throughout the day, Beggis was aware of women looking at her. They didn't catch her eye, but she caught several of them glancing over in her direction, especially Chasna, a sweet-faced blonde girl who lived two doors down from Beggis.

During the lunch break, as Beggis was lining up with the others by the brew dispenser, Chasna caught her arm. Beggis jumped. Such familiarity was not usual. 'Chasna!'

'Shh! They might hear you. Bend your head over.'

Beggis obediently bent her head and Chasna whispered in her ear. 'I'll do it. Count on me.'

Beggis squeezed her arm. A pact was sealed.

She now had to deal with the second bundle of papers, which, secured with tape inside her jacket, were presently hidden from view.

The factory next door was a manufacturing plant for the biscuits they had dispensed to them once a week. The workforce was male in the main, and the members who worked night shifts there had their own lodging house at the end of the Apartment blocks. The dogs did not make their usual morning and evening calls to this Apartment. Beggis, returning on the conveyor platform after work, clutched the papers to her side as she scurried round the side of her block towards these Apartments. She knew she would be monitored by the spy cameras. Whether anyone would then act on what they saw there, she had no way of knowing.

In the stairwell, she took out the bundle of papers, undid the string and placed them face up on the bottom stair. The words shouted at her: 'FREEDOM FOR ALL!' In smaller lettering underneath were the words 'Freedom to Leave the City! Freedom to Live Together! And Freedom to Enjoy Leisure Time!' Some rather primitive drawings accompanied the text.

From their platform, the Masters observed with interest this red-haired young woman, who apparently had no fear, leave the building and return to her own apartment. They would have to act at some point, but at present their interest in what was going on got in the way of their stopping it. One zoomed in on a leaflet.

'Freedom for all? What does that mean? Do they want to starve to death out there?'

'Possibly want the right to do that if they wish. I'll have to speak to them, I suppose.'

The next morning, as the inhabitants of the Apartments lined up for their rations, a shrill whistle blast caused the dogs to halt in their tracks. Everyone stayed still, waiting for the inevitable announcement. A booming voice came from the sky.

'Citizens of Broilerhouse Eight, it has come to our attention that someone among you has been spreading lies. I refer to the papers some of you will have picked up or seen. You already have your freedom! If anyone doubts it, I suggest they walk out of the Apartments now and leave the City. I can assure you, we will not attempt to prevent you.'

There was a pause. Beggis looked at her shoes. The silence grew. She knew it was now or never. Then she pulled herself upright, drew a deep breath and prepared to march forwards alone to the street outside. Watched by six hundred anxious eyes, Beggis took first one, then another step forwards. There was a movement at the back of the crowd. Chasna!

Chasna, with her ragged fringe and round blue eyes, came through the crowd as the curious eyes of the workers watched her sideways, not daring to show too much interest. She stood alongside Beggis, who had stopped walking, and linked arms with her. Beggis glanced at her and smiled. There was a silence in the crowd. Would anyone else come and join them?

Beggis faced the crowd. 'I'm tired of my life here. Tired and bored. I know things can be better than this. So do you.' Her red hair shone.

A man standing near her shuddered and tried to turn his face away from her. Another shouted, 'Good for you, girl.' But he made no move to come forwards and join her. Chasna challenged them with her blue eyes.

'Where'll you go?' The question came from a woman on the same landing.

Beggis replied, defiantly, 'Away from here. I know . . . I *know* that life can be different. I don't know where, or how, or what I'll eat, or where I'll live, but I just know I have to get away.'

'And I'm going with her,' replied Chasna.

The voice of the Masters boomed out. 'Here you are fed,

sheltered, given work, provided with everything essential for your needs. But if you feel you must leave it all and go, then go. Go now.'

Sensing that the opportunity would soon be lost, Beggis and Chasna took several steps forwards. The crowd, disgruntled, muttered to one another about not knowing when you were well off and jumping from the frying pan into the fire. As the two women marched slowly and with dignity out of the arena, Beggis shouted, 'At least it won't be boring! I'll be thinking of you!'

The grey, shut faces of the residents gave her nothing back for a reply. The voice from the sky bellowed, 'Go to your workstations now, residents of Broilerhouse Eight. Repeat. Go to your workstations. No more food will be dispensed this morning.' Muttering and grumbling, the residents clanged their dinner tins and shuffled back towards their Apartments to leave their tins before heading off to the conveyor-platforms.

'All because of them,' said one man, angrily, to his neighbour.

'Yes. Don't know when they're well off. They've done us out of our morning rations, they have. Wonder where they'll go?'

'They'll come crawling back, don't you worry. If the Masters let them.'

Beggis and Chasna kept on walking. Past the waiting convener-platform, past the dogs, snarling through the railings in their yard, past the factories, filling up now with workers, past the meat-processing plant with its ominous smell and stained forecourt, and out into the City limits. Before them lay the open gate to the fields where Scummo and Kelpin had passed what seemed like a lifetime ago.

'You didn't say this would happen,' said Chasna after they had been walking in silence for a while.

'I thought they'd kick up more of a fuss.'

'They called our bluff. Where are we going, by the way?'

'Search me. But I meant what I said. I'm bored. It doesn't feel like living. I want more from life than this, even if it's less comfortable. It was great, you coming with me. Thanks.'

'The question is,' Chasna said, 'what do we do now? These fields stretch on forever. I worked out here when I first arrived, with one of the outdoor work gangs. The crops change after a while, but there's nothing out here to eat.'

'No use thinking about it. I just want to get as far away from the City as I can. Come on.'

They began their long slow walk away from the only home they could remember, towards the green expanses of kale growing in a deep green sea that stretched as far as the horizon. They were forced to drink water from the irrigation ditch that evening and went without food, but they walked through the early part of the night, lit only by stars, and by midnight were utterly exhausted. They slept by the side of a large turnip clamp and slept despite rats coming and going through the night. At dawn they woke, cold, stiff and hungry, and far away ahead of them they could see the silver shimmer of the estuary.

The Masters watched with bored amusement as the two young women investigated this alien landscape.

'We may lose track of them if they cross the water.'

'Not unless they remove their ankle tags.'

'Ah yes. But the others managed to remove them.'

'We will have a new system in place soon. Implants are more tricky to remove, I think.'

'Hm. You think it's going well, on the whole?'

'Time will tell. The female with the coloured hair – is she a new breed?'

'Perhaps. We will monitor their progress. We may be able to breed from her. Even the other one might be useful like that.'

'Do we need more young?'

'As an experiment, it's always useful to cross-breed species, don't you think? The young are expendable unless they're exceptional specimens.'

'True.'

Chapter 9

The group headed by Jankin and Fanna had made themselves at home in their caves. There had been no further appearances of the eel-like creatures, though the group members were careful not to go too near the water unless there was a lookout. Flocks of gulls had begun to arrive on the shore, and from time to time the group managed to catch one with a snare. They decided early on to post a lookout during daylight hours on the clifftop, and it was while Darfi was on watch one afternoon that he spotted a small boat, some way out to sea, heading towards the part of the coast the group had abandoned. Could this be the return of Scummo and Bethyl? Darfi strained his eyes but could not be sure from his vantage point how many people there were in the boat, which was making slow but steady progress along the coast. He called down to Fanna, who was sitting in the cave entrance sharpening a stick.

'Boat on the horizon! Look, look out there! It's a boat!' He could hardly contain his excitement.

Fanna remained calm. 'Keep your voice down. Sound travels across water. If it's Bethyl and Scummo, they'll follow the signs after they land and be with us tomorrow. If it's not them . . .'

'I'm going to wave.' Before she could stop him, Darfi started dancing about on the clifftop, waving his arms. The boat rowed serenely on. He might have been a gnat for all the attention they paid. Looking down at his body, Darfi could see that his skin was brown, and his clothes, what was left of them, were also dark with age and dirt. Then he realised that the clifftop he was waving so wildly from was also brown and green. Of course they would not notice him from so far away. Dejected, he went back to his previous posture.

Fanna called up to him. 'You did well to spot them, Darfi. I'm almost sure it will be Bethyl and Scummo. Could you tell how many people were in the boat? '

'Too far away to see for certain.'

'Time will tell. We may have visitors tomorrow if it was them.'

Kelpin came running across the beach with something in her hand. 'Is it true? Scummo's coming home?' She dangled a long piece of oar weed on the sand. It snaked behind her, reminding Fanna ominously of the eel creature.

'We saw someone in a boat, Kelpin, rowing back towards the coast we left. They'll find us, if it was them. It may not be them, though.'

'Oh.' Disappointment at Fanna's words was written on her face. Then she brightened.

'Can I go and watch with Darfi?'

'Of course.'

She scampered away, still dragging the oar weed, up the steep path to the clifftop.

***

It was late the following day when Scummo, Bethyl and Andalou returned. Kelpin, who had been watching the shore and the clifftops with close attention, was the first to spot them. The figures grew in size as they approached, and when she was sure it was them, she gave a yelp. 'Scummo! It's them! It's them!'

The figures waved at them and hurried onwards. Rondi scrambled quickly up to the lookout on the cliff. Fanna waited below with the others. Kelpin ran along the rough clifftop to Scummo and flung her arms around him. For a moment, Scummo thought he might cry. He hugged her tightly, lifting her up, almost forgetting his still-painful ankle, then put her down and crouched in front of her.

'How are you doing, Kiddo?'

She gazed at him with wordless adoration. Darfi, watching them from the cave entrance, felt a pang of jealousy. Quickly, he dropped the fish he was gutting and waited for them to descend the cliff. One by one, all the group members came back into the cave opening to greet the arrivals. There was an air of great excitement. They sat by the fire, some inside, some outside the cave. Bethyl and Scummo, who were very hungry, were offered fish and some corn cakes, and everyone understood that they would not begin to talk about their adventures until they had finished. They watched the newcomer, Andalou, cautiously seat himself with them and eat. He didn't speak.

They sat, Jankin, Rondi, Fanna, Sita, Darfi, and the others, watching every mouthful, waiting for them to be done. For Andalou, so much change and new experience had left him overstimulated and at the same time, overtired. Having eaten, he curled up in the back of the cave and fell asleep at once. The others gazed at him, shook their heads and smiled.

Bethyl spoke first, waving a wishbone in one hand as she did so. 'It's good to be back. Well, we were partially successful in our mission. Scummo played his part well, and we have brought back a new member, as you see.' She pointed with the fish bone to the collapsed form of Andalou at the back of the cave. 'He calls himself Andalou, and Scummo knew him before when he lived in the City. Andalou helped Scummo to leave the City again when he hurt his ankle.'

There were sympathetic murmurs, and group members looked at the affected ankle sympathetically, while Kelpin, overexcited, grabbed it and tried to rub it. Scummo withdrew his ankle hastily, putting a hand on Kelpin's back to reassure her. He gestured towards Bethyl, his mouth still full. 'Bethyl got us out of the City. We managed to capture one of the things they use to control the dogs and a remote-control device, and we deactivated one of the mobile food wagons.'

The other group members looked mystified. He remembered that they had never lived in the City and did not know about these things.

'They have a wagon that comes round with a ration of food each day,' Bethyl explained. 'It's a way of controlling people.'

'Wish we had one.' Anga's voice came from outside the cave.

Scummo answered her. 'Anga, when I was living in the Apartments, yes, we had food, yes, we had places to live in. But I wouldn't go back. I was only half alive there. There's no warmth, no proper human contact, no . . . closeness. Kelpin's mother died and suddenly I was all she had. I can't explain it, but it was as if a light went on inside, somehow.'

Anga sniffed but said nothing. Her life felt empty just now, but she found it hard to admit that even to herself.

'How did you get hurt?' Sita wanted to know.

'Just in running away. I fell and twisted my ankle badly.'

'Was it you in the boat we saw yesterday? We spotted a boat from the cliffs.' Darfi leaned forwards, his dark, matted hair tossed back over his shoulders.

'Yes. We didn't see you, though. We met a man called Sarnon with a boat – oh, three, four days ago – at a place Bethyl arranged. We were late, but luckily he waited. We took turns to row most of the way. No wonder Andalou's exhausted.'

'So where's Sarnon now?' Sita was curious.

'He rested, then rowed back after he left us, but he'll go along the coast slowly, as we did, before he crosses the bay again.'

'Didn't the Masters try to stop you? You must have damaged their property.' Sita was interested in how Masters operated. Her curly hair was wild and tousled. Darfi noticed that her nose, with its tilted tip, was smudged with soot from the fire.

Jankin joined in. 'We have things to tell *you* as well. One of those is about the eel creatures in the sea. A very big eel came up into the pool down there, where the stream enters the sea, and we killed it. It's dangerous to go in the sea while those things are around, but they don't seem to come over dry ground. But you must tell us your news.'

The talk went on into the night and Fanna had to shoo Kelpin to bed. The nights were getting colder and the cave, though it provided shelter, was not draught-proof. Tired though he was, Andalou shivered in his sleep.

The meeting that took place the following day was to determine the future of the group. Everyone was expected to take part, though Anga and Magrab said little.

Bethyl was clear. 'I would like to lead this discussion today. This is because I have knowledge of others who may help us survive out here, and because I been able to do some thinking about how we can carry on. All agreed?'

'Aye.'

Bethyl waited until she had gained the attention of all the group members. Rondi, who was frightened of Bethyl, put down the stick he was whittling. She spoke slowly and deliberately, choosing her words carefully. 'We are divided into two groups here: those of us who were born into slavery in the City, or who were taken there as children – that's Kelpin, Scummo, Darfi and Andalou – and the rest of us, who come from the villages outside the City. The Masters tried to rule our lives, but we were in charge of more of it than the City people. We could grow our own food and make things for ourselves and had a certain degree of freedom. The Masters didn't like that and decided that we were a threat and tried to round us up. Those of us who lived further away kept our freedom for longer. Jankin and Fanna, for example, fled when the members of their village were rounded up. Imagine having to watch the dogs drive people off the cliffs to their death.'

She paused. 'The eel things came for them. Jankin and Fanna escaped. I escaped when my family had been herded and I slipped away and hid from the dogs. Anga, Doran, Magrab, Sita and Rondi' – she pointed – 'have never known what it is to be kept in an enclosure and to have your every movement controlled. What we all have in common, though, is that we're all survivors. Inside the City – am I right, Scummo? – people have shelter, food, warmth. But no freedom. Here we have freedom. But it may be freedom to perish unless we use our skills and what we learned in the past to make better lives for ourselves.'

The group was silent. They recognised the truth of her statement. Andalou, who was feeling almost rested, added something to the discussion. 'I made a deliberate decision to leave the City,' he said. 'If I were still there, I would have a warm enough place to live, a bed and regular food that I didn't have to find myself. Yet I chose to leave because life in the City is without meaning or purpose. Every day is the same as the day before. You've all been very kind to me since I arrived. Back in the City, everyone is too busy obeying orders, working, dodging the dogs or queuing for food to be friendly. Yes, I'm cold. Yes, I'm hungry, but I feel alive, really alive.'

The others smiled ruefully. Bethyl nodded at him and continued. 'We need basic things to get us through the winter. Tell us what you think they are. What's most important?'

'Clothes. Something to keep us warm.'

'A food store.'

'A toilet. The rocks up there stink of piss.'

Kelpin giggled.

Jankin looked around the group. 'You all know what we need, and you've got some ideas about how to get it, but what none of us have got are tools – we need a spade to dig a toilet. We need an axe to cut down trees. We've only got three fish hooks, and those are improvised, and there's no way we can make clothes for ourselves, and anyway, what do we make them from? We used to weave wool back in the villages, but the Masters destroyed the villages. It's not likely that any of the looms survived . . . ' His voice trailed off.

Sita gave the subject serious thought. 'But even if we can't weave, we can knit if we have any yarn, and we can try to catch more birds and rossells and use their skins and feathers.' Her homespun garments were nearing the end of their life, and gaping holes had appeared in the knees and around the neck.

Darfi said, 'We might be able to salvage something from the villages around here. I don't know – whatever we decide to do has risks attached to it – but I'd be prepared to go off on a foraging trip to see what we could find. Scummo found a dead pig on his way across country. Who knows if there are other large animals out there? Just because we haven't seen them up to now . . .'

As he spoke, Anga, sitting close to his side, looked distressed. She fidgeted and turned her face away from him.

'Anyone who goes off foraging, or hunting,' Fanna said, 'needs to be well armed and well prepared. If Darfi goes, he'll need to go with someone who knows how the villages worked.'

'I'll go with him,' Jankin said from the back.

Anga, tearful, whispered, 'I want to go.'

'So do I.' It was Sita.

The bond between Anga and Darfi had been noted by Bethyl. She whispered in Fanna's ear, and the latter nodded.

'There is something else we need to discuss.'

They all looked up.

'It would be dangerous for the group's survival if any of us got pregnant at this time. We don't have the resources to support that. Later, it'll be different.' She looked directly at Anga, who blushed, and then at Darfi, who pretended to poke the ground with a stick. Sita stared at the ground. 'Look, I know you two are keen on one another, it sticks out a mile.' Kelpin giggled. 'But if Anga gets pregnant – or anyone does – it will be a disaster for the group. Have any of you had children already?'

Magrab held his hand up. 'My w-wife was herded up with my daughter while I was away. I don't know what happened to them. You're right, we can't offer a baby anything right now.' He lost his twitch as he said this and his face was grave.

Jankin, too, had fathered three children and had watched helplessly as they were driven over the cliffs by the dogs. He broke down in tears as he recalled this. The group became silent at this point as Fanna tried to comfort him.

Bethyl called Anga and Darfi to her and asked them to consider what she had said. Anga, with difficulty, agreed not to go on the hunting trip.

'You're only young,' explained Bethyl. 'Both of you. I know it's hard for you, but it will keep.'

'If he comes back.'

'Anga, nothing is certain. You know that.'

Gradually, the group began to tackle the projects they had identified. Darfi, Sita and Magrab began to organise themselves for the hunting expedition. There were arguments about which direction they should go in. Finally, Sita proposed that they should head for a village inland some way from the village on the coast where Jankin and Fanna used to live. They felt the coastal villages were too dangerous. The others were anxious about them leaving but had to accept that it was necessary. Anyway, Scummo and Bethyl had returned safely from a much longer trip to the City itself; the members reminded themselves of this fact and said goodbye to the three who were leaving, feeling optimistic.

Their journey was slow, as Magrab, who was in front, took a wrong turning in a wood and they became lost.

Huddled together under the tall pines clumped together in the forest, they conferred. Above them, a large hawk mewed and circled, endlessly. Almost without realising it, they took their bearing from the sun, all the time listening to the sound of the wind in the trees, the rustle of leaves, the constant hum of insects above them. Then they heard it, a heavy, deliberate footfall, accentuated by a grunt. Something was coming their way, but what?

The watched, terrified, as the ferns on the forest floor began to move, heaving left and right, and birds took off in alarm over their heads, startling them. Something was charging through the undergrowth, and it was coming towards them.

'Run!' ordered Magrab, racing towards the nearest tree with low-hanging branches. The others ran after him. Magrab, first to reach the tree, grabbed the lowest branch and hooked a leg over it, quickly steadying himself and holding his hand out to haul up the others.

'Quick!' shrieked Sita, grabbing hold of the branch as Darfi pushed her up while trying to get a purchase on the slippery bark himself. The packs they had carried fell to the ground. The thing came out of the undergrowth, snorting, sharp crescent tusks flashing on either side of its mouth. It sniffed the air, using its sense of smell to tell it what its eyes could not. They had hauled themselves higher up the tree and watched it, trembling, as they clung to the precarious perches they had found.

'W-what is it?' asked Magrab in a whisper.

'I think it's a wild pig.' Sita was watching the creature as it snuffled about, looking up at the tree from time to time. Its large ears rippled perceptibly as they whispered. It grunted again. 'We'll have to wait until it goes away.'

Darfi didn't agree. 'What if we killed it? It would give us meat for days.'

'How? How could we k-kill it? I've only got a stick and the packs are down there.' Magrab gestured towards the few possessions they had brought with them, now being energetically investigated by the wild pig. The pig stopped snuffling and turned his face sideways towards them, the white lashes of its eye like wisps of straw over the orbs. They considered the question. The pig was about three strides long, lean, muscular, and heavy. The tusks now slicing through the felt of their packs <u>were</u> evidently lethally sharp. That it was unlikely to be friendly, they felt they already knew. Having rummaged and ripped its way through the packs, it collapsed on its side under the tree, and they could see its large scrotal sac. It rubbed the rough hairs of its back along a tree root, trying to ease an itch.

'Definitely a male,' said Sita, unnecessarily. 'If there were more of them they might breed. I mean, we could keep them as men used to do.'

'Do we need it for meat, though?' Darfi was concerned with their food shortage. 'I'm remembering something I heard while I was on the barge. The people who passed through used to catch animals by digging a pit. They put sharpened sticks in the bottom, with the points sticking up, then they covered it over lightly with grass and ferns. On top you put something the animal likes to eat. It goes to eat it, falls in and is impaled on the sticks. Then we finish it off.'

'Good plan. I wonder if it would work?' said Sita. 'There's only one problem, though. We have to get down from the tree before we do anything else. And we can't do that while that thing's down there. Ideas, Magrab?'

Magrab, thin, nervous, gave a careful assessment. 'We c-can't kill it from up here,' he offered. 'If we get down from the tree it'll most likely attack us. We need weapons to k-kill it with and those are all in the packs. Such as they are. We h-have to stay here until it goes away.'

Glumly, they concurred that he was right. They spread themselves out along the branches and made themselves as comfortable as they could. Sita felt sleepy and Magrab had to nudge her at intervals or she would have fallen from the tree. The pig finished his scratching and rolled over, putting his blunt forefeet out in front of him, then, levering the rest of his body upright, he gave a shake, and shreds of grass and leaves that had been clinging to his side flew off around him. He had a final nose around in their packs and began to explore the area around the tree, settling on their footprints eventually, which led it away into the forest again. They watched it go with relief.

They descended the tree again carefully and made their way in the opposite direction to the one the pig had taken. Darfi scanned the ground, looking for the sharp hoof-prints that would tell them if there were any more creatures out there. By unspoken assent, they kept near the trees, weaving a path through them that never took them far from the safety of the woods. The packs had been badly mauled, trampled on and tossed about, and the pig had eaten all their supplies. Only a knife and a stick were left.

At the edge of the wood, they came to a tree still covered in vivid yellow crab apples, glowing brightly against the gloom of the forest. Many had dropped to the ground and were now spotted with rot. There were marks in the dark ground here to show that the pigs had found it. They surveyed the area nervously, listening intently. All was silent. Sita started to pick some apples, tucking them into her waistband. The others did the same.

'Good place to dig your pit,' observed Sita.

Magrab, nervous, had to agree. Darfi considered the area. 'See if you can find me some sharp stones or sticks and we'll start digging.'

'What now? Our mission is to get to the village and see what we can scavenge,' said Sita. 'What we need to do is to mark this spot so we can come back to it. We've had to make a detour because of the pig, and if we're not careful we'll get lost. I do know these woods a bit, but it's many years since I was here last. I say we go on to the village, see what we can find and then decide if we want to try to kill the pig on the way back. Besides, it'll be very heavy to carry.'

Darfi, reluctantly, could see the sense of this. Magrab, as usual, took the cautious view. They were near the edge of the wood, and he took the knife and made a deep cut through the bark of a tree overhanging the tussocky rough ground beyond the wood.

'I remember when these were proper fields,' said Sita, wistfully. 'We need to turn to face the sun. The village is about two miles in that direction.'

They walked wearily onwards, bruised from the tree climb and weak from lack of food. Sita was remembering more now. 'Stop here a minute,' she requested. 'There may be some chestnuts here.' The chestnut tree was large and old and overhung the field. The spiky balls of chestnut cases were lying at their feet, splitting open to reveal the brown, polished fruit inside, lying like a fat unlit candle in its prickly ball. The pig or pigs had been here too, but there were some freshly fallen nuts that the three soon tucked away in their clothing. Later, when it was safe enough, they would eat them.

They approached the deserted village, cautiously, as evening advanced. Sita had been there before when she was a child. She peeped round the trunk of the last tree between them and the village. No smoke, no sound, no evidence of any human existence. The others craned their necks round her.

'Come on,' said Darfi in a hoarse whisper. 'I'll go first.'

'There's a big barn next to the church. If we can find that, we could get up in the loft – might be a safe place to stay the night?' The houses, mostly stone-built single-storey cottages, were ruined. The roofs had fallen in and there was water spilling from a blocked sink. But there was at least water. Some of the houses had been burned; most had no windows left intact. Outside one, they found a wooden pole with a rusty hoe and a shovel buried under the weeds close by. They ate what they had brought with them – raw chestnuts, crab apples, pig-nuts – and listened to their stomachs churning with hunger. It was almost dark, and the sunset inked the sky with crimson feathers. They couldn't find the barn, but the church was still standing. The door was missing, and they entered with caution, stepping over a dead pigeon disintegrating in the dust at their feet. Inside, it was very dark and smelled of mildew and mice. Magrab, exploring, found a stairway up to the belfry. The platform where the belfry had once been was still solid, and they decided to spend the night there. Almost all the light had now slipped away, but in the gloom, they could make out the hole in the roof above them.

'What was this for?' Sita whispered.

'To ring the bells,' Magrab remembered.

'What?'

'There were bells up there. You stood here and pulled a rope and the bells swung and made a noise.'

'How?'

'The clapper inside banged on the side of the bell. D-don't you know what a bell is?'

'The goats in the village had them, I think. Not like this, though.'

'Will you two be quiet?' Darfi was falling asleep. Outside, the night was ominously silent. Later, in his dreams, he heard howling from the woods they had left. He woke but could hear nothing. Unable to sleep again, his stomach clenched into a knot with hunger, and he realised something was troubling him. What if there were spy cameras in here? He could do nothing until the morning.

He spent a restless two hours trying to sleep again, but as soon as it was light enough to see, he sat up and surveyed the room. Daylight entered through a small arched window in the loft and apart from that and a few lengths of bell rope coiled in one corner; there was nothing to see. The other two were still deeply asleep, Magrab with his mouth open, moaning slightly from time to time, Sita curled up, her head on her arms. Darfi tiptoed across the dusty belfry and opened the door. Something flapped its wings and flew away. He started, waking Sita.

'It's only me.'

She rubbed a sleepy eye and looked at him. 'What was that?'

'A bird. I was looking for spy cameras.'

'Spy cameras?'

'Yeah. They put one on the barge I was on after Scummo came. I made him take his ankle tag off, but by then it was too late.'

'What do you mean?'

'It's their way of keeping tabs on us. Everyone in the City wears one. I got away from the City when I was a kid. They don't tag you until you stop growing. But all the adults had ankle tags.'

'So why do you think there might be cameras here, if none of us are wearing tags?'

'Scummo found one in a dead pig and in the hut he stayed in with Kelpin before they got to my barge. So they plant them around at random to keep an eye on things.'

Sita shuddered. 'How creepy.' She nudged Magrab, who muttered, turned over, then woke.

They could see nothing that resembled a camera, either in the church or outside. They began a search of the buildings, keeping together, Magrab going in first with a long stick. Rats slid away into the walls as they approached, and squeaking came from under the floor. Others had been here before them, it seemed, yet Magrab and Sita, who knew where to look, unearthed some useful tools, including an axe, a machete and another shovel, which were under a mouldy sack in a shed at the back of one of the buildings. The sack, though mouldy, was still usable, and they wrapped the tools in it carefully. They found some hemp yarn and some old leather saddles, but not knowing how they could be used, left the saddles behind. Investigation under a sink in one cottage kitchen revealed a rusty knife and a scraper. These were packed carefully with the other tools. By this time, it was late morning, and they had to make a decision about whether to return to the shore settlement or spend another night in the belfry.

'I'm not too sure how far it is back to camp,' said Darfi. 'But by my reckoning it should take the best part of a day. It depends whether we want to kill a pig on the way back.'

'Let's set off,' said Sita. 'This place is creepy.'

Magrab agreed. Each shouldered a makeshift bundle of tools. By unspoken agreement, they skirted the wood and talk of killing the pig ended, though Darfi was regretful. 'A bit of roast pig would make a change from endless fish or rossells,' he said.

'Never mind,' said Sita, consoling him. 'We can always come back. Better to plan it properly. The others are waiting for us to get back. Besides,' she added, 'this stuff's heavy.'

The journey back was slow but uneventful. They stopped to rest now and then and pick up any nut, fruit or berry they came across that might be edible. There wasn't a great deal. Sita found acorns but wasn't sure whether they could eat them. They tore off bracket fungus, discovered a rossell's horde of hazelnuts and ate blackberries as they went along. Finally, they were back on the top of the cliffs and being greeted by Jankin, who was lookout that day. He looked approvingly at the array of tools and other items they had brought back with them.

'You did well!'

'Yes, we did, considering we were nearly dinner for a wild pig.'

'A wild pig?'

'We had to climb a tree to get away from it. Vicious thing. It destroyed our packs too.' Darfi made his point strongly while the topic was still new. 'We should go on a proper hunting trip and try to kill one. We could do it now, with the tools we've got.'

'It would make a change from fish,' agreed Jankin. 'Let's talk about it after we've eaten.'

'What's on the menu, as if I didn't know?' Sita's stomach rumbled.

'Fish, and to follow it, more fish.'

Chapter 10

Waking after their first night of freedom, Chasna and Beggis shivered in the pale dawn light. The two women were overwhelmed by their first sight of the estuary. The smell that came off it was salty and invigorating. They sniffed it appreciatively.

'It's so big! How ever do we get over that?' Chasna was filled with awe.

'No idea. There seems to be a path here, of sorts. Why don't we follow that?'

'And then what?'

'Look, I don't know any more then you do.'

'It was your bright idea to come.'

'Shut up.'

They plodded onwards towards the water. Something moved in the dyke beside them, slapping the water onto the banks.

'What was that?' Chasna hid behind Beggis as both wheeled round to face the source of the noise. All was silent. Chasna could not resist a peep. Tiptoeing across the marsh grass, she looked closely at the clumps of reed and samphire edging the ditch. She moved closer. There was something not right about the reeds. Two sets of eyes stared back at her with unblinking ferocity from two oval, olive-coloured heads joined at the neck. Then the eel thing struck her, holding her leg and gripping it with its razor teeth. Chasna screeched with pain and fright, falling backwards onto the sticky mud. Beggis, terrified, picked up a stone and threw it at the eel thing, where it bounced harmlessly off its body.

'Help me!' shrieked Chasna, blood pouring from the wound. 'Beggis!'

Beggis tried not to panic. She pulled off her shirt and, as Chasna and the eel thing wrestled in the mud, flung it over the creature's head. It stopped writhing for a moment, and then Beggis was on it, tying the shirt around its heads. The teeth of one head were firmly fixed in Chasna's leg, but the other head was free, the jaws searching for purchase. Beggis reasoned that without sight, the eel thing might let go of its catch, but it didn't.

She held the cloth in place with one hand, while with her other hand she scrabbled about for a stone to hit it with. Chasna was corpse-white, her blood soaking the sand and running down in rivulets to the estuary. Finally, Beggis smashed a large rock sideways, knocking the thing enough to make it let go of Chasna's leg temporarily. With a sudden burst of strength, Beggis put her arms around Chasna's chest and dragged her sagging dead-weight body up onto the grass again. She could go no further. The eel thing, intent on ridding itself of the shirt covering its eyes, slithered back through the reeds into the dyke and was gone. Clad only in her trousers and flimsy undervest, Beggis shivered, partly through cold, and goosebumps stood out on her arms. She bent over Chasna. She had lost a lot of blood. Beggis took off Chasna's shirt and tied it around the wound. A large chunk of flesh was missing and what was inside the hole was dark and dreadful. She closed her eyes for a moment.

'Chassy? Chasna, can you hear me?' She prodded her friend. Chasna groaned and turned her head. 'Chassy, I'll have to go for help. I'll pull you up onto the drier ground. Are you ready?' She grabbed Chasna's arms and pulled her a little way further up the sea grass towards the higher ground. Above them, birds circled, ominously. She could do no more. Where could she go? These lands had been deserted since the Masters came. They were a long way from the fields, from the City, from anyone. Beggis knew it was useless. Chasna would not survive the blood loss or the septicaemia that would follow. Even with her lack of education, Beggis knew that was true. Chasna was unconscious, already drifting into a world where all was one. Beggis took her hand, and Chasna squeezed it so lightly as to be almost imperceptible. She waited a long time, motionless, by the unconscious body of her friend. Finally, she stood up.

'Bye, Chasna.' Tears running down her cheeks, Beggis kissed her friend goodbye and got to her feet. She would have to continue this journey alone.

Blinded by tears and exhausted by hunger and cold, she went inland a little way to where a belt of slightly higher ground, part of an old causeway, ran parallel to the sea. Pausing for a moment, she looked down at the stones of the causeway. There were fresh wet marks on them, as if someone had carried something that had dripped all the way along the causeway. Evidently, they, or it, had come from the indented salt marshes that edged the estuary. The spots of water dried as she followed them, until they were no longer visible. Ahead, the land sloped down suddenly. She was approaching a creek.

A large heron flew up as she drew near, ponderously flapping its way to the trees further along the coast. Beggis had never seen one before; in fact, the only birds she was familiar with were the City pigeons and starlings. She was awestruck at the sight of it, but its beauty lifted her spirits a little. She was right to have come. Despite Chasna's death, despite being hungry, cold and tired, Beggis was not sorry she had left the City. She felt light-headed and afraid, but she was free.

Sarnon found her later that afternoon, the colour in her cheeks now a dull ivory, leaning on a rock by the makeshift jetty in the creek. She had been waiting for him, or someone, to find her. He would have to remove her tag first, then they would see what to do. This was not the first runaway Sarnon had discovered. She opened her green eyes slowly and looked at him, too tired to protest. He took her ankle in his left hand and manipulated the band, deftly sawing through it with his hunting knife. Beggis's eyes opened very wide at this point.

'What are you doing?'

Sarnon pullefd off the tag and held it up. Without speaking, he tossed it into the water. It fizzed and popped then sank. He helped her stand and led her to the boat.

When Beggis finally reached the jetty on the coastal strip the others had landed at, Sarnon pointed her along the coast. Most of his communication with her had been in mime, yet she understood him well. Others were to be found there, and there were caves. She knew that because of the eel things that meant he could not take the boat along the shore where there was no landing place. This was the closest he could get. Beggis followed the faint path that ran along the clifftop and finally came to a dip in the headland where a stream sliced through the cliffs. A young girl was picking cress in the pool beyond, watching the distant sea as she did so.

She started. 'Who are you?'

Beggis flopped down on the bank, her bright hair dull with sweat, gritty dust and dirt and her cheeks marked with the snail tracks of her tears for Chasna. 'Name's Beggis. Yours?'

'Kelpin. You just got here?'

Beggis nodded.

'Come with me.' Imperiously, Kelpin commanded her to follow, then seeing how tired and weak Beggis was, she held her hand out. 'Hold on to me. It's not far away.' She led Beggis, stumbling and faltering, along the cliff path to where Jankin was keeping watch from his lookout post.

She had arrived.

Kelpin's Testimony

Today I have to show the others where the pig marks are in the forest. That's so Darfi and Scummo can go after them and maybe catch one for food. Darfi was told by Fanna and Bethyl that I had to go with them. They wouldn't have found the tracks on their own. Well, maybe Scummo would have. But Scummo listens to me; Darfi doesn't. Too busy playing around with that Anga. But the baby's nice, cute and cuddly. Too bad the other one died. Darfi was upset, you could tell, and Anga, well she was crying buckets until Fanna made her stop. They were told not to make babies, but Darfi didn't listen. She made such a noise when it was born, this second one, and the afterbirth was really disgusting. I took it away and buried it on the beach and the eel thing took it when the tide came in. No one knows about that except me, 'cos I saw it.

Scummo and Fanna haven't made any babies, though sometimes I think they want to. When I'm older, Fanna says, like fourteen or something, they'll let me make babies with someone. But eleven is quite big. Anyway, I might not want to make babies. Anga and Darfi's baby, Freedom, is carried around on Anga's back and he poos all the time. I wouldn't like that.

They're going pig-hunting after we eat at midday because that's when the pigs sleep when it's hot like this. I know all the places they go and I can watch them. The others don't know that.

They're all right. The only one I don't like is Rondi. Fanna says he's jealous and he has no business to throw stones at me in the woods, just because he doesn't know about the pigs and I do. Jankin's okay, sort of. Doran and Sita seem to have got together, and that shelter they made last summer was just for the two of them. Everyone noticed. They pretended anyone could use it, but no one did.

That new one, Beggis, is still sleeping. She's been here over a week now and she still sleeps a lot. She's told us what's going on in the City. A lot of people have been sick, she said. Fanna hopes no one catches anything from Beggis. We have to leave her alone until she's stronger.

The corn store in the bottom cave is finished now, and we can move the corn into it soon, though most of it's gone now anyway. But this year the corn we planted from the fields near the City hasn't grown very well so we have to keep the old stuff to plant for next year. Keeping the rossells off it is a problem, and someone has to be there in the field to stop them eating it all. Jankin said they used to use dogs, back when he lived in the village, but when the Masters took over, the dogs fought the Masters' dogs and lost and none of us were keen to have a dog after what we went through anyway. Fanna thinks the Masters' dogs are different from the ones in the villages. Maybe she's right. I just remember the ones on the landings that used to bite you if you didn't move quick enough. I feel sad thinking about my mother when I remember those times. I've forgotten her face, but

Scummo told me what she was like. He doesn't know who my father was. I wish Scummo had been my father. Or even Andalou.

Because my skin is darker than the others, Fanna said when I asked her that my father might have been a Tasker, one of the people who came into the City to sell things. You could get soap or paper from them for tokens, sometimes other things. We haven't seen any Taskers since we've been here.

This is what my day is like:

I wake up when it gets light, then I go and fetch water and bring it back to the shelters. If it's a warm day, I may go round the rocks for a swim, in the big rock pool there. The tide has to be right because we don't want the eel things coming into it when we're there. Then we eat something and talk about the day. Andalou went with Jankin yesterday to get honey. That was good, but I didn't recognise Andalou when he came back, 'cos of the stings on his face. The smoke they used didn't work very well. But the honey was lovely, all sticky golden in the jar. Today, five people are going fishing, using some baskets they made. They put them in the water where the pools are deep and the fish or the crab goes into the hole in one end and is too silly to get out. So then they pull it up and take the fish out through the door at the end and put it back in. It took them ages to make these fish traps from the willow branches last winter, but they work quite well. There are not so many fish with two heads now. Fanna says it's because they can't make baby fish, only the normal ones can breed, she says, and the weird ones are dying off. When they've gone on their fishing trip, I'll go with Darfi and Scummo to look for the pig tracks.

When we eat, it'll be cornmeal mixed with kelp or the fish the others bring back. Some days there is no food, but more and more we're learning about this. The ones from the villages know more than we do about this, and they have to tell us how to keep food so it doesn't go bad. They told me about goats and chickens and how they used to keep them. They don't know what happened to them when the Masters came. Evening is the best time, because we light the fire, and one of my jobs is to find wood and pile it up to dry. I go down to the edge of the sea to bring back the big thick seaweed stems that have been washed up. They look like monsters' mouths at the end. But they come loose from the rocks in the water and get washed up. We cook them when they're dry in a metal pan with oil from the gull stew. They don't waste nothing here. We sometimes find other things washed up, from the City. We found a body once, but it was so eaten up and covered in shrimp things as it lay just nudging the sand when the waves came under it that we couldn't tell who it was. Someone from the City, anyway, because the bits of clothes it still had on were like my old felt ones. Fanna tried to make me not look at it, but I wanted to. Once I found a lot of plastic bottles with tops on, floating. We use them for water.

My hair's all itchy now. I go to Sita and she looks through it for me, then I do hers. We pop the eggs and squash the nits. I missed her today because she was away collecting food, but later when it gets hot I'll find her under the tree and we'll do it. At night, I have a place where I sleep, next to Scummo, and now we've made some covers from the rossell skins its quite warm. We had some very cold times when I was little. Fanna and Scummo used to put me in between them and we'd snuggle up close. The others slept close together next to us to keep warm too. We could go back to one of the villages, Fanna says, but the ones who came from the villages are not happy about that. The memories are too strong. Here, it's harder for the Masters to find us.

We haven't seen much of them lately. Fanna says they're leaving this part of the coast alone. Beggis said a bit yesterday about people in the City being sick, like Minna was, so perhaps they're all dead. But the Masters won't be dead, will they? I wonder what will happen to us all.

Scummo says he thought the Masters would come after us, and they did put a spy camera on the barge, but Darfi says, no, they're just watching us to see what we get up to. Darfi found a spy camera in the village he went to when they went looking for stuff we could use in the settlement, so they're still around. Tonight, we're having a meeting, a proper one where everyone gets to talk about what we do next. Bethyl and Jankin will talk most like they always do. It's Bethyl's turn to be in charge of the meeting, so I better not be late. Bethyl's bossy, but Scummo says she knows what she's doing better than us, so I have to shut up and listen.

Chapter 11

The Meeting

Bethyl took charge of the meeting and asked everyone to sit down.

Magrab noticed that Anga was missing, but Darfi reassured them that she was settling the baby down.

Anga's voice came from the next cave. 'I can hear you from here – I'll come in and join you once Freedom's asleep.'

Bethyl invited them to find a comfortable place to sit. 'The first thing we need to talk about is our numbers,' she said. How many of us are there now, do you think?'

Jankin began counting. 'There's Bethyl and me, that's two, Darfi and Anga, that's four, Freedom, five, Scummo and Fanna, seven, Rondi, eight, Magrab, nine, Beggis, ten, Andalou, eleven, and Kelpin, of course, which makes twelve, and Doran and Sita, fourteen. Have I left anybody out?'

There was a shaking of heads as all checked round to see that all had been included.

Bethyl continued, 'These caves Rondi found have been useful. When winter comes again we could stay in them, but our numbers have grown. We need to find other shelter, somewhere warm and out of the weather where we can sleep.

I know some people have made their own shelters up here, and some people will want to stay in the caves all together, but there isn't room for all of us. The summer shelters have been useful, but we need more substantial shelters for all of us. So that's the first thing.'

Andalou said, 'I agree. Last night, Anga's baby kept us all awake. No, Anga, I know it's not his fault, or your fault, but what with that and the mosquitoes, none of us slept much. I didn't, anyway.'

Sita had been thinking about their options. 'So far, we've stayed in this area, near the caves, but we might be better going further up the coast or inland into the woods. This spot here on the top of the beach is great because there's space to sit down and the sand is soft, but we are quite visible from the sea here, even at night, when we've got the fire going. So, I suggest the woods.' She looked at the others.

'What about the wild pigs?' Magrab asked, sensibly.

Jankin thought about this. 'We may have to make a fence of some kind to keep them out.'

'Easier said than done,' replied Sita

Fanna had an idea. 'What's to stop us moving back into one of the old villages? I mean, really? I know the memories are horrible, but think about it. We'd have shelter, at least, and we could keep animals, if we can find any – even pigs.'

Rondi said, 'Yeah – why not?'

Darfi looked alarmed. 'Hang on. Anga and me, we've got the baby to consider. Anga's parents were taken from the villages and thrown over the cliffs, remember? Scummo's father disappeared in one of the villages. Jankin had to flee for his life – I think we need to be very careful about going anywhere near any of the villages.'

Various voices murmured agreement.

Bethyl called for their attention again. 'We've survived so far because some of us remembered enough about how people used to live – how to make fish traps, how to keep fish and meat from rotting by drying it or smoking it, how to hunt – and we've done pretty well at it, considering. All Fanna's saying is that since the Masters have left us alone here to get on with it, what's to stop us taking over one of the old villages?'

Scummo asked, 'You mean you think the Masters have known we're here all along?'

Jankin replied, 'I've been thinking about this a lot. I don't think we can take the chance of getting herded up by them again. But Beggis left with her friend, so did you, Scummo—'

'And me!' Kelpin insisted.

He went on, 'And you, Kelpin, and they made no serious attempt to stop them. Yet it seems as though they tried to track our movements. Those tags, for instance, the spy cameras, those were there for a reason.'

Darfi asked, 'So why have they left us alone? Why? Are they playing some sadistic game?'

'Perhaps we're special,' Doran suggested.

'Special?' said Darfi What's special about us?'

'Well, we're not in the City. We either escaped being captured or we've left. Maybe that makes us special. I dunno.'

'Doran has a point,' said Bethyl

Fanna tried again. 'So, to get back to my suggestion – if we decided to go back and re-colonise a village, what would the dangers be? And do we have a choice? Anga, you want to say something?'

'What do you mean *do we have a choice*?'

Fanna's answer was thoughtful. 'There are too many of us to fit comfortably in the top cave to sleep now. If Freedom wakes and cries, it disturbs us all – that's not because you're a bad mother, Anga, it's just how babies are. We need more space.'

Rondi asked, 'Have we given up using the bottom cave for sleeping? I don't mind sleeping down there. We could move some of the food stores somewhere else.'

'Where?' Jankin asked.

There was silence. There was nowhere else.

Bethyl said, 'Is everyone agreed in principle that we need to find other shelter? Anyone object?'

Everyone nodded assent, though reluctantly.

Jankin summed it up for them. 'This is what we propose: that we should go in couples to look at the three villages nearest to here, come back and report our findings. We need to look at the amount of building material that's left, whether there are any habitable shelters now, and things like water and storage space for our food. We've taken a lot from the village in the valley, the one we used to know as Cerin in the old days, and although it's completely ruined, it might be possible to make some of it habitable before the winter. I'd like to go back there and do a thorough search of that one. Then there's the village across the stream in the next valley, and the one on the outskirts of the woods where the hunting party went today.'

Magrab said, 'I-I don't like that village. B-but there is a church there that's still standing. There's shelter there.'

Why don't you like it?' Bethyl asked.

'B-because it's creepy. I knew it from before and there's, like, ghosts there for me. But maybe if we were all there it could be good.' They were silent for a moment.

'The village by the stream,' said Sita. 'I would worry about the eel things coming up from the sea. We don't know how far they can travel. Just because we haven't seen one inland doesn't mean they don't come along the streams.'

Bethyl said, 'Point noted. What do others think?'

Darfi agreed. 'I think it's dangerous. We haven't seen one of those things for a while – but that's because we've been careful not to attract attention.'

Rondi agreed too.

Kelpin had her own idea. 'I like the village by the wood. I went near there today, helping them track the pig. There's lots of trees there that could be really useful.'

Beggis, who had remained quiet, said, 'I know I'm still learning about all this, but I would like to live in a house again. I mean, I'm glad I left the City and everything, but I had no idea it would be so hard here. Every night I wake up scratching the fleabites or listening to Freedom crying. And when it rains, the ones sleeping next to the entrance always get wet. Maybe living in one of the villages would help us think about how to survive in the long term. I don't know. I'll go to one of the villages with someone.'

Jankin said, 'I propose we send two people, and I'd like to be one of them, out to look at the village by the wood again. I'd also like to send someone out to look at the third village, Erasil, again, too.'

'I'll go,' Magrab said. 'I'd rather go to that one.'

***

An agreement was reached. Jankin and Fanna would revisit the village by the wood, while Beggis and Magrab would make the longer trek to Erasil, staying there overnight and returning the following day. They would take a day or two to prepare. The discussion then went on to the more mundane matters of latrine-digging and fishing rotas. It was late when they turned in, and Andalou had fallen asleep and had to be nudged awake by Scummo. Kelpin, who could hardly keep her eyes open, snuggled down next to Scummo and was soon deeply asleep. It was left to Andalou to take first watch by the dying fire and to watch the white stars scatter their glitter in the skies above him as they wheeled and turned. He was comforted by their eternal presence and thought that someday he'd like to make up a song about them or share them with someone who felt as he did about them. He thought longingly of Beggis, unhappily of Sita, despairingly of Kelpin – she was still far too young. Angrily, he threw his stick into the darkness, where it slid down the cliff side with a clatter of pebbles.

Chapter 12

Beggis was not happy. Although she had volunteered to go and survey the village, she was not pleased to be going with Magrab. The next day, she sought out Fanna and Bethyl. Fanna was sharpening their few precious knives on a piece of sandstone at the front of the cave, and she was surprised when Beggis appeared in front of her. She put down her stone and ran her fingers lightly along the blade of the knife. She waited for Beggis to speak.

'Fanna, do I have to go with Magrab?'

Bethyl, who was busy sweeping the rock surface of the cave, put her twig broom down to listen. 'Why?'

'Why can't I go with Darfi or Andalou?'

'You volunteered to go, so did Magrab.'

'Yes, but he's so nervous. Always twitching.'

Fanna looked at her. 'You know, Beggis, Magrab is one of the bravest people here. Maybe you don't know that, but you will. And it's just as well you don't fancy him. We don't want any more babies just now, understood?'

Beggis blushed and her bright hair glowed against her reddened skin. 'I didn't mean that . . . Magrab's okay. I'd just rather have gone with someone else.'

Fanna looked her straight in the eye, and Bethyl spoke up from behind them. 'Beggis, Fanna and I had lovers before the Masters arrived. They died when the Masters came, jumping off the cliff. Jankin, too, had a wife and children who perished. We haven't forgotten them. It would be easy for us to take partners within the group, but none of us feels ready for that yet, neither does Magrab. When we're safe enough we'll do that, and if I'm not too old I'd like some children too, but right now we're just trying to survive, understood?'

Beggis nodded.

'We also have to rely on one another and trust each other. Magrab is one of the most honest people I've ever met, and the most trustworthy.' There was silence for a moment. 'Are you a virgin?'

Beggis nodded dumbly.

'Your time will come, Beggis, and when it does you won't be sorry you had to wait a while. Go and help the others with the fish traps now.'

Beggis, chastened and rebellious, slunk away and went to annoy Rondi.

That evening, as they met by the fire, Fanna began to sing. There was no announcement, no preparation. They were sitting as they always did in the evening round the fire and suddenly Fanna's voice rose, clear and mournful in the night air. She sang an old country song about a girl who goes walking and meets a woodcutter who takes her away from her home to a place where she is lonely and has only the trees for company. Jankin and Doran joined in. They began another song, about travelling far from home and missing it, and others joined in with the chorus, and inside every one of them something was stirred and came to life that had long been dormant. The ones that had come from the City recognised in the songs something that had been missing from their lives there: the sharing of human emotion in remembering the past. Andalou found himself stirred, and as one of the newer arrivals, took Beggis's arm as they sang in recognition of what they had each been through. Scummo felt tears on his cheeks. Kelpin, concerned, wiped them away with a grimy finger; she stood behind him as he sat and threw her arms around his neck. Nobody spoke.

This evening of the singing marked the end of the first part of the group's life together. They would move now into a village, or villages, and make a new life for themselves if they could. All were afraid of the Masters returning, yet there had been no sign of them for over two years now. Beggis had talked of sickness in the City. Whether this was what was keeping the Masters occupied, they could only guess.

Beggis and Magrab left early the next morning to begin their search, Beggis with her bright hair tied up on top of her head in a rag roll, her bundle clumsily tied against her back. Magrab carried the water bottles and a long, sharpened stick. Suddenly realising the importance of their mission, she remembered that she hadn't said goodbye to anyone. Fanna and Jankin, too, were about to leave. She waved at them, feigning cheerfulness.

'Good luck! Bet you get back before we do.'

Magrab turned to wave to the others then strode off up the track, leaving Beggis trotting in his wake.

***

Erasil was a day's journey and the paths were overgrown along the stream they followed for the better part of their journey to the village. Each wore shoes made from pigskin, which were tied with leather thongs. They kept out some of the cold, but after eight miles, began to wear through the soles, leaving Beggis, who had tender feet, wincing with pain as they pushed their way onward through brambles and nettles, not yet dead, that overhung the paths. Magrab had been to this village several times before and, blessed with a keen sense of direction, didn't falter.

Beggis stopped near a dry log to sit down and do up the laces that held her leg covers together. It was a moment before Magrab noticed she wasn't following. When he did look back and didn't see her, he felt alarm and retraced his steps at once and was relieved to find her seated on the log, her left foot pulled up into her lap as she retied the laces.

'I w-w-w-wondered what had happened to you.'

'Oh – I'm just trying to tie these up. My legs are really sore.' Beggis showed him her calf, striped across with red scratches from which blood oozed in wet scarlet beads. It was inflamed and sore.

Magrab looked closely at it. 'I-I know something that might help you.' He moved off the path and hunted for something in the undergrowth. Finally, he came back with some fleshy leaves, which he tore so that the milky sap ran down his fingers. He carefully and respectfully anointed Beggis's calf with the sticky juice.

'It wasn't quite what I was looking for, but it should do the trick. We used to give this to our farm animals when they had an infection. It seemed to work. How does it feel now?'

'Thanks, Magrab. It seems to have soothed it a little. We'd better start walking again.' Beggis still felt a little uneasy in his presence, and walking was easier than sitting still on the log with Magrab peering at her leg. She stood up, wincing a little as her feet felt the pressure of the ground again. Magrab turned and led the way. Biting her lip, Beggis limped after him.

There was so much about this environment she still didn't understand, and she often found that she was overwhelmed with the task of trying to make sense of everything around her. She wondered why she had agreed to come now. But she would have to make the best of it, she supposed. Sighing, she followed as Magrab strode through the waist-high vegetation that bordered the stream. The track had more or less disappeared over the years, though the animals continued to make their own tracks through the undergrowth. Neither dared go into the stream for fear of attracting the eel creatures. Though they had seen none for a while, they still retained a deep, basic fear of them. The stream, with its clear water and weedy pebbles, looked innocent enough. Soon, Magrab said, they would come to a pool where the stream had once been diverted, and there they would head inland away from the stream to Erasil. They should be there by early evening.

The pool, when they came to it, was deep, and there were the remains of a stone embankment at one end. There was no sign of life.

'They used to keep fish in here,' said Magrab. 'There was a grill over each end so they couldn't get out. They've gone now.' But one grill was still there, toppled sideways in the water and bearded with weeds. 'Ah, here's one still.' He climbed down the bank of the pool and balanced precariously on the rocks, unable to keep away from this potent memory of the past.

'Careful!'

'I just want to straighten it. Put it back as it should be.'

'Don't fall in.' A movement at the bottom of the pool made her cry out in alarm. Magrab leapt for the bank and Beggis hauled him up, fast, as a sodden piece of wood, a smooth tree branch, came free from its resting place in the silt at the bottom of the pool and began its slow cartwheels in the water down the stream, disturbed by the change in flow of the water. Beggis laughed nervously with relief, then cried, remembering Chasna. Magrab held her, his own beating heart gradually losing the fear that had gripped it.

'That was frightening,' she said.

'It looked exactly like . . .'

'We must be more careful. If it had been one of those things, you might not have escaped.'

'You're a good lookout.'

'Thanks.'

***

They reached Erasil as the sun was low and the light was reaching over the land with soft pink rays, while the sky was streaked with scarlet and silver clouds. Being in a valley, the village, or what was left of it, was quiet and the air was still. Insects settled on their faces as they arrived, and Beggis, who was unprepared for this, slapped and fanned them away with her hands while Magrab, whose hair was sparse, found his head the centre of the flies' attention. Calmly, he tied some grass together and used it as fly-whisk. Watching him, Beggis followed suit.

Magrab led Beggis to a house at the centre of the village, a stone one-storey dwelling with most of its roof intact. The floor was littered with owl pellets, and weeds grew from the window ledges. But it provided shelter of sorts. They gathered some sticks together and made a fire in what was the old fireplace, waiting until it grew dark enough for the smoke not to be visible. The flies, smoked out or lulled by the lack of light, departed, and Beggis and Magrab toasted some dried fish and ate the provisions they had brought with them.

Beggis was cold in the night and woke feeling lonely and depressed.

Magrab was not asleep. 'You awake?'

'Yeah. Cold, isn't it?'

'I'll warm you up.' Unused to close physical contact as she was, Beggis felt warmed as she allowed Magrab to wrap his body around hers and hold her from behind as she lay curled up beside the dying fire. It was comforting after all to have him there with her. He made no demands and seemed satisfied just to hold her, and as the night went on, she slept more peacefully than she had done since coming to the settlement. Even the return of the owl didn't waken them. Somewhere in a dream she saw Chasna. She was standing on a bank a little way from Beggis, waving goodbye, and she was smiling.

The detailed examination of the village and its buildings took up most of the morning. Grass was growing thickly around the buildings, and saplings had taken root here and there. The roofs of the buildings were mostly intact, and although the doors had been removed from some entrances, there was a basic structure inside which provided shelter. Most had been stripped of their furnishings, such as they were, but they managed to unearth a few basic tools from the outhouses. Magrab found a green stick and made a notch for every living unit that was usable. Next to the notches he carved a tiny wavy line, to show that water could be found there. Because the village was low, the well was full and the clanking old bucket and chain mechanism could be cleaned up and used. It was when they shifted the rotting wooden lid that covered the well that they found a surprise. A shiny metallic tube, set into the well wall, twisted round when they peered down and looked back up at them.

Beggis shouted in alarm, jumping back. Magrab tiptoed to the edge and peered down. The metal thing moved to face him, then withdrew into a socket somewhere in the well lining. Magrab put the cover over the well. 'I've heard about these.'

'Well – what are they? Frightened the life out of me'

'Some of sort of spy-tube. It's the Masters' way of keeping an eye on us.'

'We had spy cameras in the City. I didn't think I'd find one out here. Now what?'

Magrab thought. 'I could try to dislodge it with a stick. Push it into the well. It can't watch us anyway if the cover's on the well.'

'No, but we have to get water sometime. Anyway, it'll have sent pictures back knowing we're here. We'd better leave. I wish Bethyl or someone was here to advise us.'

'Shall we leave now?'

'How many hours of daylight are there left?'

He thought, counting on his fingers. 'I would say about six. We could get as far as the wood. I think we'd better leave, don't you?'

Beggis nodded. Wearily, they collected the few things they had brought with them and set off back the way they had come. They stopped at the pool and noticed that the grill Magrab had moved had been moved back again. There was a fresh footprint on the bank.

Beggis stared at it. 'Could that be yours?'

Magrab had big feet. He shook his head. 'Not mine.' He looked round at the grassy sides of the pool and beyond. What might be hiding in the bushes and shrubs beyond? He could see nothing but could sense he was being watched. 'Someone with a small foot, anyway. It's either one of us, or someone like us, or a servant of the Masters. Either way, it could be dangerous. Darfi said that someone came to the barge they were on and planted one of those metal things then. He didn't know who it was but he felt sure it was a servant of the Masters. They used to use people in the village to do their bidding before the Herdings – things the dogs couldn't do. They pretended to be villagers like us, but we caught them sneaking around at night and pretty quickly found them out. I think we threw one or two in the pond. They were spies. It made no difference, they just herded us up and took us to the City anyway.'

'Except for you and some of the others.'

'When I knew my family had gone, I wished then that they *had* taken me. Believe me, anything is preferable to watching your children die in the way they did.'

'In the City?'

'No. Maybe you don't know. I was away when they came and rounded up my family. My children were very young. The dogs . . .' He stopped, shaking at the memory.

Beggis laid her hand on his arm. 'You don't have to tell me. I can guess.'

'Awful. Awful. I had to bury what was left. That's why I came to this village with you. I can't bear to go back to the other one.'

Beggis suddenly saw that although her life in the City had been sterile and free from most emotional contacts, as were the lives of the other City-dwellers, here things were different. The close physical contact and cooperation between the members of the group meant that bonds formed, alliances grew and people became emotionally closer. This was difficult for those who had never experienced this before or who were unused to it. It made them vulnerable and forced them to consider their own actions. Beggis had been separated from her parents during the Herdings at the age of eight, then forced to fend for herself in the nursery until she was given her own apartment at fourteen. Since the age of eight, she had received no physical affection, had not been able or allowed to develop any close friendships and until the time when she decided to rebel and got to know Chasna better, she had been alone.

She had a sudden and unwelcome memory of her mother's face, contorted with rage and grief, as the dogs drove them away from her, leaving her shivering and fearful by a tree, where the round-up truck picked her and the other young children up. Was that what Magrab had felt? She looked at him anew. He was sitting on the bank, his brooding face blank, his hands knotted together as he remembered. She tapped his shoulder with her finger, lightly. 'We ought to go.'

He returned to the present and got to his feet. She set off back down the path, watchful and alert to any movement. He followed.

***

When they finally returned to the settlement, without any further evidence of other life, it was dark and late. Beggis had a nagging feeling that whoever it was might have followed them. The wood was almost dark when they got to it, and Magrab's hope was that if they continued through the wood, anyone following them would find it difficult to pick up their tracks. Nevertheless, the first thing they did on arriving back was to report to Bethyl, Fanna and Jankin, who were surprised to see them. They had been about to sleep, and Jankin, who was on first watch, was settling himself into position at the cave entrance. The night watch had always been from the clifftop until recently, but by some unspoken agreement, this arrangement had now lapsed. Hearing that they had come across evidence of other life, Jankin supposed he'd better go back to the clifftop again and rose stiffly, clambering over the sleeping bodies of the others to climb the little path up to the lookout post.

Bethyl and Fanna listened seriously to what Magrab and Beggis had to say.

'You must be tired,' Fanna said at last. 'Jankin will watch tonight from the top. There's nothing more we can do for the time being. Get some sleep. Jankin will tell Darfi when he wakes him for second watch.'

They turned in and slept well. They did not hear the young visitor who arrived in the night and was spotted by Darfi on the beach, trying to find a way up to the cave. Darfi left the clifftop and descended the path, causing the figure to freeze and shiver in the night wind. He put up no resistance at all. Darfi silently approached and took the young boy by the arm and led him to the fire. He had stayed by the fire then, watching the boy, who rolled over and slept almost immediately.

Kelpin was excited to see the newcomer next morning. He stretched, scratched, and looked about him. His eyes darted round the camp, taking in everything, though his body remained still. He sat cross-legged where he had slept, waiting for something. The others were curious but sensed that he needed time to accustom himself to his surroundings before anything else happened.

Jankin sat next to him and pointed to himself. 'Jankin.' He gestured towards the boy, who was silent, with a question on his face. He repeated the gesture. The watchful eyes of the boy did not flicker. Fanna approached with a corn cake and held it out to him, gesturing that he should eat it. He snatched it from her and stuffed it in his mouth as though terrified that it might be taken away. Once he had eaten, Fanna and Jankin tried again. Still, the boy remained silent. He was filthy and his thin body was covered in scratches and sores, half healed. His matted hair was full of twigs and debris from the woods and in his face, with its sharp cheekbones and weathered skin, only his eyes seemed alive. The rest of his face remained impassive and quiet.

'Perhaps he can't hear,' ventured Fanna after several more futile attempts to communicate.

Jankin clapped his hands loudly behind the boy's head. The boy gave a sudden shiver of surprise. 'He can hear all right. Maybe he's choosing not to speak?'

'Yes, maybe.'

'What shall we do?'

'Act as though he can hear. He's pretty young to be all on his own, isn't he? How old are you?' Fanna asked the boy. He did not reply. 'I'd say he was about ten or eleven, close to Kelpin in age.'

'Perhaps Kelpin could look after him. Keep an eye on him. Kelpin?'

Kelpin, who was listening keenly from the beach below, called up, pretending she hadn't overheard. 'What?'

'We want you to look after this boy for us. We don't know his name.'

'Can I give him a name? If I look after him?'

'Okay.'

Kelpin put her head on one side as she climbed the cliff path to look at the boy. The boy's eyes did not meet hers; they darted around her and returned to gaze at the ashes of the fire.

'I shall call him . . . Bouncer.'

'Bouncer?'

'He's jumping around inside,' Kelpin told them by way of an explanation.

'Well, you can show Bouncer where to wash, Kelpin. He's filthy.'

She held out her hand to the boy. 'Come with me, Bouncer.' And to their surprise, the boy got up and followed her, though he did not take her hand. Kelpin took him to the pool, now safely guarded against eel invasion, and showed him how she washed. She took off her tunic and laid it on the bank. Then, wearing only a woven cache-sexe, she stepped into the water. He was wearing the tattered remains of felt britches and a jacket that had been made to fit a much larger person. Following Kelpin's example, he took them off. He stood on the bank watching her, then slowly joined her, sitting waist-deep in the cold stream water and rubbing his body with the bundle of leaves Kelpin gave him. Naked in the pool, he shivered and clutched his arms to his chest. Kelpin's newly developed breasts were exposed to the sun and the cold water and she laughed at his discomfort. The boy looked away. They got dressed, letting the sun dry their bodies, and Kelpin took Bouncer to look for snails along the cliff.

That evening, Beggis and Magrab sat around the fire with the others and told them of the village. There was concern about the camera tube. Darfi and Scummo told the others again about the barge and how they had got rid of the spy camera there. There were raised eyebrows and questions. Clearly, some of the members felt alarm. Beggis and Magrab went over the potential accommodation and the possibilities of the village.

All the while, the boy, Bouncer, was sitting a little apart, eyes darting to left and right, thin dirty fingers opening and closing into fists at his side. The adults glanced at him from time to time.

'Is it safe to talk about our plans in front of him when he hasn't been here five minutes?' This was Sita.

Fanna answered. 'Do we have a choice? Do you really think we should make him sit somewhere else out of earshot while we decide about the village? The Masters must know we're here. For some reason, they've left us alone. I know we all took elaborate precautions when we first came here, but my guess is that they've known all about our movements from day one. Beggis and her friend left the City without any opposition. So either it means that they are watching us covertly to see how we survive, as part of some experiment, or that they actually don't care what happens to us and aren't interested anyway.'

'So why the cameras?' Darfi voiced the question. The rest were silent, considering the implications of what Fanna had said.

'They want to monitor our activities without interfering in them, I suppose. What do others think?'

There was a long discussion. A spirit of tired resignation and gloom had fallen on the group. Finally, Jankin raised his hand to speak, and the group gradually fell silent and turned to look at him. 'In a sense, it makes no difference what the Masters know or don't know. All we have is our lives now, and how we live them. We have chosen freedom – we have to abide by that. No regrets!'

'No regrets,' they echoed. But their response was tinged with weariness and the shadow of cold and hungry days and nights ahead.

M. Valentine Williams

Chapter 13

The Masters scanned the bank of monitors.

'They've gone back to the village. There's an image from the well at Erasil.'

'Were we expecting that?'

'I'm a bit surprised they left it so long. It's the best option for them now that their numbers have grown.'

'Are they still there, do we know, or just passing through?'

'I can't register them anywhere in the village, so I would imagine they've gone back to the coastal settlement.'

'What about the boy?'

'He'll follow them. The group will probably take him in – they have before with stray travellers.'

'It seems both admirable and foolish to me. Do we know why they do this?'

'Not really. They have started singing at night, too, another strange thing. They never did this in the City.'

'What effect does it have on them, do we think?'

'We are still not good at registering their emotions. We only seem able to judge things from their behaviour.'

'And has that changed?'

'Facial expressions tell us that they are mostly sad when they sing. The coordinates for sadness don't tally exactly, though. This is one of the areas we are having problems assessing. Sadness mixed with something, perhaps.'

'Keep working on it, Number Eleven. Do they smile more often now?'

'The one with the baby smiles more than the others. The young girl they call Kelpin also smiles and laughs. I would call her a key personality. If we want a survival gene, she has it, I think.'

'Interesting. Flick her up on the screen, will you? Adaptable. Seeks out safe adults. No fear in expressing opinion or feeling. Shows friendship, ability to care, practical problem-solving ability. Promising.'

'What happens now, with the boy?'

'Let us see whether he is able to respond to the situation before we call him in. We will watch him closely during the singing and with the girl-child. What has he shown us so far? Does he smile?'

'No.'

'Show fear of the others?'

'Doesn't seem to.'

'Excitement? Pupil dilation?'

'Negative. His eyes move a lot, though.'

'What does that indicate? Do we know?'

'He appears alert. A state of general arousal is detected from his readings.'

'Which is what we expected anyway?'

'Quite so.'

'Keep me informed of any changes. Number Eleven?'

'Yes?'

'Take a sample from the girl-child. We may need to use the DNA. Best to err on the side of caution, don't you agree?'

'I'll see to it, Number One.'

Chapter 14

Kelpin slept badly. They had all gone to bed later than usual because they had spent the evening preparing for the journey in the morning. Kelpin had tossed and turned, unable to sleep, itchy and uncomfortable. Something was happening to her body. Bouncer had seen it yesterday, and she had become aware of it too. Adolescence was creeping up on her. She felt moody and out of sorts. She rubbed her legs to warm them and then was aware of a sore spot at the top of her thigh, at the back where she couldn't see it. She went over to Fanna, who was giving directions to Andalou about tying up bundles.

'Fanna?'

'Yes, Kelpin.' Fanna put down the sticks she was holding. Something in Kelpin's manner meant that she needed to pay attention. Kelpin never made a fuss and was too aware of others to be asking her for attention unnecessarily at such a busy time.

'What's that on my leg? I can't see it.' She arched backwards, in vain, to demonstrate.

'Hold still. There?' Kelpin nodded. 'Looks like a bite. But it's quite large. Does it hurt?'

'I can't feel it when you touch it, at all.'

'You'd think it would feel sore.'

'Fanna, I'm scared.'

'No need to feel scared, Kelpin. It's just a bite from some insect or other. Let me look at it tonight?' Fanna looked at Kelpin and saw for the first time that her face was tense and unhappy. She put an arm round her shoulder, protectively. 'Would you like me to put some heal-all on it?' Kelpin nodded and, hiding a sigh, Fanna undid her bag of herbs and ointments and selected a skin bag containing the dry pounded leaves and roots of heal-all, which she mixed with a little water to make a paste to spread carefully across the puncture mark on Kelpin's thigh. She looked closer at the mark before she did so. The puncture wound was round and about the size of a grain of wheat. Around it was a circle of red and inflamed skin.

Fanna called over Jankin to have a look. 'Something bite you in the night, Kelpin?'

'No.'

'Well something's taken a liking to you – does it hurt?'

'No. I can't feel it at all.'

Jankin looked at Fanna. She nodded. 'Hold still now

while I put the all-heal on.'

Kelpin did as she was told.

'Enough doctoring for today. We need to get moving if we're going to reach Erasil by dark.'

They resumed their preparations, leaving behind only a faint trace of their presence in the form of small soft footprints in the sand as Bouncer, disobeying orders, ran back across the newly swept sand to pick up a strand of oar weed.

The party was moving off. Beggis led the way. Anga with baby Freedom, Doran, Darfi and Sita followed in her wake. Finally, Bethyl was left and prodded Kelpin, who was running her fingers through her hair and gazing at her reflection in the pool.

'Come on, Kelpin. We'll lose sight of the others if we don't go now.'

'Where's Bouncer?'

'I expect he went ahead with the others.'

'He didn't. He always goes with me.' They looked along the beach, scanning the rocks and sandy hummocks of the shore. The tide was out. In the flat stillness at the sea's edge, as it spread out in glassy fans of water across the sand, something was rolling. As they watched, unable to decide what it was, a broad ripple with a dark, waving shadow moving beneath it grabbed hold of the rolling shape and tugged it out to sea.

Bethyl turned to Kelpin, who, white-faced, was staring at the vanishing body.

'We can't help him, Kelpin.' She turned Kelpin's face away from the sea. After a while, she said, 'Let's go and join the others.'

The journey was made easier by the rest of the party, who chopped back the spiny branches in the woods to let them through. Jankin was waiting, as they had agreed, at the edge of the wood. Bethyl told him about Bouncer.

'Just as well we're moving,' said Jankin. 'I thought it was too good to be true, that we hadn't seen any eel things for a while. '

'He must have gone right down to the sea's edge. It was low tide and he liked to collect oar weed for us, didn't he?'

'But he must have known about the eel things? None of us would have gone down there without a lookout.'

'Bouncer was different. We don't know how much he understood, and he hadn't been with us long enough to learn these things.' Kelpin was sadly acknowledging the fact for them all. They went on their way, noting that the fish trap in the pool was untouched. Nor were there any footprints in the mud.

Now that they had decided to move back to the village of Erasil, despite the camera in the well, the group members moved forwards with a sense of purpose. It was late in the evening when they finally arrived at Erasil. Magrab and Beggis led them to the house they had camped in on their last trip. An owl flew out of the building as they approached.

'The owl says it's safe, anyway.' Jankin peered round the door.

One by one they entered, inhaling the musty smell of the damp stones. It was a long time since any of them had been in a building to stay, and it felt strange. They put their belongings down in one corner and Magrab and Darfi went outside to see if they could find any wood to burn. The darkness was by now impenetrable, and they came back quite soon, defeated. The others tried to make themselves comfortable. They had left behind the makeshift mattresses, sacks stuffed with leaves and hay, that had served as pillows and cushions, emptying them out in the woods near the beach and bringing with them only the bags, which they filled with dried fish, corn, and whatever food and clothing they had. Darfi was on first watch; the others slept. Few noticed that Bouncer wasn't with them, and it was only when the grey light of early morning shone through the grimy window that they realised he wasn't there. Bethyl waited until they were all awake and then called for their attention.

'Well, we're here. Most of us have had an uncomfortable night, so let's not be too hard on ourselves today. We need to get our bearings and look around. One of the first things we have to try and do is to disconnect or destroy the spy camera in the well. Otherwise we can't use the water, unless there's a pump somewhere. The other thing I need to tell you is that as we were leaving the caves at the beach, Fanna and Kelpin noticed that the boy, Bouncer, was not with us. They saw a body in the sea being dragged out by one of the eel creatures – Fanna, can you tell us what you saw?'

'It's as Bethyl says. Kelpin noticed Bouncer was missing. While we were looking for him, we saw something in the water, right at the edge – the tide was right out – and then we both saw something long and dark coming under the water towards the body. If it *was* a body. It pulled it under the water. I feel sure it was one of the eel creatures. There's been no trace of Bouncer, so we are assuming the worst has happened.'

Kelpin's face was sad and drawn, but she said nothing. There was some muttering among the others.

Anga spoke, restraining Freedom, who was wanting to crawl to the door and make his escape. 'At the beach we had shelter and fresh water, but the eel things were always a threat. Here we've got shelter but we may be spied upon. Not much of a choice, except that as far as we know, the cameras don't hurt you. Let's go and take it to bits, then we'll feel safer. How are we going to do that, by the way?' She grabbed the chuckling Freedom and pulled him onto her lap. 'Sit still now.' The baby sucked his thumb solemnly and buried his face in her chest, aware that the eyes of all the other adults were upon him.

'If I can dislodge it with a stick, or we can tie something round it and pull it loose, we can bury it or chuck it down a hole,' Scummo said. 'The one on Darfi's boat and the one I found when Kelpin and I first escaped, the one in the hut, were quite easy to get rid of. One I jabbed with a stick and it fell into the sea. Made a noise as it went down. The other I covered with mud so it couldn't see anything.'

They went out to the well. Bethyl told the others to stand away from the well, then she, Scummo and Magrab covered their faces with pieces of clothing. Scummo lifted the well lid and slid it to one side. Magrab pointed.

There was the camera, twisting round to peer up at them. Scummo took the stick Bethyl was holding out to him and poked the camera gently. Nothing happened. Magrab grabbed a large rock and dropped it on top of the camera. It twisted and retreated into a niche in the well side; the rock slid down and fell with a loud splash in the dark circle of water below. They put the lid on the well again.

'Ideas?' Bethyl appealed to them all.

'Cover it,' was Scummo's advice. 'Put one of the bags over it for now.' He went into the house and came out with a homemade bag, from which he had emptied the dried fish. 'Smells a bit, but this should take care of it.' He slipped the bag onto the end of his stick and removed the well cover, recoiling a little as the camera twisted towards him again. After some delicate working with two sticks, he finally managed to mask the camera with the bag sufficiently to feel satisfied that it could no longer send back pictures of any of them. 'It's a temporary measure, but it's the best I can think of for the moment.'

Kelpin, watching, was thoughtful. 'How did they put it down there?' she asked. 'We can't reach it from up here, so how did they reach down to put it there?'

Scummo peered down the dark well. There were some rungs on the side opposite the camera. 'We can climb down there. It's what they must have done. Well done, Kelpin.' She beamed with pride. 'Maybe we can dismantle it.'

Darfi offered to climb down level with it and prise it off the well wall.

'What with?' asked Scummo. They had an axe, found on a previous trip, but there was nothing else that would give the leverage they needed. They dared not risk losing the axe. Covering his face again, Scummo climbed down the well shaft until he was level with the thing. It twisted to face him. It could still see him! Suddenly, he was overcome with a blind impotent rage. He kicked the thing with his free foot, hard, and received an electric shock that made him reel. They saw his fingers stiffen, loosen from the rungs of the ladder and then he fell, while the others looked on in horror, into the depths of the well.

Andalou was the first on the scene. He lowered himself over the side of the well and climbed down the rungs before anyone had time to move. The camera thing hung limply at a strange angle and did not move. Scummo had deactivated it. He lay feebly thrashing in the water below him. They knew it wouldn't be long before he disappeared under the water. Finally, Andalou reached the bottom rung. He couldn't reach Scummo enough to grab hold of him. His face was blue and his eyes were closed.

It was Kelpin who came up with a plan. Watching from the top of the well, her face white with anxiety and shock, she remembered that in the barn where they had been sleeping there was a wooden ladder leading to the hay-loft. It was a very rustic, rudimentary ladder, but a ladder it was.

'Quick', she shouted. 'Get the ladder! The one in the barn – Andalou can put it in the water and reach Scummo that way.'

It was as if the others had also been given an electric shock, having been completely dazed by the experience of watching Scummo fall into the depths of the well, and were now free to move again. Bethyl and Darfi ran for the ladder and came back with it quite quickly. Andalou was at the bottom of the rungs, trying to grab Scummo. Bethyl went down the well and Darfi passed her the ladder. She passed it in turn to Andalou, who lowered it into the water. The well held about five feet of water, they judged. The rungs, being old, were not very strong, but with the second ladder in place, Andalou was able to hold on to Scummo.

Scummo, who had been unconscious, opened his eyes and realised that there was something in the water beside him. He floated face up, blue-lipped and barely conscious, but alive.

'We'll get you out of there,' Andalou told him. 'Can you hear me, Scummo?'

'How deep's the water, Andalou?' shouted down Bethyl. 'Can you stand up in it?'

'About five feet. I could just stand, I think.'

'Can you try? Maybe if you can stand next to him you can help him stay afloat.'

'Okay. I can give it a go. We have to get him out of here. I could use some help down here, though.'

'Doran, how about you? You're tall.'

Doran climbed over the side of the well and went down towards the water. Andalou lowered himself until he was holding on to the bottom rung and his legs and thighs were in the water. He shuddered with the cold. Holding onto the wooden ladder, he lowered himself fully until he was standing at the bottom of the well. His head was the only part of him visible to the watchers above. He pulled Scummo to him and raised his head a little. Doran descended and entered the water alongside him. Scummo's body was quite cold now. His eyes were flickering and his face was still blue. Together, Doran and Andalou held Scummo's face above the water, but they didn't have the leverage or strength to lift him clear of the surface. Doran

235

blew into his mouth, and after a moment or two, he began to lose his blue colour and breathe more easily.

Doran paused. 'I don't think he can stand up. He certainly can't haul himself up that ladder. Can you move your arms, Scummo?' Scummo moved his arms feebly. They could feel a cold current of water round their legs, and they tried not to think of the eels.

Kelpin, watching anxiously from above, had had one good idea. She didn't have another. Bethyl, meanwhile, was taking Anga's wrap off her and twisting it to form a rope. Freedom, no longer in his sling on her back, complained.

'You can have it back after,' promised Bethyl. 'I'm going to pass this down to you. If you can tie it round his chest, one of us will come down and lift him from above. You push him from below. Catch!' The makeshift rope was caught by Doran. Together, they managed to loop it around Scummo's chest.

'Scummo, can you hear me?' The eyelids flickered a little. 'Scummo, we're going to try and pull you out. We're going to push you up and Magrab will catch hold of you. But we need you to help us, Scummo. Can you do that?'

Scummo opened his eyes fully. He nodded.

Magrab came down the well shaft and the others

heaved Scummo upwards towards him.

'Put your feet on my shoulders,' instructed Andalou. Scummo summoned up some movement in his feet and gave a feeble push as Doran raised his arms under Scummo's chest and lifted him clear. With a huge effort, Magrab managed to grab the twisted cloth and hold on. Andalou and Doran, staggering under the weight and in water up to their shoulders, hoisted Scummo further.

'We need you to help us.'

Scummo extended his arms to help them.

'Now hold on. Feel the rungs? Hold on to them.'

Scummo managed to hold on.

'Move his foot so it's on the wooden ladder.' Doran moved Scummo's foot. 'Feel that? Now push.'

Magrab pulled, Doran and Andalou pushed. Could Scummo hold on to the ladder and move up it if Magrab was holding him and the other two were pushing him upwards and moving his feet slowly and carefully up the rungs? They would soon find out. It took a long time, but eventually Scummo, hauled by Magrab and pushed by Doran and Andalou, got clear of the water and managed to hold on to the ladder rungs. Doran climbed up behind him, prompting him to move his feet. The activity woke him up a bit and restored his circulation.

'You can do it!' shouted Kelpin from above. 'Come on, Scummo! You can do it!' It took time, and Scummo needed to rest at frequent intervals, but they made it to the top of the ladder, where eager arms helped them onto the ground. Scummo lay on the grass beside the well utterly exhausted. The other two were helped from the well, shivering and dripping water in pools around them.

'Let's get them into the barn and light the fire,' ordered Bethyl as the others jumped to organise it. Scummo was supported on either side by Kelpin and Darfi. Kelpin glared angrily at Sita, who had been about to help, and she backed off. Beggis ran to collect wood for the fire and Fanna made a comfortable place where Scummo could sit.

'Wet things off,' said Fanna, helping him. The other wet ones peeled their clothes off by the door. There was little in the way of extra clothing that they could replace their wet things with, so they had to content themselves with standing nearly naked by the fire and watching the steam rise from their chilly bodies. Scummo sat, head between his knees, gasping in air. Kelpin stroked his head. The others rubbed him down until he was warmer, and he was covered in whatever extra bedding they had. As the fire grew warmer, he began to relax. He had burns on his feet that would take a while to heal, and being thrown into cold water as the shock happened was a blessing in disguise, they began to realise. Kelpin kept watch over Scummo for the first twenty-four hours, terrified that he was still not safe enough to be left. As soon as he appeared to be on the mend, she wandered away to do something else. The mark on her thigh had almost healed, but there was something about it that troubled her. She asked Fanna to inspect it from time to time.

Chapter 15

The village began to look more shipshape. Holes in windows were blocked up with straw and leather to stop the draughts; floors were swept with rush brooms; stones were pillaged from the dilapidated sheds at the edge of the village and used to mend walls nearer the centre. Couples and groups staked out their territory, and although the central barn building was still used as a meeting and eating place by all members, now they also had privacy. The winter weather that loomed ahead of them when they had arrived in the autumn had almost passed, and they were all still thinner and less robust, but alive.

The village also boasted some pigs now, kept in one of the old pigsties at the edge of the village. Sita had tracked a farrowing sow to her nest in the tall reeds by the wood's edge and kept watch until the young were half grown. Leading the pigs along a path with a trail of crab apples to where they would be ambushed by Doran and Darfi was dangerous, but they managed to capture one weaner alive, while the protesting sow, dangerously angry, was driven off, snorting, with sticks by Scummo and Andalou. There were three other half-grown hogs with the sow, but Doran knew from his past experience that if they had one, and that one was a female, before long the boars would come calling to mate with her. Then they would have lots of piglets. The food supplies were so meagre that at first, they did not have enough food to give the young sow and had to extend the makeshift fences to allow her to forage in the paddock. She quickly turned this patch of earth into a quagmire, making wallows and uprooting all the bushes and thistles that had grown up there since the villagers had been herded away.

Jankin wondered where all the chickens had gone that had been kept by the villagers in the past. Most, he knew, would have been eaten once the Masters had withdrawn the food supplies. He mused about how this had happened. The villagers had taken care of themselves for years, growing vegetables, barley and fruit, keeping hens and pigs and two or three communal cows. They had fishponds, pigeon lofts and warrens full of rabbits close by. Food was always available, in some shape or form. In his village by the coast, fishing had always provided the villagers with the food they needed. After the fish started to be pulled from the nets with two heads, or other deformities, the villagers did not want to eat them, and the eel creatures began to appear in the coastal waters. It was odd, how it all began.

One morning, the villagers had found large sacks of field beans, corn and barley left outside the main building. No one had seen them arrive and no one knew who had left them there. Were they a gift from another village? They didn't think so.

Warily, the villagers approached the sacks and investigated the contents. There was no writing on any of the sacks or any indication of their origin. When the villagers opened them and realised what the contents consisted of, they took the sacks into the communal storehouse and kept them for the winter. They remained suspicious and watchful. Jankin himself was very fearful, sensing something going on that was beyond his understanding. Several weeks later, there was another delivery. This time it was fruit: one sack of apples, one of pears and one of sweet chestnuts. As these items were things that the villagers already grew and made good use of, they simply stored them away with their own produce. Most of this was kept in a communal store. Now having a surplus of apples, the villagers made more cider and gave out the pears for everyone to eat. The villagers did not like to feel under an obligation to someone they didn't know. The senior villagers were mainly concerned by the fact that no one ever saw the sacks arrive.

After the third delivery, the people in the village began to be extremely anxious. Who was leaving these sacks? Would they want something in return?

That winter was a hard, cold one, and the villagers began to depend on the extra rations they were receiving. Finally, the older villagers decided that they had to find out who was making these deliveries. Accordingly, they kept watch night

243

after night until, at last, their patience was rewarded. One dark night, when the man on watch was almost asleep, a vehicle, moving smoothly and without sound, glided smoothly along the track, and a hooded figure seated on the back pressed a lever. Silently, three sacks slid onto the ground in the middle of the track, and the vehicle reversed, going back the way it had come. The watchman could hardly believe he had just witnessed it, so swift and silent was the operation.

'It was a sort of machine,' he told the others. 'One that just slid along and then the front sort of came down and the bags slid off. No noise at all.'

'Could you see who was on it?'

'Someone was on it, but they had a kind of cloak around them. Small, they were. I couldn't see them properly.'

Despite pondering over it for some while, they could make no sense of it, and having ruled out the other villages around, who they discovered had also been receiving food from an unknown source, they were at a loss to know the source of these unsolicited gifts.

Some of the villagers wouldn't touch the gifts, thinking that they might be poisoned, but after a while, when others had sampled them without ill effect, they grew bolder and began to help themselves. As time went by, they began to depend more and more on these gifts and to talk about their mysterious benefactors as gods.

One bright spring morning, when most of the villagers were going about their morning tasks, they heard a loud crackling sound, followed by a voice that penetrated even the farthest corners of the village.

'Good morning, people of Village Seven,' the voice croaked. The villagers looked around to see where the sound was coming from. 'You have been the lucky recipients of our gifts these last six months.' The villagers continued to look in every direction to find the source of the sound. 'Now we are requesting something from you. We are asking you to make three of your members available to us. This will involve very little and the three will be away from the village for only a few hours. The procedure is entirely painless and all three will be returned within the day. Please select the three who will take part.'

The villagers were completely taken aback. There was a long silence as they looked at one another for clues as to what was happening. Finally, Bagdun, self-nominated leader, shouted back, 'And if we do not wish to take part? What then?'

'You have two days to think about it.'

'We didn't ask for your gifts. We'll pay you for them if that's what you want, though it seems hardly fair.'

'We are only asking that you cooperate with us a little. That is your payment. We will be back in two days.' There was more crackling and then silence. Fear, panic and anger spread like a forest fire through the village. Some blamed the village elders for having taken and made use of the gifts.

'So what should we have done? Left them outside to rot?' Bagdun was as panic-stricken as the rest. 'We have no knowledge of these people – if they *are* people. All we know is that they cannot be seen by us. Does anyone want to volunteer?'

No one did.

When the second day came and the voice once again boomed out over the village – 'People of Village Seven, have you decided who should accompany us?' – Bagdun shouted back, 'We are not willing to be tricked in this manner. We will pay you for the gifts in some other way. That is all.'

'You do not appear to understand, man from Village Seven. You have no choice. If three of you do not choose to come with us, we will select three ourselves.'

Bagdun stood his ground. He spread his arms between the other villagers and where he assumed the voice was coming from, shielding them. They heard barking in the distance, which drew closer and closer until the villagers could see the dark shapes of the mastiffs advancing down the lane towards them. The dogs, directed by inaudible whistles, cornered three villagers and drove them, terrified, out of the village and along the track towards the woods.

The three villagers returned several nights later, unable to talk about where they had been or what had happened. All had tags around their ankles.

They appeared to act as they had before, but something about them had changed, and they were treated with suspicion by the other villagers. All attempts to remove the tags failed. Bagdun, who felt responsible for what had happened, was blamed by the rest of the villagers.

Then the senseless notices appeared: YOU MAY WASH YOUR CLOTHES HERE on the trough by the village pump, YOU ARE PERMITTED TO MEET IN THIS ROOM, and, strangest by far, YOU MAY CONTINUE TO FEED YOUR ANIMALS, and YOU ARE PERMITTED TO FISH HERE. There were no more gifts. At first, the village people tore down these notices and carried on as they had always done. Some of the villagers did not want to do the things they had been given permission to do. They would not give in to the unseen beings out there.

The three people who were taken away were shunned by the other villagers. Bagdun, feeling himself scorned by the others, who felt he should have offered himself as a volunteer, tried to get closer to the three but found them to be flat and unresponsive since their encounter and unable to remember anything about their time away. They carried on their work as before, but it wasn't long before Bagdun gave up trying to gain information from them. Little by little, the Masters encroached upon the daily lives of the villagers. Gradually, more and more of their lives were taken away from them as the Masters gained control. It was impossible for the villagers to fight an invisible enemy. The commands that came from the sky blasted messages out to the bemused people day after day. Some of the villagers tried to ignore the orders and the restrictions being placed upon them; some jumped to do their bidding.

Jankin was already trying to decide whether to leave the village with his family, but felt the risks to them all were too great.

The responses from the Masters were unpredictable, and because they could not see who was issuing the commands, it was impossible to see if they were pleased or not. Some people did leave the villages and disappeared, heading for more distant destinations where they hoped the Masters could not reach them. The people became more careworn and harassed-looking daily as they scurried about, trying to obey the edicts, one of which stated that all chickens must be kept in a communal pen. This meant that villagers had difficulty deciding which bird belonged to which family, and separating a broody hen from the others so she could sit on a clutch of eggs was almost impossible. People quarrelled among themselves about it. Finally, the day came when the dogs arrived, big slavering mastiffs, and the villagers were herded like sheep along the lanes that led through the countryside to collecting points, where they were driven into holding pens and kept there by the dogs until the transport came. The homes they left behind were theirs no longer. Many of the villagers cried when they realised that they were leaving the only life they had ever known. It was then that the unexpected rocket attacks on the Masters happened, destroying the ferry that would take the villagers to the City. Driven over the cliff-edge by the savage dogs, most perished, while Jankin was forced to watch the slaughter from his hiding place on a boat moored in the bay.

Some of the homes in the villages were deliberately demolished by the Masters, while others were left standing but uninhabitable. Once the people had gone, life as it had been in the villages had gone too, and the buildings quickly fell into disuse. Any animal left behind in the village that had not been attacked by the dogs either escaped into the woods or stayed where they were and starved to death. Fairly soon, the countryside became a wasteland. Because the people were separated, it was difficult for them to keep in touch with one another. For those who escaped the Herdings, or who had run away from the villages before them, some were lucky and joined forces with others; others perished, eaten by the eel creatures, savaged by marauding dogs or dying from exposure and starvation.

Life in the City was miserable for many of the villagers. They missed the freedom of the countryside. There were no fields to walk in, no animals to tend. Most of the work that they had to do went on in the factories around the City. The Apartments they were put into were cell-like and sparsely furnished. As before, there were these senseless rules and regulations they had to abide by. If the breakfast wagon came round and they were not there in the line, they went hungry. They had no holidays. No sports were permitted. It was not really allowed to visit another's apartment, though quite how they could prevent this, no one knew, and there were liaisons between people despite this edict. Many villagers envied those who had run away before the Herdings and wished they had done the same.

Every morning and evening the dogs prowled along the corridor checking that everyone was in their apartment. No one dared to remain outside on the landings. The thought of those savage fangs bared in a snarl and looking for an excuse to seize a leg or an arm with bone-crushing force was enough to frighten people into staying indoors. Residents became lethargic. They stopped thinking about or caring for one another. Most looked forwards simply to their rations being given out and to the games on Sevenday in the arena. Some of the people questioned why they had been brought to the City, but there was no one to ask about it. Most simply rose in the morning, went to work and came home in the evening, with the only highlights in a day being the arrival of the food truck.

Residents, finding their lives empty of meaning, retreated indoors and passed their time away, apathetic, depressed and, without knowing it, bored. Gradually, they became aware that there were different groups in the Apartments. One such group were the Gelds, who were plump, feminine men who came and went from their apartment block at frequent intervals that coincided with the trips to the Jamarama.

Families had been separated during the Herdings and were kept apart by ensuring that the residents were housed in different sections. Sometimes an old neighbour was spotted in the distance as they boarded the hover-platform, but there had never been time to talk.

***

Now the time had come for *them* to return to the City. For weeks, the thoughts and the planning arising from this decision had taken up their waking hours. Bethyl, Fanna and Jankin, together with the other older members, had tried to make a decision that was in the best interests of them all.

While they realised that the City could offer material goods they badly needed, in particular clothes, food containers and bedding, the villagers began to grow restless and could not decide whether to return to the City, armed with the dog-controller Scummo and Darfi had taken, or to stay in their village. During hunting trips, they came across several bodies, located by their smell, which they kept clear of, and a young woman who was clearly sick and on the verge of dying. It was this encounter that helped them decide to return.

The young woman, when they came across her, was sitting under a tree, her head lolling forwards and her straight hair covering her cheeks. When they approached her cautiously, she flopped forwards even further. They called to her, watching her bone-white hands flutter as they spoke.

'Hello.'

No response.

'Are you sick? Do you need anything?'

The young woman raised her head a little. Her voice was breathless. It was an effort to speak at all. 'Fever. Stay away. All dead now.'

'Can we do anything for you?'

'Water.'

Darfi undid his water bottle and pushed his stick through the handle, holding it out to her. Weak as she was, she could not undo the top, and Darfi did not know what to do for the best. Finally, he took a deep breath and held it as he unscrewed the bottle top and placed the bottle in the woman's hand, before jumping backwards to what he hoped was a safe distance.

The woman put the bottle to her lips, swallowing water with an effort, then was silent for a time.

'All sick in the City,' she informed them. 'Finished.'

'Are you sure we can't help you?'

The woman shook her head sadly, then slumped over onto her side.

'Are you going to leave the bottle?' asked Sita, watching the water slop into the ground from the relinquished container.

'Have to,' he replied. 'I don't want to be responsible for bringing the sickness back to the village.'

The others agreed. They stood and watched as the woman slumped further onto the woodland floor, her head masked by the crisp dead leaves and brambles there. They knew there was nothing more they could do to help as the body ceased to move, the soft breath having left it as it fell. Shaking their heads sadly, they left the scene and went on with their hunting trip, though with heavy hearts. They knew that if they returned another time, the body would either be gone or it would be half eaten by the wild animals that were beginning to build up their numbers in the woods. The woman's death haunted them for several days and they talked about her at the meetings they held in the evenings around the fire. Bethyl felt strongly that they should go back to the City to see what had happened. If – and it was a big if – they could go back there without risking dying themselves, they argued, they would know better how to plan for the future. Eventually it was decided that Bethyl and Scummo should go back to the City and see what was going on. Kelpin was not pleased with this arrangement. She did not want him to put himself into any situation that might be dangerous; she had not yet quite recovered from the incident at the well.

Their relationship had stayed close ever since the death of her mother, and, young though he was, Scummo had taken responsibility for her and kept it. At times, it was as if he was the father she had never known and she was his infuriating but adored adolescent daughter. She was fiercely protective of him and jealous, though she did allow herself to become closer to Fanna as time went by.

She went to talk to Bethyl, whom she admired but was scared of. 'Bethyl, why does Scummo have to go to the City? Why can't one of the others go instead?'

'Because, Kelpin, he offered,' replied Bethyl lightly. 'And of all of us, Scummo knows the City best. Beggis does not want to return, ever, and Andalou, though he offered, was relieved that Scummo was going with me. You are worried about his safety?'

Kelpin nodded miserably.

'There are no guarantees, but I personally intend to return here in one piece, and I know the same is true of Scummo. We are going on a reconnaissance mission; that is, to see what's going on. We are not going to get involved with anything in the City, only try to find out what's happening there. Understand?'

'But what if the Masters catch you?'

'The strange thing is, Kelpin, that they have never tried to capture us here. They could have captured you and

Scummo when you first left the City, at least I imagine they could have, but they didn't. When I went back before with Scummo, when Andalou joined us, I'm sure they could have caught us with the dogs, but again they didn't. And Beggis and her friend were able to leave without being stopped. We don't know what their plan is, if there is one, but I do know that unless we take a chance and see what's happening, we may regret it in the year ahead.'

'Why?'

'Because there are all sorts of things in the City we need. Things we could make good use of. And if the City has been abandoned, as Scummo seems to think, there will be people alive there still who may need our help.'

Kelpin had to be content with this.

Chapter 16

Nothing about the City was as Scummo remembered it. Yet it was still the same in essence. Gone were the hover-platforms, gone the running feet of workers up and down the stairways. It was quiet everywhere. They kept their distance from the empty buildings, not knowing who might be there. Some sort of enforced quarantine had been organised, it seemed, as the Apartments they peeped into showed evidence of a hasty move. There were no bodies. Scummo looked around the building he had lived in. It seemed like a lifetime ago. The dull green stain on the balcony wall where his neighbour had spat continually was still there; the grey, dirty, ugly buildings were all still the same. Slowly, they crept from corner to corner of the block, along the walkways, searching. Had the Masters really abandoned the City? Where were the bodies, and if there were any survivors, where were they? Bethyl went in front of Scummo, silently listening, looking, checking. They covered two blocks in this way, then passed the next two, feeling there was little point to searching each one when there were no sounds or signs of anyone. The last block was slightly detached from the others.

Scummo had never been inside, but he knew there was a nursery on the ground floor, the one Darfi had escaped from. Otherwise, his knowledge of the layout was nil. Something told him that if there were survivors anywhere, it would be here. Bethyl nodded when he said that, and they began to walk to the far end of the arena, hopeful that they might find some of what they'd come to seek. As they drew under the shadow of the forbidding building, Scummo noticed the arena had not been swept for a long time, and neither was there any evidence of the dogs. Suddenly, Scummo caught a movement out of the corner of his eye. A thin wispy shape was standing like a scarecrow on the balcony above them. He nudged Bethyl. Had they been spotted? She whispered that they should stand out in the open and address the man. They stepped out into the arena. A wave of nausea-inducing stench wafted over them.

'Hello-oh,' Scummo called up softly.

The figure lowered its head and looked down, up again and then seemed to collapse at the knees. They heard a faint sound. 'Help us.'

Scummo and Bethyl looked at one another.

'Us?' Bethyl repeated.

'How many of you are there?' Scummo called. But there was no reply. He was about to ascend the concrete steps leading to the floor where they had seen the man when Bethyl stopped him by grabbing his arm.

'Hold on,' she said. 'We have to know we're safe before we can help them.'

The man on the balcony had staggered to his feet again and then appeared to be sitting on something. He called down. 'About fifteen of us left. The Masters gave us an injection. We haven't died like the others. There is no food here. The Masters have gone.'

'When did they leave?'

'Ages ago. Three weeks. More. I don't know.'

Scummo's mind was full of questions he dared not ask. What were they eating? What would they find up there?

Bethyl turned to face him. 'What do you think? Is it safe to go up there? Yes, I think it is. He seems to be saying that the ones still alive are all survivors, so they can't infect us. Or can they after three weeks?'

'We haven't had the injection, whatever that was.'

'No, true. What should we do? If we go back to ask the others, by the time we return all these people will be dead if they stay here.'

They debated it this way and that, uncertain what to do.

'At least we can leave them some food,' offered Scummo. Then other figures appeared on the walkway, slowly and with shaking bodies 'Can you walk?' he called to them.

'We're weak,' answered one. 'How far?'

Scummo conferred with Bethyl. It was clear the people were too weak to walk any distance.

'We'll try and find you some food,' Bethyl called up to them. 'We'll come back.'

'Help us,' implored the figure on the balcony.

'We'll come back,' Scummo insisted. 'We have to find food for you.' No dogs, no Masters, just these few survivors too scared or weak to help themselves.

Bethyl was moved by their plight but found it puzzling. 'Why are they still there? Why haven't they left and gone to search for food themselves?'

'Good question. Though I know people were pretty apathetic when I was here. They just sort of got on with it, I suppose. I would've done the same if it hadn't been for Kelpin, poor kid.'

'You had a purpose. Something suddenly caught hold of you and made you take the risk of leaving.'

'Yup.'

They had gone down a narrow street at the back of the Apartments. When Scummo lived here, there were factories along this street and meat-paste-processing plants or felt-making works. There had been a constant noise of machinery and workers chattering. Some of the buildings had been warehouses for storing beans and grain. They stopped outside one. Would there be any food still stored inside? The metal door was firmly closed, and though they pushed and pulled at it, it refused to budge.

Bethyl pointed upwards. 'That window is open,' she observed. She was light and muscular, and by standing on Scummo's shoulders. she could just about manage to lever the window open and wriggle through the narrow gap, where she fell, unable to turn around enough to hold on to the narrow sill, landing on several sacks of beans and knocking over a pair of scales. *Lucky*, she said to herself. In the gloom inside. she looked around. She had fallen about eight feet.

'You all right?' called Scummo from outside.

'Nothing broken.' Bethyl stood up. Then she unfastened the door, which had been bolted from inside. *There must be another way out of here*, she thought. Scummo came in to join her. Together, they examined the sacks and found the beans to be shiny and fresh, slipping through their fingers easily.

'They'll need soaking and boiling,' said Bethyl, remembering.

'Well, it's a start,' said Scummo. They uncovered some bins of round grains.

Bethyl sniffed them. 'No idea. You?'

'Could be couscous or tapioca,' guessed Scummo. 'Or it could be rat poison.'

'Rat poison?'

'It's probably grain, but we've no way of knowing for sure.'

'Shall we mix it with some water to see?'

They took a small scoopful to the tap and filled it with water. The granules swelled up and became translucent. Bethyl sniffed at it. 'Tapioca!' she said triumphantly. Was there still a supply of gas in the Apartments? Scummo wondered. If so, could they cook some of this stuff and feed the residents with it? A further search led to the discovery of some white powder that looked as if it might be dried milk and one pile of wrinkled turnips.

'This won't restore their health, any of this,' said Bethyl, 'but it will do for a start.'

Getting back to the City had been harder than they imagined. The fields were ragged and overgrown. The field workers who formed a large number of the City-dwellers had been among the first to fall ill, and without them the land soon returned to its natural state, once the Masters had left. Scummo had seen rusting combines and machinery in the fields. Bethyl, who did not know the City as well as Scummo, had noticed changes too. They discussed them as they scooped out some of the dried milk powder ready to take back to the survivors. They hoped that milk mixed with water would give back some of the energy that the survivors needed. They took half a sackful of beans, some tapioca and the milk powder back to the Apartments. This time, despite the overpowering smell, they went up to the first-floor landing, where the survivors were waiting for them.

'How did you get into the warehouse?' asked the old man they had first met. 'We've tried to break down the door, and we've been all along that street trying to find a way into some of the other warehouses. We knew there must be some food inside that big warehouse, but it was too difficult to get inside and we were very weak.'

'We had to break in,' said Scummo, pouring scoops of the white milky liquid into mugs in order to give each a drink. He told them about the beans in the sack. 'If you eat these now you'll be very ill, but if we can soak and cook them thoroughly you may be able to eat them later.'

Bethyl added to this wisdom. 'There was some stuff in a sack that we thought might be tapioca. We've only brought a little of it with us, but there's more in the warehouse. Have a look – maybe you can identify it for us.'

The man looked at the grains Bethyl held out, sniffed them and put one in his mouth. 'Not sure,' he said. He turned on the water and filled the remaining mug, adding the grains to it. They started to swell and become transparent. 'You're right,' he announced. 'It *is* tapioca. They used to feed us on it when the beans ran out. If you give it to me, I'll put it in this tin and cook it with some of the milk.'

Just then, a skinny figure emerged from inside the building and snatched the tin from him and drank down the mixture. Suddenly there was chaos as the other residents woke up and clamoured to be fed. Scummo backed away hastily, uncertain what to do.

Bethyl looked alarmed. 'Stop that!' she called to them. 'There's enough for everybody.'

A woman close to her muttered slyly, 'Some of us have had more than our share already, eh, Tinsit?'

'Shut your mouth. We all did what we had to do to survive, you included.'

Bethyl called them to order. 'Anyone who eats this tapioca uncooked will be very sorry, I can promise you. We have done our best to help you, now you have to help yourselves. You' – she pointed at the man who snatched it – 'will have a stomach ache so bad you'll wish you were dead.'

As she was speaking, a half-starved teenage boy behind her had hauled himself upright and was trying to get into her backpack. Bethyl removed his hands and turned to face him. 'You will all get some food very soon. Scummo, have you got more of that milk mix?'

He passed it to her and she held the dirty can to the boy's lips. 'Not too much. Your stomach can't take too much in one go.'

The boy's head lolled back, half-dissolved milk powder round his lips.

When all the survivors had been given a milk drink, and the tapioca mix was nearly cooked, Bethyl pulled Scummo aside.

'Something's going on here. Some people are much weaker than others. I think the stronger ones have been forced to eat the ones who died.'

Scummo, who had wondered the same when they arrived, nodded gravely. 'What do you think is causing the smell?'

'Don't ask. Let's get out of here. Two of us can't control all of them and I'm scared they might take our supplies if they get any stronger. You saw what that boy tried to do.'

'It wouldn't help them if we starved too. We've done what we set out to do – checked for survivors and found them food. If we bring back some more stuff from the warehouse and then leave them to it, I'd say we've done a good job.'

'I'm glad you agree.'

They were halfway down the stairs when the residents noticed they were leaving. A young woman fell to her knees, imploring them not to go.

'Don't leave us! We'll all be dead! Take me with you!' She sobbed despairingly. Scummo felt heartbroken, as he had when he had found Kelpin with her mother dead all that time ago.

He turned to Bethyl, whose face was sad but set. 'We're only going to get more food for you. We'll be back soon.'

Scummo patted her on the arm, trying to reassure her. Still she howled and beseeched them. Bethyl nodded to him. Time to go. They walked resolutely away from the

Apartments and back towards the street they had come from, the groans of the survivors echoing in their ears.

They were about to re-enter the warehouse where the beans were stored when Scummo had an idea and tried the door of the paste-processing plant next to it. It opened easily. He waved to Bethyl to stay outside, but she refused. A gory mess met their eyes, of bones and hair and sticky blood around the hopper that fed the paste-grinder. Backing away hastily, Scummo tried not to vomit. Bethyl went deathly pale. A dark sticky paste had been scraped away from the grinder mouth, but the floor and the stained containers told their own story.

They left the building and stood silently outside, trying to put into words the horror they had seen.

'We both thought this might be the case,' said Bethyl at last.

'The plant was used to make meat paste for the dogs,' said Scummo, 'but we never asked what kind of meat it was.'

'Those were human bones, human hair,' said Bethyl. 'The point is, did they kill the sick ones that died and feed them through the machine, or did they maybe pick on a weak one and kill them before dragging them here? There is a difference. We may not want murderers in our group.'

Scummo was silent for a while. 'People fought one another to the death when I was here,' he said. 'It was our only amusement.'

'Ah, the fights in the arena?'

'Yes.'

'And did you take part?'

He shook his head. 'No. Luckily my name was never put on the board. But others did.' He did not mention Andalou and the fatal stone he had thrown. 'People behave badly when they're desperate,' he concluded lamely.

Lugging the second round of beans, rice and tapioca was tiring, and they stopped for a moment to have some of the dried fish and biscuits they had brought with them, anxious not to show these to the residents.

The beans were swelling in the sink where Scummo had tipped them when they climbed back up to the first apartment. All the milk and tapioca had gone.

'Who is going to be leader here?' called Scummo, tired of being pawed and anxious to be on his way. The man called Tinsit emerged from the next apartment, followed by the older man they had first seen. Tinsit had a weak, always-open mouth and misshapen ears.

'I will be. Name's Tinsit.'

The older man looked as though he were about to say something, but then stopped himself.

'Okay then,' said Bethyl. 'You're in charge. I shall put these new supplies here and I shall personally hold you responsible if it is not divided up fairly. We are going back to our camp now. The warehouse is open, so you won't starve. The ones who recover best with what we've given you must fetch more for the others. There's still beans and tapioca and milk in there, plus some turnips.'

Tinsit gave them a sideways look. 'Only beans and tapioca and milk? You've got food on you, I'll bet, better than that. What we need is meat, isn't that right?' He looked around him and the residents hung their heads. Some nodded. Bethyl gave a warning glance across to Scummo and both turned and fled down the stairway, pushing aside the weak inhabitants who clung to them.

Once safely down in the arena again, Bethyl and Scummo walked swiftly until they were well out of range, too absorbed in getting away to talk. Far in the distance, they could hear frenzied barking. The dogs were loose once more.

M. Valentine Williams

Chapter 17

They had come to the City by the long route around the estuary. The boatman who had provided such a useful service to Beggis and others had long since gone, recalled by the Masters. They could not go back the way they had come. Bethyl instead led Scummo to the safe house they had visited before. It was empty and the door had been smashed in. The trapdoor was still intact and hidden beneath an old wooden chest, and they made their exit through this secret stairway, knowing that the dogs would find them but be unable to follow unless they had help. The dogs, however, hungry and thin, were only searching for food, and having escaped from their compound, went all out to search for it. The meat paste factory was their destination, where they licked up and chewed anything that was edible before going in search of other prey. The surviving residents heard the dogs return with dread and despair. They tried to barricade themselves onto the landing by pushing a dismantled shelf bed across the stairwell, but it was a temporary measure only. Slavering, red-eyed and emaciated, the dogs prowled along the landings, sniffed out the survivors and growled ominously. Shut up in their Apartments again, there was little the survivors could do but wait.

Scummo carried the dog-dazer he had stolen on their last visit to the City. It had become a talisman now, and he had no idea if it would still work. The dogs would have to get too close for his liking before he could try it again, but it was comforting to know he had it. As they pulled aside the chest and opened the trap door, Bethyl, out of breath from running, pushed Scummo down first.

'No light,' he said, suddenly more worried about being underground with nothing to guide them than frightened of the approaching dogs. Bethyl climbed down and, reaching up, closed the trapdoor over their heads. There was almost total darkness. They were both silent for a moment.

'Take my hand,' said Bethyl. 'I'll lead the way. We'll have to go by touch, but remember – I have been down here before with you. We must not get separated. Her left hand on the tunnel wall, her right behind her holding on to Scummo, Bethyl slid her feet carefully along the floor. It was slow going. and after a while they stopped and tied a length of homemade twine from their packs between them. With both hands free, they made better progress.

'Something moved under my foot,' said Scummo in alarm after they had gone fifty yards. They stopped.

'Feel with your feet.' Something crunched under Scummo's foot. 'Cockroach?'

'Could be. At least it wasn't an eel.'

'Scummo?'

'Mm?

'Do you think we'll ever be like we were? I mean – our lives were basic and happy in the villages, weren't they? Until *they* came. Sometimes I think I know why Shaful went back; he couldn't bear the hardship.'

'Bethyl, I've known both, and believe me, what we have is better. It's what we make it, for one thing. In the City there's no freedom, or there wasn't. I've felt more alive, more myself, since I left. Yes, it's hard, yes, it's challenging and tough, but it is better. You really have doubts?'

'Sometimes,' she replied honestly. 'Don't you?'

'What would your ideal life be like then?'

'To know you weren't being watched and controlled. To have somewhere of my own to live with others and to have enough food, warmth and shelter so I could think about having a child. Not to have the endless search for food and the bickering that goes on in the group. It's understandable, but you can't get away from it. I'd like to keep chickens and a cow, maybe grow more food too. You?'

'Same as you, mainly. Only I'd like it to be interesting. Have a bit of fun from time to time.'

'Do you remember the harvest dances, or had they stopped in your village when you were a child?'

Scummo thought carefully. 'I have a dim memory of someone playing the pipes and people dancing out in the square. I think it must have been the harvest dance. My mother could dance. I remember when I was quite small, she picked me up and my father came over, and together they held me and danced around to the music.' Scummo suddenly stopped, overcome with emotion. 'What a lot we've lost,' he said at last.

Bethyl, treading carefully, was unable to see him in the darkness, but his words echoed mournfully in the dank passageway. In the darkness, Scummo was glad the tears that ran down his face were hidden. They trudged on slowly until Bethyl's hand felt only empty air on one side. She felt with her foot until she found a stone.

'We turn here,' she told him. 'There are three places where the tunnel forks and we go left, left and then right.'

'I'm glad you can remember. It's all a blur to me. My ankle was so painful I couldn't think of anything else. We had a light of sorts then, didn't we?'

'Yes. Something I stole from the Masters. It doesn't work now, so we're on our own.'

On they trudged, groping, shuffling, Bethyl leading Scummo into the darkness; he was aware that things might creep up behind them. They stopped to rest. The food they had brought with them was almost exhausted, but they drank from the bottle they had filled at the Apartments and hoped it would last them. It was very silent below ground, but they could hear water dripping somewhere and the damp floor of the tunnel seeped moisture into their clothes so that they became cold and miserable. They rose and groped their way onwards. At some point, perhaps when they rose again after their rest, they missed a turning, or perhaps it was that Bethyl could not remember whether the turning they had reached was the second or third tunnel exit. Disorientated and confused, they stumbled forwards in silence, each blaming the other.

Eventually they saw daylight creeping along the walls of the tunnel towards them. Their eyes took a while to adjust to the light. They hoped they had reached the storm drain exit they had arrived at before. As they drew closer, Bethyl gave a cry.

'It's blocked! Someone's put a grill over it!' They came closer. The black metal bars of the grill imprisoned them. Scummo almost wept again. Bethyl rattled the bars, and Scummo put his face close to the grill for a better look. Left and right he could see nothing locking the grill in place. Above and below were strange fittings in a semi-circular groove. Nowhere could he see a lock.

'I wonder . . .' Scummo held the bars in both hands and tried to rotate the grill. The fixings moved slightly, then more as the whole grill rotated. But it still wasn't open. 'This does something, but how?' He and Bethyl examined the grill. Should they push it? Pull it? They tried both. Nothing. Bethyl, exhausted, sat down to think. *Calm down. Think logically about this,* Scummo told himself as he carefully worked his fingers around the edges of the grill. Finally, his fingers found some bolt heads by the fixings, and these he pushed, hard. The fixings began to rotate, freeing the grill, which swung open.

'You've done it!' exclaimed Bethyl, jumping to her feet. 'Well done! I thought for one awful moment we would have to go all the way back again.' She staggered out into the fading daylight. 'This is a different exit. We must have gone wrong back in there. Still, at least we're out.'

It looked much the same as the exit they had arrived at previously – a gully to collect water off the land and channel it away. But there was no box of food for survivors, no wood in the distance. All they could see was a gently sloping field, now overgrown, that ended with the pale fish-green sky of evening. The ground was quite dry here, and they decided to rest until it grew light enough to see. They had been cold and hungry in the underground passage, disorientated and weak from their flight from the dogs and the fear that kept them moving; now they were hungry and shivering but relieved to be in the fresh air.

They could not keep awake long enough to keep watch and slept back to back, propped up on their packs. The stars scattered their points of light high up in the inky blackness above them. Somewhere, a craft fleeing from this world was speeding onwards into the endless cosmic space, loaded with data and recordings, reporting back.

When day broke, Scummo and Bethyl discussed which direction to set off in. Either side of the gully were faint tracks leading along the base of the ridge, yet they felt they would have a better idea of where to go by going to the top of the field, which was higher than the gully bottom. They could hear no dogs, no people. Was it safe? They didn't know, but they went on regardless, walking through the rough grass until they reached the top of the hill. On one side the estuary glittered in the sun; on the other were woods and something they could not make out clearly. Bethyl's eyes were better than Scummo's, and she was able to pick out some buildings – were they ruins? – across the valley near the trees.

'Erasil. I'm sure that's Erasil. Look, there's the reservoir we passed last time.'

'It's a long way off. But yes, I think you're right. Let's go.' Heartened, they set off. There was a track of sorts that led over the brow and down over the rough grass to a valley beyond. Bethyl caught her foot on something and tripped. Scummo stopped. Hidden in the grass were the bleached bones of a human body. Ants crawled over it and had filled an eye socket with fine particles of grit. He watched them, fascinated.

Bethyl, still rubbing her knee, pulled him gently away. 'We don't know if they died of the sickness,' she explained. 'Better to be careful.'

They came across other bodies as they travelled – and stayed away from them. They had eaten all their rations now, and although they had water to drink, they took care when they collected it. Eels might be anywhere in the maze of dykes and ditches, streams and rivers that crossed the land. When night fell, they found themselves close to the reservoir. Bethyl had found some earth-nuts, Scummo some turnips growing wild. They ate these in silence and the cold, crunchy vegetables gave their stomachs something to work on. Then Scummo was violently sick.

'Indigestible food after no food at all,' said Bethyl, passing Scummo the water to clean his face. 'Never a good idea.' She felt nauseous herself but quelled it. Scummo felt better after a while. They found a place to spend the night on rough ground under some low trees. Tomorrow evening, all being well, they would be back at their village.

***

They had been away almost three weeks by the time they arrived, dishevelled and dirty, at the village. Kelpin was overjoyed to see Scummo safely back again and clung round him until even he was irritated and asked her to stop. They had hidden caches of food along the trail, using glass jars and clay pots to store nuts, dried fruit and the seeds of a plant they had discovered was good to eat. Some of the food was mouldy by the time they got back to it, but there was enough edible food for them to manage on. As they travelled, they had picked fungi from the woods, for it was now early autumn, and added this to their diet. The villagers were very keen to learn all about the City and voiced their anxiety about the sickness. Settling down in front of the evening fire, Scummo and Bethyl waited until all were present before they began their story.

'Well,' started Scummo, 'as you know, our main mission was to see if there were any survivors. Then, if there were, how we could help them without getting sick ourselves.'

Then Bethyl answered their unspoken question, which annoyed Scummo slightly. 'You should know that there are survivors.'

A murmur of interest came from the group. He glanced at Bethyl and continued. 'The survivors were given a vaccine to prevent them falling sick. But they were starving to death.'

'And we managed to find enough food for them to be going on with—'

'—but they're too weak to walk far, so we couldn't bring them back here.'

'Besides,' Bethyl went on, 'Scummo and I felt that we might be in danger if we stayed too long. You know how desperate people can behave.' The group nodded. They had seen this for themselves.

'How many are left?' asked Darfi.

'They told us fifteen. We did wonder . . .' Her voice trailed off.

'What?' they wanted to know.

'Whether they had been forced into eating one another.' A collective shudder went through them as Scummo said this.

'We went into the meat-processing plant,' he explained, his nose remembering the smell as he grimaced. 'There were human remains in there that had been fed into the machine.' He recoiled, as they did, at the thought. 'The Masters have definitely gone, but the dogs must have been chained up or locked in somewhere. As we were leaving we heard them barking and had to run for it down the secret drain. We were lucky to get out.'

'We didn't hear the dogs at all on the way in,' said Bethyl. 'It must have been the sound of us, or the smell of the meat paste plant that gave them the energy to break loose.'

'Let's hope they don't leave the City and come looking for us here anyway. What do we do about the survivors? Fanna? Magrab? Any of you? We need to decide this properly.' Scummo wanted to have the matter settled.

Jankin was firmly against the survivors joining them. 'There's likely to be more of them than there are of us,' he pointed out. 'We've had a hard-enough time of it trying to feed ourselves. From what you've been saying, it doesn't sound as though the folk in the City have much idea about fending for themselves. Scummo, did I understand from you that they may have taken to eating each other?' He said this with revulsion in his voice.

'The meat paste plant we went into with all the hair and teeth lying around certainly made me think that's what they'd done. I didn't like a couple of them; it seemed to me that they had exploited the others and they were keen to get our rations off us, even after we'd given them food.'

Beggis, still feeling an outsider, took the City-dwellers' side. 'I'm not sure about that. What would you or I have done in that situation?'

Darfi joined in the debate. 'If you make an enemy of the person who comes to help you, they won't come back if they've got any sense. Scummo and Kelpin were desperate when they found me on the barge, but they didn't make me feel threatened. I think now that they've got means to feed themselves, at least for now, we should leave them to it. What do you think, Anga?'

'I don't like the sound of them,' was all she would say.

Then Bethyl remembered the woman who had implored them so piteously not to leave her. 'Perhaps we're judging all of them by the couple we didn't like. Tinsit was the name of one of the untrustworthy ones.'

Beggis sat up at hearing this name, her bright curls bobbing. 'Tinsit! Nasty piece of work. He used to be my boss when I worked in the sewing factory. I wouldn't want him here.'

Bethyl was thoughtful. 'In the past, the people who didn't want to be with this group took the boat and left. All of us who stayed have pulled together and worked hard to see that all the group members survived.'

'Except Bouncer,' Kelpin interjected, in a small voice.

'I don't want anything to threaten that,' Bethyl finished.

Fanna added to the debate. 'They might challenge how this group is led. It seems to be Bethyl who takes the leader's role most of the time, with others filling in. Would they accept Bethyl as a leader? I mean, they'd have to at the start if they were going to make use of what we've got and our knowledge and everything.'

Although there were arguments in the group from time to time, it did seem that as long as the three older members, Bethyl, Fanna and Jankin, operated together, the others were more or less content to go along with what was decided.

Jankin felt he needed to state his position. 'As a man, I suppose I was used to being in charge in the village I came from. But losing my family knocked the energy out of me, and personally I was glad when Bethyl came along and took on the role of leader. We all have a say in what happens, just that she somehow steers us in the right way. That's what I think, anyway,' he ended, sitting down with a thump next to Sita. 'What do you think, Magrab?'

'I'm h-h-appy with Bethyl as leader. It's autumn n-n-now,' stammered Magrab. 'If they come here and they need nursing, we won't have enough food for ourselves through the winter. How much have we g-g-got stored up?'

'If we kill the pig in the new year, we should have enough if we can carry on fishing. The smoked fish lasts a good while. We've got the corn we dried as well. If we had salt, we could do more, of course.'

'How do you mean?'

'Before the Herdings, some of us filled crocks with salt and salted down pork and vegetables like beans. They keep like that. We got the salt from people over near the marshes who looked after the salt pans. They won't be there now.'

'How do we know?'

'Everyone was moved away during the Herdings. It's not likely they escaped.'

'But the salt pans may still be there.'

They discussed this and the possibility of saving more food for the winter to come, then they returned to the real question. Did they want these survivors, an unknown quantity, to join them and threaten their way of life? Jankin went round the group, asking each member what their views were. The survivors, if they made it back to the villages, whether helped or by themselves, would bring their own problems, but on the other hand they would also bring much needed manpower. They decided to do nothing for the present, as it was felt that the presence of the dogs made going back too dangerous. Darfi and Andalou offered to make a trip to the salt pans to see if they could collect enough for their needs.

This was over a day's journey, and neither had been there before so their travel was guided by the landmarks they could see from the village, the direction of the sun and whatever other clues they might pick up. They had, by this time, begun to make crude clay pots, which they baked on the fire, and despite many broken pieces caused by the impurity of the clay, they had collected a few that were used for storage. Anga, hindered by the toddler, was the chief potter, and coiled snake after snake of greasy clay in circles until the pot was made, smoothing it with her fingers as she went. Kelpin and Rondi made pinch pots, good for small measures of food, and it was these that Andalou and Darfi took with them.

Not all the members were happy with the decision to do nothing. Beggis, despite her dislike of Tinsit, felt for the survivors keenly. Scummo, too, remembered the woman who had clung to him, and the boy who reminded him all too vividly of himself at that age, parentless and abandoned in the City. One evening, they both voiced their anxiety.

'I still think we ought to help the survivors,' said Beggis when the subject was brought up again two weeks after Scummo and Bethyl had returned.

'How?' Bethyl asked.

'We ought to go back with Scummo's dog-dazer and lead any survivors back here. They can live in their own village; they don't have to live here with us. I can't believe we would just let them all die.'

Fanna brought common sense to bear. 'It seems to me that what we all have in common is that we have escaped, one way or another, from a way of life we didn't want. We can't impose freedom on them. Bethyl and Scummo gave them the means to survive. Whether they escape or not is up to them now. They know others have, because they've seen the evidence. Of course, it's true that they don't have all the information about the secret passageway, but they don't need that to escape. What they need is some protection from the dogs, if they're still loose, and a general direction to go in. They can take food with them, if there's enough. Some like us will know how the countryside works. But the biggest task they face is in looking after one another. In the end, it's the most important thing there is.' She said this with such conviction that everyone was silent.

'I'm not sure they have that ability,' offered Scummo. 'At least I didn't see any evidence of it, did you, Bethyl?'

'I must admit that I did feel that there'd be fighting after we left. With no one looking over their shoulder to see that the food was handed out fairly, the strongest would take it all for themselves. And without a leader to insist on equal shares, the strongest members, in this case the males, would deprive the others in order to get more. I'd like to be wrong about this, but I think that's accurate.'

'So how come this doesn't happen here?'

Nobody knew the answer to this. There was none, except that they were a family and they cared about one another. Also, the female members of the group were, for once, in control.

Chapter 18

The wound on Kelpin's thigh, which had reopened, was causing the group some concern. Fanna noticed it and ordered Kelpin to lie down so she could look at it properly.

'It hasn't healed up yet,' she explained to Kelpin, who was sulkily prostrating herself on the hay-filled sleeping pad in the main room. 'Keep still.'

'Yes, Kelpin, keep still. It won't hurt,' mocked Rondi from the doorway.

'Rondi, do us a favour and clear off. Or I'll send you to collect acorns again. Come to think of it, you can go with Beggis and do some picking anyway. Hazels, chestnuts, acorns – anything you can find. Okay?'

Rondi muttered and went away from the building to find Beggis, who was drawing patterns with a stick in the clay dish Anga had made. She sighed and went to find the woven basket they took with them on these trips. Free of interruptions, Fanna turned her attention back to Kelpin. The mark on her thigh was redder, and the wound more open. Fanna bent down close to look.

'I think there's something in the wound,' she said, pressing gently around it. Kelpin squealed. 'Sorry, Kelpin. I think we need to get this out. Stay there.'

Scared, Kelpin lay down again, her smooth muscular brown legs tense and restless. Fanna came back with Bethyl and Jankin, and Kelpin looked alarmed.

'Kelpin, I've asked Bethyl and Jankin to help.'

Kelpin had no time to object. Before she knew it, Jankin had pushed a wad of soft leather in her mouth between her teeth and bound it there, while the others had taken her arms and tied them together at the wrists. Fanna took the knife they used for gutting fish, washed it and thrust it in the fire, then withdrew it, holding the wooden handle carefully so as not to burn herself. Cooled a little, she very carefully put the tip of the knife blade into the wound, ignoring Kelpin's desperate writhing.

'Keep still. We have to do this. Be brave now. Bite the wad in your mouth and hold onto Jankin. This will be over in a minute, I promise you.'

Fanna enlarged the wound a little and put the blade tip into the oozing red sore. Kelpin shuddered with pain. Applying pressure to the sides of the wound, Fanna's nerve nearly failed as she looked at Kelpin's wild beseeching eyes. Suddenly, a black pellet popped out of the wound and Fanna brushed it into a square of cloth and kept it safe.

'We got it!' she announced, applying heal-all to the wound. 'Untie her hands, Jankin, please.' Bethyl came in with water.

Kelpin sat up. 'What was it?' she wanted to know. Fanna showed her. 'Who put it in me?'

'We don't know. I seem to remember it happening round about the time Bouncer arrived? You showed it to me then, remember?'

She did.

'Sorry to have to do it like that, Kelpin, but at least it's out. I'm not sure what we should do with it, but I have a strong instinct to take it to a deep place in the sea and drop it down there. Like the spy-tube things, it must be something to do with the Masters. I've got it out safe, so don't worry about it. Okay?'

Word got around the rest of the villagers that something had been discovered in Kelpin's body and removed, and later that day there were a number of body inspections as anxious people checked their own legs and arms for evidence of foreign bodies. Although Doran found a large tick from the pig nestling in his groin, and the others found a variety of thorn punctures, sores where clothing had rubbed or unsightly warts, no more wounds such as Kelpin's had come to light. All were agreed that the tiny pellet should be taken to the rocky promontory along the coast and Andalou should throw it as far as possible out to sea.

The pellet was dropped into a stone with a hole in it, then sealed inside with clay. Andalou took it with Kelpin to the headland. 'Ready?' he asked her.

'Ready,' she replied.

He stepped back, brought his arm back, summoned all his strength and threw the stone with the pellet far out to sea. It fell with a distant 'plop' into the water and was gone. When Fanna inspected the wound the next day, it was closing over and a healthy-looking scab was starting to form.

'Do you think Bouncer did it?' asked Kelpin, disbelieving.

'We'll never know for sure, but its seems like too much of a coincidence to me. He may have been directed to do it and not even known. He was rather strange.'

The others felt anxious and at the same time relieved that the alien object had been found and removed. Rondi treated Kelpin with cautious respect. 'Why did they choose you?' he asked.

Kelpin shrugged. 'I don't know. Maybe we'll never find out.' Secretly, she was upset and went to talk to Scummo, who was annoyed that he had not been informed of their plans to remove the object and was upset that she had been hurt.

Kelpin reassured him. 'They had to do it,' she insisted. 'It was a good opportunity and they did it really quickly. It did hurt a lot, though.'

Slightly mollified, he gave her a squeeze and went back to mending his nets.

The problem of what to do about the survivors in the City would not disappear. Beggis was troubled by it in particular. Several weeks later, the villagers were woken by the sound of dogs howling far away. Kelpin sat straight up with frightened eyes.

'The dogs!' she shouted, unable to keep silent. The others woke and listened as the howling and barking went on and on, causing them to shiver where they lay and bar the door with extra wooden staves. Gradually, the sound diminished and became further off until it vanished completely. In the chilly dawn light, the villagers crept together and huddled round the remains of the fire. Someone was missing.

Doran had been woken by the sound of the dogs and gone outside to climb the church tower to see if he could make out where the sound was coming from. The villagers had not had a night watch for some time, preferring to sleep together in the big hall and bar the outer door to strangers. Doran knocked to be admitted and they all looked round to see what had happened.

'They were quite far away,' said Doran. 'The sound was coming from a good way off, maybe from the estuary.' Realisation dawned. Andalou and Darfi were out by the salt pans. They should now be on their way home.

'What happens if Andalou and Darfi meet up with the dogs?' asked Anga, worried.

'I'm sure they'll be able to look after themselves,' replied Bethyl, with a certainty she didn't feel. 'Have you still got the dog-dazer, Scummo?'

He had.

Anxiety hung over the group. They were afraid for themselves, for their animals tethered outside and for the two missing members. They shut the sow and her piglets up securely every night after this, but they went about their work with their ears straining to catch any sound that might indicate the dogs were getting closer. Finally, three days after they should have returned, a very weary and distraught Darfi stumbled into the village and collapsed inside the main room, where Anga, bathing Freedom in front of the fire, jumped up and gave a scream of joy and relief.

'What happened?'

'Let him recover first.' This was Jankin, offering water.

Darfi took a while to recover his wits enough to speak. 'Need help. Andalou,' he panted. 'He's alive. Dogs came. Split up. Needs help to get back. Barge.' He breathed long and hard. They tried not to hurry him.

Kelpin came through the door, as ever alert to any excitement or news. 'Our barge? The one you lived on?'

Darfi nodded. Finally, he was able to speak clearly. 'Andalou and I found the salt pans and even collected some salt. No one's been near the place for months. Then we found the barge, washed up on the mudflats. You can imagine how excited I was.'

They nodded.

'So we spent a while trying to refloat it when the tide came in, and we had almost succeeded when we heard the dogs. Andalou was on the barge. I was on the mudflat and the tide was coming in fast. Well, things looked really bad, I can tell you. Then the barge floated off and I was left on the mud and we could see the dogs getting nearer. Andalou couldn't reach me. I thought I'd swim for it, try to reach the barge. Then I thought that no one would know where we were. While I was trying to make my mind up, the dogs came down to the beach and started barking. The bit of mud I was standing on was surrounded by water. The dogs tried to reach me but the mud put them off.'

'So how did you escape?' Almost all the group members had arrived and were crowded round him, eager to hear the story unfold.

'Well, I could see Andalou and the barge disappearing into the estuary. The tide had come in so that the sandbank I was on was under the water. It seemed to be a bit firmer where I was standing. I was expecting to sink down, but I didn't. There were a few rocks and I stood on those. I shouted to Andalou that I would come back here as soon as I could and to stay on the barge and hope it washed up further along the coast. So he's on the barge.'

'And you? How did you escape? What about the dogs?'

'They tried swimming to get to me, but they're so heavy that they couldn't get a purchase on the mud enough to get out of the water. I knew if I could stay on the rocks long enough, the tide would turn and I'd be able to leave. Remember, I lived on the estuary for years. They got tired of trying to get me eventually and went away. I had to wait for the tide to go out again before I could leave. By that time, Andalou and the barge had completely vanished.'

'How many dogs were there?' Bethyl wanted to know.

'Five altogether. One was limping badly. Three were neutered males, I think, though it was difficult to see properly.'

'And the journey home?'

'Difficult. I had to leave the salt behind. I tried to keep near trees, so that if the dogs came I could get up out of their reach. It's taken me ages to get back.'

Anga had made Darfi some food while they were talking and she handed over the porridge to him now. He ate hungrily. The others thought about the situation. Andalou was missing. The barge might be anywhere. And the dogs were loose.

Scummo got the attention of the group. Brandishing the dog-dazer, he called for quiet.

'Darfi, can you draw us a rough map of the route to the salt pans and the direction the barge was going in when you last saw it?'

Darfi got a burned stick and drew a map of the estuary and the salt pans on the floor.

'The barge will be carried inland on the incoming tide, and if it's washed ashore or grounded on the flats, it will end up near where we go fishing from the headland. But the tide can also carry it back out to sea again. I think that's unlikely, given the shallowness of the estuary and the sand bars. What is likely to happen is that the barge is grounded once again on a sandbank out in the estuary with no means of getting off. If that happens, Andalou will need help to get to shore.'

'What about if we sent a search party out with Scummo's dog-dazer, well armed, and begin a search of the coast from the fishing rocks back towards the salt pans?' Fanna was keen to help Andalou.

'We need to think about how we rescue him once we find him – if we *do* find him.' Doran was thoughtful. 'What we need,' he said, 'is a coracle. A light boat we can carry on our backs. Perfect for the estuary.'

'But we don't have one. Fanna started to make one but it's more difficult than it looks.'

They sat in puzzled silence for a while. Then Kelpin had an idea. 'Can Andalou swim?' No one knew. 'Who can swim well here?'

Doran and Magrab raised their hands.

'If we can swim out to the barge when we find it, and take a rope with us, we can tie the rope to the barge and hold onto it coming back.'

'We've only got that rope up in the belfry, if the mice haven't eaten it. It's not long enough.' Fanna was thinking it through.

'Well, we won't know how long it needs to be until we find the barge. Can I go?' Kelpin asked.

Fanna nodded.

'Anyway, he might have been washed up close to the beach. He might be on his way back to us right now.' This was true, though optimistic. The estuary was wide and shallow for the most part, and it would take a very high tide to wash the barge up onto the mud and shingle beach. A party of five – Kelpin, Doran, Rondi, Fanna and Scummo – armed themselves with hunting spears, rope and rations and set off for the fishing rocks. Darfi stayed under the watchful eye of Anga, while Beggis, Magrab, Bethyl and Sita prepared themselves for a long wait.

Reaching the fishing rocks, Rondi climbed to the top and looked out over the estuary. Nothing except the rippled expanse of grey-green water came into view. The tide was still rising. They made their way along the cliffs slowly, in single file, ears tuned to the possible sounds of dogs howling or barking in the distance, but all was quiet. Finally, in a sheltered creek, they found the barge. There seemed to be no one on it. Several very muddy sticks were pushed into the mud as a temporary mooring. They called his name, but Andalou did not appear. Around the barge, the water was lapping, but the now receding tide showed the mud to be thick and sticky. Had Andalou managed to reach the shore? It seemed likely that he had. Then where was he?

Kelpin searched the shoreline for clues and found a footprint. 'Someone's been here.'

They came to look. 'His foot size. Where is he?'

'Here!' Andalou burst out of the bushes halfway up the slope, dishevelled and with leaves sticking to his clothes. There was laughter and some teasing. He had been short of water and left the barge at low tide to find a stream to drink from. He was greatly relieved to hear that Darfi was unharmed.

'Did you see any eel things?' Kelpin wanted to know.

'No. We haven't seen any for a while now, have we?'

'Doesn't mean they've gone, though.'

'No, true. Look what I've got!' He showed them two crocks full of white gritty stuff, hidden on the shore. 'Darfi and I had only just begun collecting salt when the dogs came. But we did at least get some.'

He was certainly pleased to see them and had been about to make a decision whether to wait for the rescue party or make his way back. The memory of the dogs was still strong in his mind.

'We brought Scummo's dog-dazer with us,' Rondi reminded them. 'And we've got spears.'

'Let's hope we don't need them,' replied Doran, gloomily. He, more than any of them, remained aware of how vulnerable their little group was. His heavy, weather-beaten face scanned the horizon anxiously at regular intervals; his thick-lobed ears were constantly alert to the sound of the land they lived in, the sea they fished in.

They began to walk back towards the village, heading inland where a line of trees appeared, always mindful of the possibility that the dogs could come back. It was an anxious journey, and it took them over a day to reach their village. They had to spend the night up in the trees like roosting birds, out of the way of the dogs, who were heard howling far away on the other side of the estuary.

It was only when they got closer to home that Scummo signalled fiercely to them.

'Shh!' They all stopped still. 'Dogs! Can you hear them?' They could, and the barking was coming from the direction of the village. The group tightened their grip on the spears they carried. Scummo felt for the dog-dazer. They would have to confront the dogs some time, and they were as prepared now as they would ever be. They crept closer and heard the sounds of excited barking and yelping growing louder with every step they took. They stopped at the last stand of trees and watched for a moment.

The dogs were outside the main building in the village, snarling furiously. They seemed to be fighting over something, but what that something was, they could not make out. Could it be the pigs? There was no sign of the sow in the small pig yard. The piglets, too, were nowhere to be seen.

Andalou picked up some stones. Kelpin, trembling, held her spear with a firm but quivering hand. Doran, silent, was thinking of a plan. Fear and alarm gripped them all.

'One of us should creep down to the pig yard. Then we make a noise to attract the dogs. Once the dogs are inside the yard, we attack them.'

'And what about the person in the pig yard?'

'He takes the dazer and uses it as soon as the dogs come near him.'

'Or her,' corrected Kelpin.

'Do we know if the dog-dazer still works?'

'Only one way to find out! Anyone volunteer?'

To their surprise, Rondi put his hand up. 'I can jump on the roof of the pigpen from the back,' he told them. 'I've done it lots of times when the old sow's been a bit nasty. I'll do it.'

Rondi, armed with the dog-dazer, crept through the wood, running silently from the last tree to the pigpen, where he vaulted easily onto the roof. The others crept a little nearer.

The dogs were making such a noise as they fought over their meal that he was unobserved by them. He stood up and gave a loud, shrill whistle. One of the dogs stopped eating and looked towards him, sniffing the air. It began to trot towards him. One at a time, the other dogs dropped their meal and followed. The group held their breath. Rondi waited until the dogs were just inside the entrance to the pen and pressed the control on the dazer.

Nothing happened. The dogs, scenting their quarry, jumped up at the roof, barking loudly. Rondi tried the dazer again. Some faint signal on it reached the dogs, who stopped for a moment but then continued their commotion. The group charged down the slope, yelling loudly, and attacked the dogs with spears and sticks, while Andalou picked out the leader and aimed a stone at its head. One dog caught Kelpin's spear between its teeth and would not let go. Doran, quick to respond, stabbed it through its eye with his spear. Even in death, the dog would not loosen its grip.

Scummo and Fanna fought off three dogs by jabbing the spears into their open jaws. Then the remaining dog, which had Kelpin cornered, was dispatched by Rondi, who had been watching from the roof of the pen, when he leapt down and cut its throat. Fanna had been badly bitten on her arm. The others were bruised, scared, but unhurt. The other villagers came out to have a look, stepping over the dead, mauled pig outside their door.

Fanna fainted and was caught by Doran, who, dazed, was stumbling towards the others. A dog whined horribly as it died. Rondi, still clutching the dazer, was the last member of the group to reach the safety of the big room, and the door closed behind him, shutting out the dead and dying dogs, the dead pig and all the horrors of the last few days.

'Are we all safe?' questioned Darfi. They counted heads. Everyone was present. 'How long had the dogs been here?'

'Six hours. Luckily, we heard them before we saw them and got inside quick. There wasn't time to protect the pigs.' Anga spoke for them all. Others took up the story.

'But catching the pigs took them a while and it took their attention off us . . .'

'. . . so we were barricaded in here with them outside and hoped you didn't come back while they were here.'

'Just as well we did, though. Five dead dogs. Let's hope there aren't any more roaming about. We need to get on and skin them, Bethyl,' Andalou said. 'Pity about the pig.'

The loss of the sow was bad. They had had to release the half-grown weaners back to the forest as they nothing to feed them with. They organised themselves with the various implements they had, and Scummo and Darfi skinned the dogs, washing and scraping the bloody pelts over the next few days before hanging them to dry. Fanna's arm looked bad. She lay with her sallow face set and drawn with pain. The mark of the dog's jaws, with its punctured skin, was livid and swollen on her arm.

Bethyl ran to find her herb box and the honey pot, and before long, Fanna's arm was bathed in herbal tea and bandaged with a honey poultice. Kelpin watched this operation, holding Fanna's other hand, with keen interest. Fanna moaned.

'Will she be all right?' Kelpin asked Bethyl anxiously, out of earshot.

'I can't tell you that. The honey I put on is an antiseptic, but dogs' teeth are nasty things and they've gone in deep. The bone in her arm may be cracked. We need to keep a close watch on her and look after her well.

'Can I do it?'

'Of course.' She squeezed Kelpin's shoulder. 'I think Fanna would like that.'

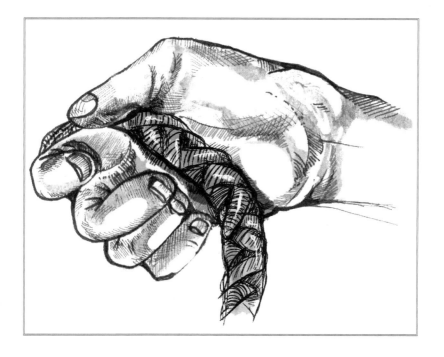

Chapter 19

The talk round the fire that evening was subdued. Fanna lay in a corner, her face turned towards the wall, her injured arm propped on a hay pillow.

As the events of the last few days were discussed and they took stock of their situation, it was clear that Fanna's quiet, firm presence was a real loss to the group.

'What do we do now?' asked Anga.

Sita, who had kept quiet until now, spoke up. 'We still haven't decided what to do about the people in the City. If they left – if the dogs didn't get them – they'll be roaming the countryside. Sooner or later they'll find us . . .'

'Or we'll find them,' Rondi finished grimly.

'So we need to decide whether we welcome them or not. If we rescue them or not. What do you think, Scummo?'

'I think they'll have left the City by now, if the dogs didn't get them.'

'Do we wait for them to find us?'

'What else can we do?' They gloomily agreed that after nearly a month, any survivors would either be dead, perilously close to running out of food, or would have taken their chances in the open countryside. Scummo had the greatest reservations about the survivors, if there were any, joining their group. If they lost Fanna, there would be a period of instability. This would make the group less stable. He was aware that the City had marked him, Beggis and Andalou as different from the others. They had had a different experience. Newcomers from the City would have to learn about the way of life in the village. He had learned a lot: how to collect firewood, light fires and keep them burning at a steady heat for a long time; how to collect food from the land around them; how to locate the nests of wild bees, smoke them out and collect the honey; skin animals, fish. He could weave fish traps from willow, make crude clay pots, find crabs, make useful spears, follow tracks. He could make a shelter from saplings and was starting to build a coracle with Fanna's help. He sighed, weighed down by the thoughts of what would be needed if the City survivors joined them. Discipline was the key, he thought, but the discipline that freedom imposes – discipline from a place deep within himself that was to do with loyalty to the group, love, kinship. Not the imposed discipline of the Masters. All this had started with Kelpin, he realised. He looked at her as she gazed at Fanna's drawn face. She was almost grown up.

The group member he was most attracted to was Beggis. For a long time now, he had tried to gain her attention. Beggis would shake her bright hair and look at him sideways, but he knew she was interested. Kelpin was jealous. Darfi had Anga and their child, and Sita seemed to be interested in Magrab, especially since they had escaped from the wild pig together. Bethyl, Doran, Jankin, Andalou and Rondi, who was still young, were without partners. They had lived hand to mouth since they had been together and were only now able to think about the long-term future of the group. There were not enough women, he thought. Not enough of anything, in fact.

Beggis remained anxious about the survivors. There were days when she regretted her impulsive decision to leave the Apartments with Chasna, but those days did not come often, and when she looked at the others in the group and the concern they had for one another, she knew deep down she'd made the right choice.

The other group members were also secretly worried about the survivors too, and a week after the killing of the dogs, Beggis brought the issue up again. Fanna was no better and the bite had become infected; her arm looked greenish, stank, and she could feel nothing with her hand. Bethyl went about with a serious face and Kelpin found herself weeping more and more frequently at Fanna's side. Then Fanna, delirious, slipped in and out of consciousness. Bethyl and Doran spent a while discussing the situation.

'You know what this means?' asked Bethyl.

Doran nodded glumly. 'She loses the arm or her life.'

'She's not strong enough to survive an amputation, even if we could do one.'

Bethyl agreed. 'She's been ill for a while, before this happened. She doesn't have the strength to fight the infection.'

They had no idea how to carry out an amputation.

'How long has she got?' Doran asked.

'Another day at most, I think. Best warn the others.'

They were all upset to hear what they already half-knew. The bite on Fanna's arm had cut to the bone and the infection was grave. She was not expected to live.

It was then that Beggis decided to tell the group she was going back to the City to see what had befallen the survivors. A shocked silence greeted her.

Bethyl, too concerned about Fanna, couldn't stop her. The others tried half-heartedly to argue her out of it, but her mind was made up. Only Scummo appeared to understand.

'It was only when I went back with Bethyl the first time that I understood what I'd left behind when Kelpin and I left the Apartments. Nothing had changed. I knew I'd made the right decision to leave. I needed to go back to realise that. Good luck. I'll tell you about the journey if you meet me later.'

'Thanks, Scummo.'

Leaving Bethyl was not so easy. 'I can see why you want to go, Beggis, but I wish it wasn't now, when we'll have to lose Fanna. And to lose you too . . . There may be more dogs roaming around out there; have you accounted for that? Still, we don't keep prisoners here. Good luck on your journey.'

Beggis was upset but her mind was made up. The route Scummo mapped out for her was around the estuary, a longer journey, but it was agreed that Beggis could not take the underground route through the storm drain alone. She listened carefully, aware that now there was no ferryman, her life depended on remembering the information she was being given. She left without saying farewell to the others, who were saddened by her leaving. Her own sadness was more than she could bear.

Fanna died the next night, and there was much mourning and ceremony as they laid her to rest. Kelpin was especially affected by her death and clung to Scummo as she had as a child.

Gradually, they put their lives back together. The sow that the dogs had killed and partly eaten had been cut into portions, salvaging what was edible, for nothing could be wasted. All the piglets were dead. With some difficulty, they decided to eat one of the dogs, but some of the villagers wouldn't touch the meat and, when they were unable to eat any more, the remaining dogs' bodies were eventually buried outside the village. Andalou's salt was useful in preserving some of the meat, though there were impurities in it. The coracle was finished and tested on the water, where it was found to leak a little and had to be brought back while they tried to think of a way to waterproof it. Fanna would have known how to do it, but she was gone.

In the past, the villagers had looms on which they wove woollen garments, buying the spun wool from inland farmers in exchange for fish, baskets and pots. So much had been lost in the years since the Masters arrived that there was little left that could be used. They had unearthed some basic tools from the villages they had explored, but these would not last forever, and their food stocks were only just adequate for the months ahead. They needed clothing, rope, axes and knives, and more importantly, the means to make them. All these issues were discussed at the meetings round the fire, and a growing air of frustration took hold of the group as they realised again how difficult their lives had become.'

Sita was the first to speak. 'We've decided we need clothing. But how do we get it?'

'We've used rossell skins, pigskin and feathers, but we need something else. Okay, we can use the dog skins when they've cured – *if* they cure – but there must be something else.' Jankin was thinking it through.

Bethyl said, 'We used to use wool, but I don't know if there are any sheep left.'

'I haven't seen any. Where were they kept?' asked Scummo.

'Up on the hills, inland from here.'

Kelpin had another idea: 'Is there anything else we can use? I found this fluffy white stuff when we went to the salt pans.'

Bethyl smiled 'Kelpin! Well done! It's bog cotton. We can collect that and try to spin it into a thread . . .'

'If the dogs aren't around . . .'

'We'd never collect enough of it,' said Scummo. 'But it's a start.'

Jankin had been thinking. 'I remember older people in my village collecting nettles.'

'Nettles?' Doran asked. 'What did you do with those?'

'They put them in a pond and soaked them . . .'

Magrab was curious: 'A-a-and what happened?'

'It stinks,' said Jankin, 'but the green stuff rots away so you're left with the fibres. Then you can spin them into yarn.'

Bethyl asked, 'Does it work?'

'Seems to,, said Jankin. 'They did it every year.'

Scummo asked, 'Are there any nettles growing round here? What do they look like?'

'They're the plants that sting you. There are some by the far field, if the pigs haven't dug them all up,' Bethyl replied.

Magrab volunteered, 'I know where there's a big patch of them, on the edge of the wood. They'll be dying off now, but we could pick what's left.'

'I'll go, if someone will come with me. Magrab? We can take the spears if that's all right, Bethyl?' Scummo was keen.

Glad at last to have a plan, Scummo and Magrab took a large basket and went off to the woods, while Kelpin and Rondi set out for the salt marsh near the fishing place, which was nearer than the salt pans. It was a three-hour walk there and back, but when they returned they had enough bog cotton to be able to start stretching and twisting it between their fingers. Once a length had been made, they tied it to a stone and let it drop and twist until it formed a tight but uneven thread. The men were scornful of this activity.

It was becoming more apparent now that without Fanna to back up decisions, Bethyl's leadership was in question. The male group members were happiest when they were hunting, or fishing, and these activities took them away from the village a great deal. Bethyl did not enjoy the domestic tasks of food preparation and sewing, though she was a good potter, and she particularly disliked basket-weaving. This was usually left to Anga, who could watch Freedom as he played in the dirt, making marks in it with a stick, or chased insects. Pot-bellied and runny-nosed, Freedom was fussed over by the adults, but he was lonely with no other children to play with.

***

Weeks passed, and Beggis finally reached the City. It was very very quiet. The first thing she noticed was that the path she had walked with Chasna so long ago as they defiantly left the City was thigh deep in dead grass, brambles and dry flowerheads. She approached the Apartments slowly and with caution.

Something had changed, but there was no one to be seen. Leaves drifted across the arena, orange and russet eddies, mixed with rags, papers, dead grass.

'Hallooo!' she called, suddenly tired of the silence and heedless for her own safety. Somewhere a door blew shut, a gate swung, and there was a sound, the faintest of patters, from the stairwell to her right. 'Who's there?' Another patter of light feet. The owner must have been diminutive to hide so well. Beggis spun round, trying to catch a glimpse of whoever it was. 'You can come out now,' she called. 'I won't hurt you.'

A face peeped round the stairwell, big eyes alert to danger. Beggis kept still. The small person crept closer – Beggis could see it was a girl – keeping her eyes firmly fixed on Beggis. Then, without even thinking about it, Beggis threw her arms open and the figure ran into them, burying her face in Beggis's cloak. It was a while before either of them could speak. The girl was not as thin as Beggis expected, but she was extremely dirty. Beggis thought she must be about fourteen or so, not quite fully grown. A conversation began then that continued as the girl led Beggis to her hiding place on the roof of the Apartments. They had to climb over a gate at the top of the stairs to reach it, hidden as it was inside an old ventilation shaft. She had been safe from the dogs in here, but what had she found to eat? The girl, who had lived with her mother in an apartment, had watched her mother die from the mysterious illness. Then, frightened by the surviving residents who chased her and whom she didn't trust, she survived alone, raiding the food warehouse and foraging outside the City for food. Twice, she had been seen by the dogs and had to climb to safety on the City walls, but nimble and light-footed, she had managed to make a route for herself across the roofs and walls of the City and had escaped to her eyrie each time. Then came news that shocked Beggis.

'The Masters came back. Did you know?'

'When was this?'

'Fifteen days ago. I mark the wall with this bit of burned wood every night. When something happens, I put a special mark beside it so I can keep track of it.' She showed Beggis the dirty wall with its scratchings. 'They took away the ones who were left. I stayed up here.'

'Do they know you're here?'

'Don't think so. But the others might have told them.'

'Did you watch them leave?'

'Yes. They didn't put up a fight or anything. Just went along. The dogs herded them into a transporter and then they left. The dogs went too, in another transporter.'

'Did the Masters say anything? Give out any of their orders from the towers?'

'They told the ones still left here to prepare to leave. They were going to be taken to a much nicer place where they would have food and shelter.'

'And you weren't tempted to join them?'

The girl looked wistful but shook her head. 'I knew someone would come. I watched two others come the first time and give food to the people who were left. I knew they'd come back.'

'I don't know your name. I'm Beggis, by the way.'

'Polla.'

'Well, what do we do now, Polla? Would you like to come with me and we'll see if we can make it back to the village I came from? Life there is rough and difficult but the people are good. I think so, anyway.'

Polla nodded. 'I'd like that.'

'What can we take back with us? I've got some supplies of food left in my bag, but they won't last us long. It'll take time to get back, about ten days at least if we don't have any problems. Got any food we can take?'

'A little. Some dried corn and some of the tapioca from the warehouse. Lucky I got to it first, or they'd have taken it all. I also found, in one of the other stores, a few boxes of dried apples and prunes. There's only a handful, but maybe they'll help a bit.'

'We need to think about water. The group told me about where to get drinking water on the way, but there's not much between here and the estuary. Have you got any water bottles or anything we can fill?'

'I get my water from one of the empty Apartments on the way down the stairs. I found this' – she fished out a green glass bottle – 'in there too. I usually keep it full.'

'Great. We'll fill it on our way out and take it with us. I'll fill mine too.' They collected up their few untidy belongings, now tied in bundles. Beggis hooked her bundle over her stick. Polla had little to take but tied her glass bottle to her waist with rags. Together they set off, down the grey anonymous stairways and the dismal landings, passing the open doors of Apartments that had once been home to thousands of people who were now dead or disappeared. Relics of peoples' lives – food cans, buckets, decayed mildewed mattresses, crumpled shoes, torn down paper notices instructing the residents of Broilerhouse Eight, Nine and Ten to attend for vaccination and reminding them of the rules of the establishment –

littered the empty rooms. Beggis could not imagine how she had survived here, but here she was, leaving it once more and taking with her the last surviving resident. *I needed to come back to say goodbye,* she thought. Chasna hadn't made it, but she and Polla would go back and take up the life she had begun with the group. It would not be the same without Fanna, but in time, the group would grow and they would learn to cope with the hardships of the weather and the erratic food supply.

Chapter 20

It was later that year, when winter was beginning to bite hard and when the stocks of dried fish and salted meat were running low, that the Masters appeared once more.

As it had begun before, so it was again. Food was left by the entrance to the village: a sackful of dried beans and a smaller one of apples.

Jankin was the first to find the mysterious offerings. 'This was how it began before,' he said. 'This is the Masters' way of coaxing us to do what they want us to do.'

'Can't we eat the food?' questioned Anga.

Bethyl came on the scene. 'Jankin's right. This is how it began before. We take their food and it puts us under an obligation to them. Polla?'

'Yes?'

'Did the Masters do this with the people left in the City? Did they trick them?'

'They tried. Then they rounded them up and took them away. The dogs too.'

It had happened so suddenly, so unexpectedly, that the villagers were unprepared. Polla and Beggis had returned safely and the situation in the City was discussed by all of them, but there was little they could do except carry on with their lives.

They stood guard over the sacks in case one of them should be tempted to take some of the food and waited to see what would happen.

On the fifth morning, an all-too-familiar voice boomed out of the sky above them.

'Citizens of Village Nine! Pay attention! You have shown remarkable resilience and powers of self-reliance. We wish to reward you for your efforts. We have new quarters for you, furnished with warm comfortable beds and with meals provided free to you every day. There you can lead useful and productive lives free from anxiety about your food supply or other matters. Clothing and all material goods will be supplied to you. You have until tomorrow to make your decision.'

Anga and Freedom were terrified and clung to Darfi. Scummo, helpless, tried to comfort Kelpin and the others. If only Fanna were here!

It was silent again. Bethyl listened long after the voice had stopped. The villagers, unsure whether they could be overheard or not, followed Jankin and Bethyl out of the village and into the wood. They sat under a huge beech tree, dead leaves all around them, shivering in the chill.

Kelpin was clear. 'I'm not going back, not ever.'

Darfi said 'Nor me.' Anga got very close to him. He put his arm around her.

Jankin was cautious. 'We may have no choice. Think what you'd be giving up by staying here.'

'Think what you'd be giving up by going back,' argued Bethyl.

They thought. The arguments went one way then another until Polla felt her head was spinning.

'I'm not going back,' she announced. 'Never.'

Regretfully, they all came to that conclusion.

'What happens now?' asked Kelpin, reasonably.

'Whatever happens, happens,' answered Scummo. 'We have to accept whatever follows on from our decision.'

He looked at Kelpin. She was slender, dark and beautiful. A young woman with her mind made up. She looked at him with eyes full of love, hope and longing, and he understood that he could not protect her from this. She understood this too.

'We're a family, right?' stated Beggis. 'Families stick together, no matter what. We all have to choose the same, I think.'

'Who thinks we should consider the offer?' Bethyl asked the question. There was silence. Then she asked each of them in turn what they wanted to do. Magrab was certain, but regretful, Sita doubtful. Rondi was hesitant, Darfi clear.

'What if they use the dogs again to move us? What if we stay and they break up the village?' Rondi asked.

Magrab was adamant. 'We die here, if we must. We have to resist them.'

'It's all right for you, but I've got the baby to consider,' said Anga, patting her belly. There was another life in there just beginning. Freedom squirmed in Darfi's arms. Darfi did not look at Anga.

Scummo said, 'You think the Masters would let you go back and keep your children?'

'Kelpin survived. So did you,' said Anga, defiantly.

Scummo said, 'The Apartments we came from are horrible places, Anga. They kept Kelpin with her mother for a reason, not out of any sense of kindness.'

'What reason?' Anga wanted to know

'I don't know,' Scummo said. 'They were interested enough in her to put that implant in her leg.'

Anga was quiet.

Sita joined the discussion. 'And if we stay here, what power do we have over our lives if they can come back and do this again?'

None of them knew the answer to that.

Finally, Bethyl spoke again. 'All those proposing to stay here and work together to defend our territory, no matter what, raise your hands.' Scummo and Kelpin raised their hands. Polla followed. Bethyl's hand was already raised. Jankin and Magrab raised theirs with Beggis. Rondi slowly raised his, followed by Sita. Darfi and Anga raised their hands and the decision was made. Bethyl asked Sita what had convinced her. Sita told her that it was because Scummo and the others who knew the City were the most definite about not going back there.

'They should know what they're talking about,' she said.

'What do we do tomorrow,' asked Bethyl, 'when they come for our decision?'

Magrab stepped forwards. 'I will t-tell them our decision,' he said, his eyes steady and bright, his hands clasped in front of him.

'And then what?'

'We take the consequences.'

Sita hid her face in her hands and wept. Anga held Freedom tightly. Kelpin went to Scummo, who put his arm around her. He had protected her as much as possible from danger in the time he had known her. Here, he was helpless.

None of them slept that night. Instead, they sat round the fire talking about old times and gaining strength from one another. Bethyl started to sing, an old, old song that they had sung before, and gradually their voices joined hers in the chorus.

> 'We are the first and last men,
> Diggers and planters of seeds
> Here when the world began And we are all agreed
> We are the land
> We are the land, my people, we are the land.'

***

The control tower heard and received the singing and the discussions.

'Do they mean to turn us down, Number Six?'

'It seems they may, Four. It hardly matters. We've got the information we came for.'

'Looks as though our mission will end early if they will not be persuaded to return to the City.'

'It can't be helped. The other colonies beyond the estuary may choose differently, of course.'

'Ah, yes. I'd forgotten about them.'

'You shouldn't. They attacked us with rocket-fire last time we tried to round them up.'

'Really? Before my time. What happened?'

'The rocket destroyed the boat they were going to be transported on and the dogs drove them on up to the top of the cliff. They fell off or jumped and the eel creatures did away with them. A bit gruesome.'

'Did you see it happen?'

'I watched some of it from the tower. The screams carried over the water to where we were. I think the orders after that were slightly more reasonable.'

'What happens to the dogs now?'

'There aren't many left. The ones left will soon be tamed by the villagers, if history repeats itself. They've still got the dazer. They should be safe.'

'The girl, Kelpin, why is she of special interest to us?'

'One thought that of all the subjects identified, she had the most promising survival gene. Besides, she has a different genetic make-up to the others. We don't know who her father was. If she breeds in the next timespace, One may want to look at the offspring to see if they might be good breeding stock for the next protocol.'

'Interesting. And SCUM04? The one who left with Kelpin? What happens to him?'

'Again, nothing. They all either survive using their wits and their ability to look after one another, or they perish. We'll never know. The City will be dismantled, so they will not be able to return there. After we've gone, the planet's future belongs to them. Nothing to do with us.'

'The experiment worked very differently where I came from. I don't think anybody left the City; they were all too frightened of what lay beyond the walls. But they'd been in the City longer than these people. For them, the City was home, just as the villages are for these people.'

'Having the survival gene yourself – has that made a difference to the way you view these people? Would you want to come back to see how they're getting on, for instance?'

'Hmm. I'll have to think about that. I still can't quite understand what keeps them together. The women being leaders, I think, particularly those two women . . . Pity that one died.'

'Yes. But they seem to be able to carry on without her.'

'Sign of good leadership.'

'Really?'

'Oh yes. Right. Is everything ready?'

'Affirmative.'

'Well, let's say goodbye to them.'

M. Valentine Williams

Chapter 21

Morning came, and the villagers still sat around the ashes of their fire, half asleep. Bethyl called them to order. 'Well, this is it, everyone. Let's prepare ourselves and go out into the courtyard—'

'No, make them come to us!' It was Rondi shouting. 'Why should we dance to their tune? We are free people, are we not?'

The others, awake now, held each other close in a last embrace. They filed out of the main hall. Sita and Beggis straightened their long, tangled plaits of hair. Doran stood behind Sita, his arms round her shoulders. Anga wiped dirt off Freedom's face, and Darfi took his son and put him in a sling on his back, where he squirmed and then settled. Anga played peekaboo with him to make him smile. Bethyl looked at them and felt her heart would break. She stood next to Jankin. In a line, they waited for the Masters to arrive, dirty, thin, dishevelled, but with bright eyes and proud bearing. The Masters observed this. The voice came booming from the sky.

'People of the village, we wish you to tell us your decision. Who is your spokesperson?'

Magrab stepped forwards. 'I am,' he said firmly.

'And the decision is?'

'We all, without exception, wish to stay here, undisturbed, and lead our lives. We may have little, but we are free people and we do not wish to change that.'

'And this is the will of all of you?' The villagers nodded, and murmured assent. 'Does anyone disagree?' The villagers looked at one another, at the headstone by the square marking Fanna's grave and at their homes. They did not waver. There was silence.

'So be it. The City will be dismantled and we will have no presence here after Sevenday. We wish you farewell, citizens of this place. You should know that you are not alone; there are other colonies beyond the estuary, on the other side of the City as you knew it. They, too, have opted to remain. No doubt you will make contact eventually. Farewell.'

Something in the sky shifted, telescoping away from them, and was gone.

'You were brave, Magrab,' said Sita admiringly.

The others were silent. They stood and looked at one another. This was it, then. Now they were really on their own. Anything they needed they had to make, any food they wanted they had to grow, or find, any problem they had, they had to solve. Fanna, who had a gentle wisdom they had all respected, was gone.

Bethyl took Jankin by the hand. 'We are one people,' she said. 'Will you have the two of us as your leaders?'

'Aye, we will,' they called back.

They debated whether to eat the food the Masters had tried to bribe them with, but when they looked in the sacks there was nothing but smelly mush. They really were on their own.

***

Now it was winter again. The little settlement by the wood had changed. The villagers now had more pigs, which they let loose in the woods when food was scarce to forage for themselves. There were pigeons too, in the loft over the main hall, and a fish pond which they stocked with carp and trout, caught in fish traps in the river. Although the hall was used for meetings and was a convenient communal space in summer, in winter it was cold, and villagers had to huddle round the hearth. The cow byres and cottages that could be repaired were partitioned with wattle and daub hurdles to make sleeping spaces for the families, who used hay from the summer meadows to insulate the spaces a little. They began to make bricks with the clay they dug from the fish pond, mixing straw in with the clay to bind it. These they baked in the old bread oven where they fired the pots.

Gradually the rossells and two-headed eels and strange fish had died out, unable to reproduce, and other species began to reappear. Deer were seen in the forest; rabbits and beavers populated the streams and clearings, and in the village, babies began to be born. Anga, never thin, produced another child, a daughter this time, with Darfi. Sita and Doran were about to become parents, and Rondi and Polla had formed a pair. Polla was still young and thin and unlikely to be fertile, but Bethyl, fearing an early pregnancy would kill her, took the young couple aside and gave advice to Rondi and bitter herb ointment to Polla. They ignored this advice, thought better of it, and proceeded to make love as before, but with more attention to the consequences.

Scummo, Magrab and Andalou were left as solitary males, as Jankin and Bethyl, heads of the tribe, remained together. Kelpin and Beggis were females without a mate. Beggis respected Magrab, but was really interested in Andalou, who was frightened by her hot temper. Finally, the day came when Bethyl, tired of the moody sparring between the three men, and the restlessness of the girls, called a meeting.

Bethyl addressed the group. 'The time has come for us to make a decision about the future of our group.'

Kelpin asked, 'Why?'

'Because if we are to grow and become strong as a community, we need more mates. Who is going to mate with Kelpin? Who with the others? Perhaps some of the unmated ones would like to choose from the others. Beggis?' Bethyl was to the point.

Beggis was very embarrassed by being singled out.

Bethyl persisted. 'Who would you choose, Beggis, if you could?'

'I would choose him,' said Beggis shyly, pointing to Andalou.

'Andalou?'

He looked at Beggis. She sat, with her red gold ringlets around her shoulders, looking forlorn and unhappy. He was touched. He reached across and patted her arm.

'I agree,' he said. Then they both smiled and their faces lit up with sudden happiness. Magrab looked away.

'And Kelpin?'

Kelpin looked down.

'That's not fair,' interrupted Scummo. 'You can't make her choose like that. We have a different relationship. If I had a daughter like Kelpin, I'd be delighted. In fact, she *is* like my daughter. Magrab and I are too old to mate with Kelpin. Besides, it doesn't feel right.' Kelpin avoided looking at anyone and concentrated on watching an ant crossing the floor instead. When she spoke, it was slowly and carefully.

'Scummo means more to me than anyone. But he's right. I don't want to mate with him. Or Magrab. Not that I don't like Magrab, I do, but . . .'

'I have a suggestion,' said Bethyl. They waited. 'If we make contact with other villagers, we may be able to find mates for those without. We know there are some others on the far side of the estuary.'

Before she could continue, Magrab broke in, 'I do not w-want a mate,' he said, shyly. 'I will help Sita and Doran with their baby when it comes. I do not want my own family again.'

They discussed the need to make contact with other groups, the risks, the rewards, all unknown, that such a meeting might offer.

A party of three set out from the village in the spring: Bethyl, Scummo and Jankin. They had all nominated

Magrab as spokesperson in their absence. They made the long journey around the estuary on foot, skirting round the remains of the ruined City, all the while looking for signs of life, footprints and smoke that might indicate the existence of other beings. Spring was well advanced when they first found the signs they were looking for.

It was Jankin, with his acute hearing, who first alerted them. From far across the valley lying before them they heard the sound of a woman singing.

'Do you know the song?' Scummo whispered to Bethyl.

'Shh! It's one of the songs we sang. I think it's called "Far from Home."'

'How shall we approach? Jankin?'

He thought hard. 'We can leave a message at night in their camp – but that's risky.' His eyes lit up. 'I know, we can creep closer and tie something onto an arrow and fire it into the camp.'

'Won't that seem like an attack?'

'Not if we make sure it doesn't hit anyone. We can send a message on it.'

'Saying what?'

'I don't know. 'Peace', maybe, or 'Friend?''

Bethyl had the arrows, Scummo the bow. How could they write a message? Bethyl took a curl of bark from a silver birch and scratched 'Friend' on it with her knife. She lashed it to the arrow with plaited dried grass. All this took a while, and the others grew restless. Finally, she was ready. They moved forwards until they were within range of the settlement and Jankin took the bow from Bethyl and took aim.

'Too late!' Scummo yelled, as a smoking ball of burning pitch hurtled towards them. 'We've been spotted!' The grass in the clearing was set alight and the three had to run forwards to escape the bitter smoke.

'Fire the arrow!' yelled Bethyl to Jankin. He aimed above the clearing where they had seen the woman. There were other shapes moving about there now. The arrow flew up in a graceful parabola and, losing speed, came down just short of the clearing where they had seen the woman. A figure darted from the bushes and snatched it away.

'Now we wait,' said Bethyl.

They sat on the dry tussocky grass and waited. Around them, they could hear movement in the bushes. Jankin very much wanted to stand up and kept his bow taut with its second arrow in case they were rushed. Finally, he could stand it no longer. He motioned the other two to rise and they stood, back to back, their spears, stick and bow ready. Out of the bushes stepped a ragged bunch of people, who surrounded the three and kept them in the centre of the circle with their sticks and spears.

'Who are you?' demanded one.

'Where have you come from?' cried another, a man with several broken teeth.

Bethyl stood tall and firm, her grey eyes scanning the figures surrounding them in case of a sudden attack.

'We have come from the village on the far side of the estuary. The Masters told us of you. We are peaceful people and we wish to talk with you.'

'Throw down your weapons.'

'You must also throw down yours.'

The snaggle-toothed man looked at her with more respect. 'Do women always give the orders in your village?' he sneered, looking at Jankin and Scummo. They held their ground and stared back. There was a pause. Finally, 'We will talk,' he pronounced, turning on his heel. They followed him.

These people had erected shelters from bundles of brushwood on a wooden frame and roofed them with turf. They had stuffed clay and moss into the cracks and the shelters blended in with the surroundings. In many ways, their settlement appeared further advanced than Erasil, and the three travellers looked around with interest, making mental notes of what they observed. They were beckoned into the largest hut and asked to sit on dry logs arranged around a central hearth. There was no fire. All had left their weapons, such as they were, outside.

First, they exchanged names. The snaggle-toothed man was not the leader, it seemed; this title was given to a very broad, tall man, who introduced himself as Wesney. Wesney had a special cushion and lowered himself down onto it with some difficulty. His knees appeared to trouble him. He asked how many settlers there were in Erasil. Scummo answered him and asked the same question back.

'Twenty-three, in all. We fought off the Masters during the Herdings by firing missiles at their boats. They took most of us eventually, but some here have never been to the City.'

'Like us. And how have you survived the colder months during that time?' asked Jankin.

'We have these shelters, and we keep some animals which provide us with enough rations to manage through the winter months. We are some way from the sea here and we've not yet developed ways of fishing for our food. At the beginning, some of us tried that and the eel things in the water attacked them. So we gave up. What about you?'

Gradually, the atmosphere became more friendly between them, and the talk widened out into a description of how they had killed the eel and how they made fish traps and used bait to catch fish lurking in the deep water by the cliffs. They talked about the new fish pond and could see Wesney's eyes widen with interest. They talked about crabs, kelp and shrimp, which they had learned to catch by using pottery scoops with perforations in them. In shallow waters this was quite successful. Their hosts hung on their every word.

In turn, Bethyl, Scummo and Jankin told of their forays back to the City, their attempts at making a coracle, the pigs they kept, the crops they tended. All the while, Bethyl was aware that the information they were sharing could be used against them. Knowing they had stores and stone dwellings might entice these people to join them, or worse, raid their territory, and all manner of problems might arise. But she could see no alternative.

'We have a choice,' she concluded finally. 'We can set up in opposition to one another, or we can share our knowledge and trade with one another and both prosper.'

'Or we can take you prisoner and force you to disclose all the information you have or make you take us to your village.

You've left out that option.' Immediately the atmosphere changed. Wesney was enjoying this.

Scummo came back with a quick response. 'That wouldn't be a very intelligent thing to do, though, would it?'

'Why not? Seems reasonable enough to me.'

Scummo thought hard. 'Because we'll tell you and show you what we've learned for free anyway. If you keep us prisoner you'll have to feed us. And you'd have no way of knowing if what we told you was correct. If, on the other hand, we come to some agreement, we can show you how to make fish traps, for instance, and we can trade prawn scoops, or salt or something else for things you produce.'

Wesney's deep-set eyes shifted back and forth as he thought his over. Bethyl was filled with revulsion for this large, unfriendly man, whose flesh was ringed with dirty smudge lines in the creases of his arms and neck.

'And why exactly have you come here?' he asked. 'You must want something.'

'We have begun to raise children in our settlement,' said Bethyl. 'Some of us do not have mates. We came to see if there are members of your tribe that might wish to find a mate from our group.'

'I am one of those who as yet has no mate,' said Scummo, quietly. He felt their eyes upon him.

'We have one woman as yet not spoken for,' said one of Wesney's aides. Wesney signalled to him to fetch her. He came back pushing a girl ahead of him who was so terrified they could not see her face for the curtain of dirty hair that hung down around her.

'You can have her,' said Wesney. 'Useless female. Fights like a tiger if anyone comes near her. I'd be glad to see the back of her. We'd want something in exchange, though.'

Bethyl was holding back her own thoughts about this transaction but could keep quiet no longer. 'Do we know what *she* wants?' she asked, pointing to the terrified girl. She addressed the quivering girl gently but directly. 'This man' – she indicated Scummo – 'has no mate. He is gentle and I know him to be a good man. If you agree, we will take you back with us and you can be his woman. Have a good look at him—'

'Wait a minute,' interrupted Wesney. 'We might require him to live here with us. He can be useful to us.'

'That way we lose Scummo and gain nothing. Think again.'

The girl raised her head. Something about her looked familiar to Scummo. Then she spoke. 'I want to go with him,' she said, clearly.

Wesney shrugged. 'So be it. And what do we gain?'

'What do you want?'

'Well not any of you, that's certain. She's too old and the other one is not the right sex. We take women as we want them. There's only one prefers his own sex, eh, Barco?'

The man referred to as Barco tittered and was silent.

'So what do you want?'

Wesney thought hard. Finally, he had an idea. 'You must stay for three days and show us how to make traps to catch fish. Agreed?'

They looked at one another and nodded. 'Agreed.'

The three days that followed were difficult for the three visitors. Bethyl had to bite her tongue continually at the way women were treated in this place. It was clear that the men used them, owned them when it pleased them, lent them out when it didn't. The women were all very thin and only one had conceived, but the baby had died shortly after birth. Bethyl was shooed away from the eating place when she attempted to sit down with the men. The other women steered her into a separate shelter and gave her some of their food. She'd noted that the men were eating meat while the women made do with broth. The women were not asked to take part in any of the decision-making, and the young man assigned to Bethyl, who was to learn pottery-making, clearly did not like being shown what to do by a woman. They all three slept together, at least, but the shelter they were in was shared by several others and they did not feel able to compare notes. The young woman attached to Scummo shadowed him closely, careful not to let him out of her sight. The fish baskets were made, copied, finished, and used in the river, and by the third day they were ready to set off back to Erasil. Bethyl had to leave the shrimp scoops to dry out, hoping that her instructions about firing them had been understood.

Wesney did not really want to let them leave and on the third day tried to persuade them to stay, but they were adamant.

They left on the morning of the fourth day, Jankin in the lead, followed by Bethyl, with the young woman, who referred to herself as Grantis, between Scummo and Bethyl. She said farewell to no one in the settlement and walked with her head held high. Again, Scummo was aware of something familiar about her. What was it?

They had not travelled far before Jankin called to them to stop.

'I think we're being followed,' he whispered. 'We'll keep going and aim to lose them when we get near the estuary. The water will help hide our tracks.'

'They'll still find you,' said Grantis. 'They always do.' She said no more. The other three were impressed.

When they came out onto the sea meadows by the estuary there was no more cover, and whoever had been following them kept still and hidden and watched. Aware of this, the group skirted the edge of the water until they were in a small inlet. This they jumped across, leaving a footprint in the mud, then veered sharply inland, taking care not to step on places where a mark might be left. Finding a wood, they camped under a low yew tree when night came and kept watch but saw no one. Their food was running out and their feet were raw by the time they arrived back at Erasil.

Chapter 22

Kelpin saw them arrive first. She had been hiding up a tall tree in the woods, looking for wild pigs. When she saw three of them returning, her heart beat very fast with anticipation. The other person with them was a woman. Scummo's new mate! She watched them cross the rough land south of the village as they made their way slowly through the thick, tangled grass. The horror of sharing Scummo with an unknown woman made her shudder. She dropped lightly from the tree and ran back to the village.

'They're coming back!' she called. 'There's someone with them!'

Everyone came to see and as they waited, the three figures finally emerged from the path by the wood and came towards them.

There was a great deal of curiosity about the other village and the people in it. Grantis listened carefully and although the others looked to her to add something to what they were saying, she felt inhibited. Later, she felt, she would talk, but not now.

Kelpin greeted her cautiously. 'You know Scummo and I came here together?'

Grantis shook her head.

'Well, we did. Scummo rescued me after my mother died and brought me here.'

There was an unspoken question on Grantis' face. Very softly she said, 'I am to be Scummo's mate.'

Kelpin looked down, her mouth moving as though she wanted to spit something out.

Grantis went on, 'Will you help me? You know him better than anyone.'

Kelpin was nonplussed. Finally, she found her voice. 'He doesn't like mushrooms, he doesn't like to be woken up too early and he coughs a lot in the winter,' she blurted.

Grantis put her hand out. 'I'll do my best to look after him. Will you tell me if I get it wrong?'

Kelpin nodded vigorously. 'He'll look after you too,' she said. 'He did with me. And he tried to with my mum.'

For the first time in a long while, Grantis smiled.

It took a while for Scummo to recognise Grantis as the skinny girl who had clung to him on the balcony long ago when he had made his second trip back to the City. She had recognised him immediately.

Grantis was cautious at first. This village might be the same as the one she'd left. Only time would tell. She was treated warily, but with respect, and when, after supper that first night, Scummo took her to the space he had made for himself and Kelpin and indicated a third area for her to sleep, she was thankful to rest undisturbed. There was none of the tension here that had existed in the other village, and the males were quieter and gentler with one another. A few days later, Scummo told Kelpin not to follow them and gave Doran the task of seeing that she obeyed him. He took Grantis into the woods and they were gone a long long time. When they returned, she was smiling.

'Grantis has consented to be my mate. We are hand-fasted,' he told the villagers that evening. Grantis nodded. 'We will have a feast to celebrate! Who'll come on a hunting party with me?'

Kelpin sulked and went off to annoy Rondi. Grantis ignored her and while Scummo was off hunting, she took the old bedding outside and burned it. The fleas that had kept her awake were popping on the fire now. She made a clean bed out of bracken and some new hay and covered it with skins. Kelpin would have to sleep somewhere else. At fourteen, she would soon need her own mate. It was not proper for her to stay too close to Scummo now that he was hand-fasted.

The hunters returned later that day with their spoils: two large rabbits, a pigeon and a bag full of mussels. There was just enough for a celebration meal.

It was while they were roasting the last of the rabbit that Magrab, who had been thoughtfully chewing the meat, which was altogether too fresh, heard something moving about outside in the yard. It was early evening, and the night watch hadn't begun yet. All the villagers were in the main room, eating and talking about the hunting party and the knowledge of the village Grantis had come from. Suddenly, Magrab raised his hand, gesturing to them to be quiet. Alarm showed in their faces as Magrab and Jankin, who were nearest the door, silently rose to their feet and crept towards it. They opened the door together, sticks at the ready, and were surprised to see a young goat rooting around in their hay store. The goat, a female, scampered off before they could capture it.

'Try to follow it!'

'It's heading for the woods!'

'Don't shout! You'll startle it even more.'

They walked swiftly and stealthily after the disappearing goat, which kept up a steady pace until it was lost in the long grass beyond the wood, and they could no longer see to follow.

'We'll track it in the morning.'

'Did you see? It's a young nanny. Not much use on its own unless there's a billy around. But it's a young one, so it must have been born last year, or early this year . . .'

'So that means there are more of them!'

'I wonder if the other village knows about them?'

'I'll ask Grantis.'

Grantis knew about the goats. There was a pen at the back of her village, which Scummo, Bethyl and Jankin had not been allowed to see, and where livestock were kept.

'There are five goats there,' she told them, 'though one escaped while I was there because Sarli didn't shut them in properly. They beat her cruelly for that. The ones that are left aren't cared for well.'

'So could the one we saw be one of theirs?'

'Yes, it's possible.'

They waited until the next day and set out early to track the goat from where they had seen it last, armed with a net and some shrivelled crab apples. Capturing it alive would be difficult, but they had to try. Magrab, who had kept goats many years ago before the Masters came, thought that the goat might respond to human voices, and that if they could only get nearer to it, they might be able to coax it to come back to the village. There it would be a great deal easier to enclose it in a pen or tether it. They followed its sharp hoof tracks through the soft ground of the wood edge and out onto the rough ground where they had seen it disappear the previous evening.

'This is w-where we last saw it.' They scanned the ground closely and were rewarded by finding a pile of fresh pellets.

'These droppings are fresh – look, there's steam coming from them. Let's sit down and wait to see what happens.'

'Shh . . .' They sat, aware of the dampness of the ground seeping through the thick, dead grass, and the rain-sodden scent of the earth. They kept silent, ears straining, for almost twenty minutes. Then Magrab nudged Jankin and gestured silently. Beyond the matted tussocks of grass, something was moving. There was a rustle. Then another.

Cautiously, the goat put its head out to have a better look, then withdrew it. They held their breath. The goat did it again. This time they could see the yellow eyes, with their vertical pupils, observing them. They continued to sit, unmoving, while the goat became more confident. One false move on their part and they knew it would scamper off into the bushes and their efforts would have been in vain. After a while, Magrab thought it was worth taking a chance. Without moving, he called the goat softly, gently, over to him, using the memory of his own goat as a guide.

'Here, nanny. Here. Over here!' The goat watched him suspiciously but did not run. Very slowly, Magrab felt in his bag and drew out some crab apples. He threw some, with the minimum of movement, towards the animal. Jankin was fascinated.

The goat started, drew back, then approached again, sniffing the apples. Magrab called again to it. The goat came towards them and sampled an apple, then another. Magrab knew they had won. He beckoned to Jankin. Very, very slowly, they stood and backed away from the goat, watching it out of the corner of their eyes. Magrab let a couple more apples drop. The goat watched him and followed.

It was slow, and they had to be patient. Jankin would have liked to rush the goat and capture it by throwing the net over it, but something about Magrab's face and approach told him Magrab was in charge here and knew exactly what he was doing. Although immature, the goat had horns that were sharp and pointed. Jankin didn't fancy being butted by it.

Finally, they reached the entrance to the village. Magrab signalled to Darfi, who was cleaning a skin, to keep still. No one else was about. They managed to lure it into a pen and it settled down quite peacefully to eating some hay. Magrab jumped out of the pen, grinning from ear to ear.

The addition of the goat to their small collection of livestock – two semi-wild pigs, some pigeons and rabbits – cheered them all greatly. They stood around the pen watching it and commenting on every move it made. The goat seemed happy enough and watched them through its narrow yellow eyes as it chewed the hay. Their enthusiasm was tempered with caution. They knew that a female on its own was useless. This one was young and had not been mated, so they would have to feed and house her in the hope that a male could be found. But it was a start.

It was eight days later when three of Wesney's men arrived with him at the village. Wesney came straight to the point, wheezing a bit as he spoke. 'We've come for the goat.'

Magrab stepped forwards. 'What goat?'

'Very funny. The one you stole. The one that's rightfully ours.' He pointed to the pen in the barn.

'We do have a goat. We found it one night outside eating the hay. We didn't take it from you.'

'Doesn't matter. Small female goat, am I right? Stupid woman in the village let it out. Been missing since the autumn. Ask the one you've got here, Grantis. How is she by the way? Got her pregnant yet, have you?' He stared at Scummo.

Bethyl stepped forwards, conciliatory. 'Good to see you again, Wesney, though somehow I expected it. Come inside and we'll discuss the matter. How did you know we had a goat?'

Wesney did not reply and, with his followers, entered the hall and sat down on the hay sacks provided. Their eyes roamed over the building, with its solid stone walls and mended windows. Wesney had difficulty sitting down and was helped by two followers. Doran, solid as ever, stood next to Sita, who was holding the new baby. Anga and Darfi joined them, with Freedom asleep on Darfi's shoulder. Gradually, they all came into the hall and viewed the newcomers, who were equally curious about them. Only Grantis hid herself, not wanting to be seen by the villagers who had once been her fellows.

Scummo understood. 'Stay here. I'll come and find you when they've left,' he said, and Grantis nodded. She was in their sleeping space, ready to hide. Scummo stood at the entrance to the hall, wanting to be sure no one was roaming around the village without their knowledge.

Seeing the babies, Wesney began, 'Your women breed well, I see.'

'We have been fortunate. Do your women not have children?' answered Jankin.

'No. Skinny bitches, all of them.'

'Maybe that's why?'

Wesney looked curious. 'Think so? We make them work hard. Think if we fattened them up a bit they'd be better at breeding?'

'You speak as though they were animals.' Bethyl could keep quiet no longer.

'Yes. Well. Our men like to be men, don't we, eh? Leave the women to work in the settlement while we do the important stuff. '

'I see there are no women with you today.'

'That's right. They're where they should be, keeping the village tidy and tending the animals. Which reminds me. The goat.'

Kelpin had been listening with close attention and decided to speak up. 'Even if it *is* your goat, I have an idea.' She turned to Bethyl, who nodded.

Before she could continue, Wesney butted in. 'This one's only a kid. What does she know?'

Bethyl ignored this. 'Kelpin?'

'You've said that our females breed easily. That's because they are cared for. We could look after your goat, feed her properly, and you can lend us a billy so that she has kids, then we can share the kids and build up our herds. There are people here who used to keep goats and who know how to look after them properly.'

Wesney looked suspicious. Magrab continued, backing Kelpin up. 'After all, the goat is no good to us unless we can breed from her, and no good to you if she's mated but still doesn't carry live young. Have you got a billy back in your village?'

'Yes, but he's not up to much.'

'What do you mean?'

'He was one of the wild goats. They used to live on the mountains and when we caught him he was already quite old. Bit lame as well. Stinks the place out. We keep him tethered away from the village. But like you say, one goat's no good on its own.'

'And are your goats breeding well?'

'Nah. That's why we want this one back. The three we've got left don't seem to want to breed.'

Bethyl thought before she spoke. 'So what's the answer? What's going to work for all of us?'

One of Wesney's followers stepped forwards, a lean man with a vivid scar on his cheek. 'I say we just take the female back with us. It's ours by right.'

'And how would you take it?' Bethyl was icy cool.

'We can take turns carrying it on our shoulders.'

'How long did it take you to get here?'

'Four days.'

'And you can carry the goat all that time? Since it came here, it has put on weight.'

The men looked doubtful. Wesney, aware of his painful joints, was considering the journey. He had found it arduous, as it had rained hard during the night while they were travelling and they had been forced to shelter in some caves along the shore. They were afraid of what might come out of the sea and afraid of what might come out of the caves. It was an uncomfortable night. Perhaps carrying the goat was not a good option after all.

Bethyl tried again. 'What if we brought the female to you in a few weeks when the weather is better? If the billy is, as you say, too old to travel well, this would be a better solution.'

'And how will you bring it?'

'It will take longer, but we will lead her gently, feed her well and with luck on our side we should be with you two full moons from now.'

'That's a long time. Too long. How do we know we can trust you?'

'Because it's in our interests. And yours.'

Wesney and his men could see that, but they didn't like it.

'If you really w-want to carry the goat all that way, don't blame us if she won't feed properly or dies on the way. It's too far.' Magrab, who had kept goats, spoke with authority.

Reluctantly, the men had to agree.

***

Jankin wanted to know how Wesney and his men had discovered them. As they were reluctant to disclose this, they assumed that they had been followed back by one of the men with Wesney now. They realised that they had become lax in their keeping watch. There were spies in the woods, maybe a spy in their own village. Jankin looked around at the others. Surely they would not betray their own friends and comrades? He remembered Shaful. You could never be sure.

Wesney was not keen on returning empty-handed. He felt he needed something to take back with him to guarantee the return of his goat. What could this be? His eyes glanced at Kelpin, Beggis, Sita and Anga. There'd be a fight if he wanted to take any of these. Where was the woman he had given Scummo, the one they called Grantis?

He couldn't imagine his own men making such a fuss about a woman, but in his camp, women were not in charge, while here it seems they were equals. It was all very puzzling.

'What security can you give me?' he asked.

'Security? You have our word,' Bethyl answered

'I'm sorry but that's not good enough.'

'Do you have something else in mind?'

'What have you got?'

'All we have is ourselves. We're not trading our people. We've suffered many hardships together and we're a close community. Here we are equals. With you it is different.'

Wesney nodded. 'Well how about the one who knows about goats coming with us now? He can tell us how to care for our other animals. Deal?'

Bethyl and Jankin looked at Magrab. 'You don't have to agree.'

Magrab was deep in thought.

'We'll treat him nicely,' offered the scar-faced man, with a leer.

Magrab looked up. He spoke this time without a stutter. 'I will come with you and show you how to care for your animals. Then, in two full moons, the nanny will be brought back to your village, mated, and I will stay until the kid is born. When it is weaned, I will return to this village, with either the kid or the nanny. Agreed?'

Bethyl was concerned. 'Magrab, are you sure about this?'

He nodded, his mind made up. Sita and Kelpin noted the expressions of Wesney's men and didn't like what they saw. Sita came forwards until she was standing in front of Wesney. 'If any harm comes to this man' – she pointed to Magrab – 'I will personally undertake to come after you and kill you.'

'Oh I *am* afraid,' sneered Wesney. 'Hear that, men? This little lady is going to come and kill me if anything happens to . . .' He paused. 'What did you say your name was?'

'Magrab.'

'Magrab here. That's quite a promise.'

'And one I'll keep,' Sita asserted. 'I owe this man my life. And you are fools if you underestimate what I can do.'

Wesney allowed one eyebrow to arch. Boorish bully though he was, he knew determination when he saw it. Perhaps it might be best to play it their way. Let the goats mate and see what happened next. He liked the spirited way these women defended themselves. It was a change from the subservient females – he could hardly recall their names – who did the work in his own village. Maybe they did have something to teach them after all. The group were fed and rested that night, and though Andalou and Doran kept watch, the men slept peacefully on their hay sacks. Grantis stayed out of sight. The villagers were sad to see Magrab go. Under his cloak he carried a pigeon, one he had raised. He had a handful of corn in a pouch to feed it with. He would send it home when the time came. Wesney and his men thought he was being sentimental.

'I have a purpose for this bird,' Magrab said, stroking the pigeon's back. But he would say no more.

They set off early in the morning, Wesney relying on a stick, which slowed the party down. They had inspected the nanny goat and noted reluctantly that it did indeed look fit and in better condition than when they had last seen it. The men themselves were not in good condition. Years of barely surviving in the City had weakened them, and they had lost teeth and their cheeks were sunken through malnutrition. The villagers at Erasil, more skilled at foraging and adept at fishing and keeping livestock, had fared better on the whole. Though they were lean, they were strong. They had learned to cooperate and work together and to look out for one another.

Chapter 23

Magrab went back with Wesney and his men, and the villagers of Erasil missed him. They told one another that it would not be for long, but their hearts were heavy. One month passed, and the nanny goat thrived and grew fat. Finally, the time came to make the journey to Brasto, as the other village was known. Doran, Darfi, Grantis and the other villagers had spent the time working on their land. They had an extensive garden now and young corn was sprouting, linseed and beans were growing and the stock in the fish pond they had dug was increasing. The pigeons Magrab had looked after strutted and cooed in the warm sunshine. They watched to see if his homing pigeon had returned, but there was no sign of it. Then, one morning, the pigeon appeared, a binding around its leg. There was no message. Had it fallen off?

'It's a sign,' said Kelpin. 'Trouble is, we don't know what of.'

'I think it's a sign we should set off with the nanny goat,' said Bethyl.

The party set off the next day, consisting of Jankin, Rondi and Scummo. Scummo carried with him Magrab's pigeon and a bag of corn. Grantis was tearful at saying farewell. Before they went, she shyly told the group much that they needed to know about Brasto. She drew a map with charcoal on parchment. It was spring weather, and the woods were alive with birdsong and the paths soft with mud when they set out. A journey that had taken Wesney and his men four days on foot took the men a great deal longer. The goat began to understand that she would need to walk in order to be fed and became more docile, allowing Scummo to lead her. Sometimes, when she slowed right down, he carried her. Eventually, they found themselves near the village.

When they arrived, they found Magrab thinner but faring well despite being the butt of jokes by Wesney's men. He was delighted to be reunited with his pigeon. The billy goat was in better condition and had been well tended by Magrab. A group of women came to watch as the nanny was led into the enclosure next to where the billy goat was standing, chewing the cud and eyeing the approaching nanny with a lustful eye. Magrab led the female in and then shooed everyone else away. He observed from a distance, understanding that the animals needed peace and quiet in order to mate. The nanny, tired after her long journey, was not interested in mating. Magrab knew she would come into season soon and that all that was needed was patience. Delighted to see his friends, he showed them the other animals with pride.

'They've got the livestock, but they don't know how to look after it,' he said, as they looked at the sow and her piglets.

They moved on. The goats had been rehoused on Magrab's instruction in an outdoor yard with a shelter. He had found salt for them to lick, and there was sweet hay in a willow basket for them to eat, with nettle cuttings and dandelion. The three nanny goats turned their heads to look at Magrab, whom they recognised, and went on chewing the cud.

'They'd been keeping them tethered out here,' Magrab went on. 'They had no proper food, only what they threw into the pen. They looked pitiful when I arrived. They've got salt now, which they need. Wesney knows nothing about caring for animals, neither do the others. You can't bully animals into breeding and being healthy.'

'Watch your tongue,' said the man with broken teeth. 'Don't let Wesney hear you say that.'

A boy of around fifteen appeared from the village. 'Wesney wants to talk to you,' he said, indicating Magrab and the others.

'Thanks, Codron. He, b-by the way, is my main helper. I'm training him up to be a herdsman, aren't I, Codron?' The boy nodded, pleased. Magrab turned and went to the main hut, followed by the three others.

Wesney's large, heavy and decidedly smelly body took up most of the space in the main hut. His followers crowded in the doorway as the four sat down.

Wesney lost no time in getting straight to the point.

'Your man here, Magrab,' he said, pointing. 'He seems to know what he's talking about. You' – he pointed at Jankin – 'have kept your word. I hear the nanny goat has been well looked after.'

'Sh-she's waiting to be mated with your ram,' said Magrab.

'How long do you think that'll take?'

'A day or two. Then we can try the other nannies again and see if we can encourage them to breed.'

'That old billy won't know he's born,' chuckled Wesney.

'About our deal,' continued Magrab. 'When the first kids have been born and weaned, the agreement is that I take some back to Erasil.'

'*Some?* You can take one.'

'And if it's a billy?'

'We'll have to bring our nannies to you. Do it the other way round.'

'I have another idea,' said Magrab. 'If I stay here and care for your goats, you can pay me with kids, one of each sex.'

Wesney didn't like this idea.

'By that time I'll have trained the lad to look after them and they'll be healthy and strong. Good breeding stock.'

Still, Wesney wasn't won over. It all sounded much too reasonable.

Meanwhile, in a separate hut, some of Wesney's men were discussing ways of taking over Erasil and its inhabitants.

'How many men they got?'

'These three, plus the one who came back with them first time, Magrab. That's four. There were some others there when we went. I'd say no more than six or seven all told.'

'If we take them by surprise, we could kill them easy.'

'Or make them work for us.'

'Yeah. Follow them back and kill them.'

'And then what?'

'We take over their houses and their women and all their stuff.'

'What about Wesney?'

'He's getting too old for this. Time he was moving on. He can't stop us.'

'And who says he has to be leader anyway?'

They muttered on, unaware that Codron, who was stacking wood outside, was listening to every word. The villagers of Erasil left Brasto the next day, without their goat. Scummo felt they might have made a huge mistake, but Magrab assured him that all was for the best. Still, Scummo wasn't happy.

'We've given away our goat for what?' he asked bitterly of Jankin on the way back. 'We've got nothing in return. Promises made by Wesney's lot aren't worth the paper they're written on.'

'We'll see. Seems to me that Magrab's doing fine. If the goats breed well he'll be back with a couple of kids before you can turn around.'

'You're very optimistic, Jankin.'

'We spelled out the value of what we can trade with them. They don't have knowledge or skills in husbandry or fishing. All they know about is how to kill things. Their huts were good, I have to admit, but that's about all. Think how much Bethyl knows about plant medicine. Think about the skills we have. They would be stupid to compromise all that.' He paused. 'I shall be glad to get back to Erasil.'

'Me too.'

Rondi, who hadn't said anything, now spoke. 'I got

talking to the boy who helps Magrab. He says they're jealous of us and they think we're stupid.'

'Who's jealous?'

'The women, mostly. They have a hard life and the men treat them badly. They wish they'd been like Grantis, so the men would let them leave.'

'Do *you* think we're stupid, Rondi?'

'A bit. But I don't see what else we could have done. The way our village works is that either you cooperate and help one another or you die. Seems simple enough to me. But I'm not sure Wesney and his men see it like that.'

They walked on, glad to be away from Wesney, his unpredictable men and sad, skinny women. That night they lit a fire in the forest and huddled round it, wrapping their clothes around them. Two days later, they reached Erasil. Here there was good news. The sow had farrowed and produced a litter of eight piglets in their absence. Bethyl had spotted deer in the forest, quite close to Erasil, and there were now trout in the pond.

Sita was keen to hear about Magrab and how he was faring. At the evening meeting they discussed events. Bethyl, too, was unhappy about the loss of the goat, but felt it was the lesser of two evils.

Nine days later, Magrab's pigeon arrived, and that changed everything. A note was tied to its leg which read simply: *B attacks E soon. Beware.* Kelpin found the bird and untied the note. The villagers heard the news with alarm. There was no doubt in their minds that the B and E stood for their villages. Panic set in.

Bethyl and Jankin called them to order. Jankin gave the orders now. 'Sita and Anga, take the babies to the caves. We'll let you know when it's safe to return. This is a serious threat. Keep calm, we have to think this through.'

This was easier said than done. The two women prepared to leave with heavy hearts. Both knew their men would stay and defend the village. There was only just enough daylight left to make the journey. Kelpin, quick as ever to spot the unusual, unthought-of option, offered her opinion.

'We may have to shoot them. We've got the bows Doran made, and Darfi and Scummo are good marksmen. We could make a trap.'

'We'll need more than that. Arrows are fine, but if they capture one of us they can threaten to kill them unless we give in. We've got to stay together to stop that happening. We need lookouts who can climb to the highest treetop to spot them before they get here. They don't know we've had warning.'

'What about Magrab?' Sita was asking, bundle and baby on her back, ready to leave. They had forgotten Magrab.

'We can't do anything about Magrab. If he sent the message, as I'm sure he did, he'll be looking after himself now. We just have to trust that he's all right.'

They considered how to defend the village. The woods grew to the north, and that was the direction the men had come from before. To the east was the fish pond, beyond that a stream with steep banks. Westwards were the rough pasture lands that they had started to cultivate. No one could approach from this side or from the east without being seen. To the south was rocky, hilly land with a track leading to the coast. This land was covered by gorse and heather and was a possible hiding place for Wesney's men. The woods to the north would provide the best cover, and it was here that the lookouts, Rondi and Andalou, took turns to watch.

If either saw anything moving in the distance, they were to throw a stone at the metal roof of the pigpen.

'We could barricade ourselves into the main hall,' said Bethyl. 'They'll smoke or starve us out eventually, though.'

Kelpin had an idea. 'Why don't we light the fire in there, and all but one of us leave, then the one who's left fastens the door like we do every night? Then they get out through the small window and down the shed roof when they hear voices outside.'

'And then what?'

'They'll batter the door down and be caught like rats in a trap.'

'Ah, I see. The minute they get into the hall we're there outside with our arrows trained on them. And what then?'

'If they fight, we fight. But we give them the option to go peacefully.'

'So they can come back and do it again, when we're not prepared? I don't think so.'

'Where will we hide then?'

'Opposite the hall doorway, in the hay barn where the goat was.'

'Let's hope we get some warning.'

'They'll probably come at night. The lookouts may not have much time to warn us.'

They built a hiding place for themselves in the barn and placed their weapons there within reach. Magrab's message had arrived in the nick of time. Halfway through the second day they heard a clatter from the shed roof. Alarmed, they all stopped what they were doing, ears straining to hear anything unusual, but all was silent. The lookout shinnied down the tree and reported to Rondi.

'Saw a group of them,' Andalou told him. 'Three, I think. Coming over the rough ground. Should be in the wood by now.'

Only Bethyl kept calm. Light was fading. They would normally have been cooking an evening meal. 'I'll stay in the hall and start to cook. The fire's still going, luckily, but I'll make it give out more smoke. If you hide with the weapons in the barn, I'll give a signal, but don't attack until I do.' Bethyl was insistent. 'We may need to wait quite a while. We want them to come right into the hall.'

'Do you think we could deal with this peacefully?' Jankin said gravely.

'I want to try.'

'You're risking your life. Possibly ours too.'

'Think of the alternative. If we kill them we'll be at war with Brasto for all time. We may have to kill them, but if you're waiting outside for them it gives us some safeguard.'

Grantis stepped shyly forwards. 'I am waiting with Bethyl,' she asserted. 'I know these men. It may be that I can say or do something to help matters.'

379

Scummo was alarmed. 'You hid from them last time,' he reminded her.

'I know. I wasn't ready to meet Wesney again then. He tried . . . he tried . . .' She couldn't go on. Scummo was at her side, arm round her. They knew what she was trying to tell them.

Kelpin looked appalled. 'Hope you kicked him in the bollocks.'

Scummo pulled Grantis closer to him. 'You don't have to tell us, Grantis. We saw for ourselves how they treat women over there.'

'Stop chatting. And be quiet. Get to your stations, all of you.' So saying, Bethyl entered the hall with Grantis and placed the wooden bar across. 'Come and learn how to make millet cakes. We need to keep calm and act normally.'

The two women mixed and pounded the millet, added water to it and set the hot stone ready for the millet cakes. All the time, they were listening. The millet cakes steamed and spat and gave off a good smell. The women clattered a few pans and talked of this and that. In the hay barn, the others were fidgeting. Darfi's nose was tickling with the dust and he had trouble keeping himself from sneezing. Suddenly, Kelpin gave him a nudge and pointed. Over by the wood they could see shadows moving. They kept very still; Darfi's nose was tickling even more unbearably and he held his nostrils pinched tightly together until his eyes watered.

Then three men came out of the shadows, down the track and banged on the door of the hall, trying to open it.

Grantis dropped something and let out a yell of terror. 'Who's there?'

'Open up and find out.'

'Give your names. Who comes calling at this hour?'

Calmly, Bethyl went to the door and put her hand on the wooden bar. 'Grantis, serve out the cakes please.' She gestured to Grantis to get out through the window. There was a shoving and banging as the men tried to get in. 'All right. I'm opening the door.' She held her spear more firmly in her right hand, while in her left she used a stick to lift the wooden bar. The door burst open inwards and would have sent Bethyl flying had she not moved back just in time. She faced them alone, unflinching, spear at the ready.

'Where are the others?' demanded the leader as he looked around the empty room. Bethyl kept silent. He was a thin, hungry-looking man she recognised as Hargin. He had sneered at her attempts in the village to teach him how to make fish traps. She realised now she had probably humiliated him in some way, so venomous was his expression.

'Why don't we kill this one anyway? Make an example of her,' said the second one, a dark-haired youth whose name she didn't know.

'I've got a much better idea,' leered Hargin, knowingly. 'Teach the bitch a lesson. Put the weapon down, there's a good girl, and give us some cakes.'

The third man stood in the doorway, his spear at the ready. Of the three he seemed the most uncertain about what to do now they were in their opponent's camp.

Bethyl stood her ground. 'If you come any nearer you'll get this through your chest.'

'Ooh we are scared, aren't we, boys?' sneered Hargin. But he made no move to go towards her. Looking round at the empty room, he demanded, 'Where are the other ones, anyhow?'

'Behind you,' yelled Scummo.

His arrow flew from its bow. The man in the doorway took the arrow in the small of his back and fell to the ground in agony. The others rushed behind Scummo through the door with their weapons at the ready. The fallen man was writhing in the doorway and they had to step over him. Then what they had dreaded happened. Bethyl was overpowered by Hargin, disarmed and taken prisoner. The shorter man held her arms firmly behind her back while Hargin held a knife at her throat. The others held back, appalled at what had transpired.

'Your companion is dying,' said Bethyl through clenched teeth.

The man who held her looked at the injured man and wavered.

'If you kill her, we will surely kill you. You gain nothing. We will not allow you to leave this room.' Jankin's voice was clear and commanding. Kelpin, at the back of the group, looked at him with surprise. 'If, on the other hand, you want to talk, set her free immediately.'

'And spoil my fun?' Hargin drew his knife tip across Bethyl's throat, raising a thin, vicious, red wound. He stood aside. 'Want her to have more of the same?' As he spoke, a figure appeared at the small window behind him and a knife thrown with great accuracy caught him in the back of his skull. Grantis. He clutched his head, blood pouring from the wound, and the knife he carried clattered to the floor.

Bethyl wrenched her hands free from the man holding her, who had temporarily released one hand so he could pick up the fallen knife. Scummo, Jankin, Darfi and the others advanced and overpowered him.

'What happens to him now?' demanded Kelpin once the man was lying face down on the floor with Darfi on top of him and his arms tied behind his back. Bethyl was wiping blood from the wound in her neck. Jankin checked outside to make sure there were no more intruders. When he returned, Hargin was still sitting, stunned, on the floor, with blood pouring from his head. Andalou stood over him with his spear, ready to prod him if he so much as moved an inch.

Andalou knew what he wanted to happen. 'I say we kill him. That way no one can go back to Brasto and tell tales. Besides, they would have killed us.' The others nodded their agreement.

Bethyl looked at the man on the ground with an arrow in his back. He was still alive, though clearly in pain. She felt faint then and had to sit down. The thin red wound on her neck was beginning to swell.

'I say we finish the job,' said Doran, enjoying the excitement. 'Kill all three of them.'

'Yeah. Kill them,' Andalou demanded, wanting to inflict pain.

Bethyl, who could hardly speak with her damaged throat, tried to get their attention. She looked imploringly at Jankin to stand by her. Jankin was not in total agreement with Bethyl about what should happen to the men.

'Bethyl thinks we should show them mercy,' he said. 'The problem is, if we let them go they'll only go back to their village and plan another attack.'

'Even if we treat their wounds?' enquired Polla. 'Isn't there any other option? If we kill them it makes us just as bad. You.' She pointed at the man holding his still-bleeding head. 'What would stop you coming back and attacking us again if we let you go?'

Surprised at the question, the man took a little while to answer. 'Staying here with you, I suppose,' he said eventually.

Polla seemed surprised by this answer. 'And what about the wound you've inflicted on Bethyl?'

The man looked down. His expression could have been one of shame or regret; it was hard to tell. They waited silently for him to speak. He could think of nothing to say.

'Kelpin, can you fetch the medicine box for me?' Bethyl asked, with an effort.

Unable to say much more, she watched as Kelpin fetched the wooden box and the men, still reluctant, began to mutter among themselves. With a sigh, Jankin and Doran took charge of the wounded men, cutting one man's clothing away from the arrow and staunching the flow of blood from the head of the other. The arrow tip was embedded in the muscle to the left of the spine, but it didn't appear to be a deep wound. Perhaps he would live if they could remove it.

Scummo, too, had mixed feelings about this. It was his arrow that had pierced the man's back and he was both proud, ashamed and frightened at how easy it had been to fire it. But the excitement he felt was also invigorating and brought back memories of his days in the Apartments and the Sevenday contests. Bethyl, holding a wad of Kelpin's bog cotton to her wound, delegated Polla and Kelpin to remove the arrow. They placed a wad of material in the man's mouth.

'Bite on this,' ordered Kelpin. The man struggled a bit. 'We're going to take the arrow out.'

The wound hadn't bled a great deal, but as they worked and extricated the metal head, cleaning the wound with salt water and applying a herbal compound as directed by Bethyl, the man fainted with pain, and when he came to was astonished to realise that he was sitting up, being offered a drink by Polla. The man Grantis had injured simply sat on the floor, rocking, his hands on his head. There was blood everywhere. They attended to him next.

'What do we do with them now?' Jankin asked of Bethyl when they were out of earshot. 'We've treated their wounds, but if we let them go . . .'

'. . . they're a danger to us. Or are they? Polla's question was a good one. They probably would rather stay here.'

'Yes, but do we want them to?'

'We need to discuss this together, without the men listening.'

'The one Scummo shot is in a bad way. He's not a danger to anyone right now. As for the other two, I say we lock them in the barn while we decide their future. Agreed?'

All the members were summoned. They were all very tired now as it was nearly midnight, and they sat, lay and sprawled in the hay barn as they discussed the matter. Finally, they decided to guard the prisoners until morning and to release Hargin, if his wound allowed it, and the other man, while waiting until the third man with the arrow in his back either recovered or died. When fit enough, he too would be released.

The villagers were not optimistic about a sick man finding his way back, alone, to his village, but the three men were using up valuable food, and when a vote was taken, no one felt that Hargin was trustworthy enough to stay with them in the village. They were less sure about the other man, who, uninjured and vocal, was making a fuss about being tied up.

Bethyl, recovering a little though still sore and shocked, was unable to help with the decision very much. They kept guard over the three men for the rest of the night and in the morning found that the man Scummo had shot was feverish and there were angry red lines on the skin of his back. Kelpin inspected them.

'Not good news,' she said.

Polla agreed. The man groaned as they touched him. His skin was hot and inflamed and the hole in his back looked angry. As they cleaned him with salt water, washing out the wound, he called out in agony. Scummo winced, knowing he had inflicted the wound. Hargin's head was swollen and tender, but he was not feverish. The third, uninjured, man was demanding breakfast.

'You've got a nerve,' said Beggis. 'You came here ready to take over our village. You hurt Bethyl and now you want food? What would Wesney say about that?'

The man looked shifty. 'Wesney doesn't know we've come,' he said. 'He thinks we're on a hunting trip. Anyway, Wesney's old now. He doesn't make all the decisions any more.'

'You mean he decided everything before?' Beggis was aghast. 'Doesn't anyone have a say in what happens?'

'You take your orders from a woman,' he sneered.

'Bethyl doesn't give orders. She and Jankin have the most experience, so they were chosen by all of us to be our leaders. We all have a say in what happens.'

'How did you know we were coming? Seems like you were ready for us.'

Hargin looked up. 'Yes, how *did* you know? Who warned you? I bet it was that one who came to look after the goats. What a job for a man! Not that he's much of a man, is he? What's his name, Magrab?'

The villagers kept silent, knowing that Magrab's life might be in danger. They had not thought about what would happen to him if the men returned. Doran and Andalou exchanged looks. Darfi saw the silent interchange and nodded. He would help them in what they had to do. Rondi ran to the caves to tell Sita and Anga that they could return.

Bethyl was still sleeping when Darfi, Doran and Andalou took the two men away into the woods.

'Where are you taking us?' demanded Hargin.

'You'll find out,' was all Darfi would say. 'Keep quiet and keep walking.'

'My head's hurting.'

'Tough. Keep walking.' Eventually they came to a deep quarry, filled with stagnant slime-green water. The sides were steep and rocky; anyone falling in would have a difficult time getting out. The men were made to stand on the edge.

'Jump or we'll push you.'

Hargin was terrified. 'I can't swim,' he whimpered.

'What about you, Ratface?' Darfi was icy cold.

'I can't either.'

'Time you learned,' said Andalou, and with that he gave both men a mighty shove before the others could stop him. There was a loud splash as both men toppled over backwards and fell into the pit below.

'Perhaps we should fish them out,' said Darfi, as splashing continued below. They peered over the edge. The men were both standing shoulder-deep in water, trying to gain a foothold on the steep rocky side.

'Too late. See that?' They looked at where he was pointing. Three huge snake-like forms were gliding through the water towards the men.

'Saint Emilia! I wouldn't have wished that on them.'

There was nothing they could do to save the men once the eels had them. In any case, they had not thought about how to climb down to the quarry bottom, and the only possible route was round the far end of the quarry and down a track. It would take too long.

When they arrived back at Erasil, Bethyl wanted to know what they had done with the men. They looked shifty to begin with.

Bethyl knew at once something was wrong. 'We had not reached a decision,' she protested. 'What did you do with them?'

'You were asleep,' Doran told her. 'We decided on our own to act before they caused any more trouble.'

'So where are they? You didn't kill them?'

'No,' said Darfi truthfully. 'We tipped them into the quarry way over in the woods. They could get out, only . . .'

'Only what?'

'The eel creatures were in the pond.'

'So the eels had them? They're dead?' Bethyl was trying to take in this information.

'Yes. We're all responsible. How's the one who got the arrow?'

'Not well. I think it pierced his kidney.'

Andalou looked at her long and hard. 'Bethyl, if he dies, it'll be for the best. Taking the other two to the quarry was my suggestion. They would only have gone back to their village. Magrab would have been in danger. As it is, they may come looking for the three men here once they fail to return. You're not always right about these things.'

Bethyl turned away from him. 'I have always tried peace, tried to help people think for themselves without the need for violence . . .'

'. . . and they would have raped you. *Did* cut you, in fact . . .'

'They had no chance to listen to what we had to say. How do we know what might have happened if they had stayed with us for a little longer? Even Hargin—'

'—would have done anything in order to gain a foothold here. He thought we'd be a pushover, that all they had to do was to walk in here, take over the place and kill a few of us while they were at it. Bethyl, I'm sorry, but what's done is done, and I for one can't say I regret it. The question is, what do we do with number three, if he lives?'

Andalou went outside into the sunshine, leaving Bethyl to rage inwardly at what had happened. Doran and Darfi found jobs to do outdoors. Their women would be back soon. The presence of the two women added a different balance to the group. Andalou, in particular, was aware of the excitement he had felt, the sense of victory. He couldn't wait for Beggis to come back from the river so that he could tell her about it.

Chapter 24

It was later in the year when they heard from Brasto, and the messenger was Magrab once again. This time he had not sent a message; he had come himself, bringing three goats. He was tired, for the journey had been a long one as the goats had been driven from their pasture by the estuary to Erasil by a circuitous route. He had brought something else back with him: two duck eggs which he intended to incubate. He gave one to Anga to keep between her breasts. The other he kept under an armpit.

'As soon as they're warm enough they'll start to develop,' he told them. 'I took them from a nest by the river. They're live eggs all right.'

Kelpin looked at the egg with wonder, and envied Anga her custody of it. She did not have enough body fat to keep the egg warm and was aware of it. Meanwhile, Magrab told them the news from Brasto.

Wesney was dead. There was fighting within the village and several of the men were vying for leadership. There had been many stories told about what had happened to the three men who had not returned. Some said they were prisoners in Erasil; some that an accident had befallen them on their hunting trip; others that they had gone back to the City to see for themselves what remained. Magrab was interested to hear the account of the raid. They glossed over the incident at the quarry, but he guessed what had happened.

'And what happened to the third man? The one Scummo shot?' he asked.

'I'm still alive, though it was a near thing,' said a man who had been seated in the dark corner of the inglenook. He came over to introduce himself to Magrab. 'I'm Arlon. I remember you from Brasto.'

Magrab took his hand. 'I don't understand why you're still here.'

'He was ill for many days. Then when he recovered he didn't want to leave,' said Kelpin, nosing into the conversation.

In fact, there had been many bitter arguments about this third man, which eventually he had won by saying simply, 'I am really not a threat to you. I just want to stay here and get on with my life. When the other two suggested this trip, I had a bad feeling about it – I knew Hargin of old, but I really didn't think they'd act as they did. Wesney tried to rein them in but they wanted to come here and take over, then take prisoners back with them. I have been well treated here and I have no wish to cause further trouble.'

Magrab was the centre of attention for several days after his return, especially when the egg he was holding so carefully in his armpit hatched out. Anga's egg hatched soon after and one of her children was given the task of minding the ducklings. The villagers got on with their daily routines, each member choosing and being allocated other tasks. Jankin took more control over the meetings, as Bethyl's power seemed to decline after her wounding by Hargin. The shallow cut had healed well and left only a thin white scar, but it was Bethyl's inner being that was most damaged. The other women tried to help her restore her confidence, but things were not the same.

Sooner or later, it would come to light what had happened to the men from Brasto. Sooner or later the unbearable need for violence, which was like a drug and which she had fought so hard all her life to avoid, would appear again. Maybe hunting wild pigs would give some vent to it. Maybe the influence of the women would win. She had tried hard enough to give them the power to run their own lives, and they were all capable, proud and confident in themselves, except Grantis, and now she was pregnant her status was improving every day.

Kelpin was the daughter Bethyl had always hoped for but was now too old to have. Practical, quick-witted and robust, Kelpin was almost fully grown, and had learned everything Bethyl could teach her. Again, she thought of Fanna. What a loss she had been to their community!

With a small herd of goats, and the possibility of some ducks, the villagers felt optimistic now Magrab was back with them once more. As Scummo was occupied more and more with Grantis, whose pregnancy was not going well, Kelpin often found herself lonely and seeking companionship. Although many years her senior, Magrab was the one person she respected and chose to be with. He had skills the others had not yet learned, to do with animal husbandry and livestock, and Kelpin was keen to learn all she could from him. She became his willing assistant and main helper.

Polla spent most of her time with Rondi when he wasn't out hunting, though she would often accompany him as he searched for signs of the animals that had begun to populate the forests again. When she was in the village, she and Kelpin would often talk as they ground the grain or weeded the vegetable garden.

'You know Magrab?' Polla began.

'What about him?'

'He seems, you know . . . lonely, don't you think? Out of all of us . . .'

'He and I are the ones still unmated. So?'

'Nothing.'

'Look, I *do* like him.'

'You spend enough time with him.'

'I know. I like him. I like his company. Scummo spends all his time with that Grantis so . . .'

'Magrab fills his place? You can't blame Scummo for looking after Grantis. She might lose the baby yet. Don't be jealous; it doesn't suit you.'

'Mind your own business. Anyway, who said I was jealous?'

Polla didn't reply to that, but went on, 'Magrab is one of the most trustworthy people here. Also the one who's lost most, though Jankin and Bethyl also lost people in the Herdings . . . You'd be good for one another.'

'He's too old. Forget it.'

'He's – what – ten years older than you? More sensible than Rondi, not as solemn as Jankin. All the others are spoken for.'

'I don't have to mate with anyone if I don't want to. Anyway, you've missed out someone – Arlon.'

'Yes, Arlon. Can we trust him do you think?'

'Search me. Why do you think I need a man anyway?'

'But Kelpin, on those long hot summer nights, don't you just want someone to . . . You know?'

'I suppose. But Magrab? Hmm.'

'Ask Bethyl her advice. Or Beggis. Or Sita.'

Kelpin hated to admit it, but Polla did have a point. She moped around for a few days before talking to Bethyl. She was washing some samphire Rondi had picked on the marshes, removing bits of grass and debris that had got tangled with it. A pile of boiled crabs sat in a crock ready to be shelled next to her. When Kelpin came closer and Bethyl sensed she wanted to talk, she gestured to her to sit down and passed her the crock and a sharp stick.

'Help me with these, will you?'

Kelpin broke each crab body away from its shell, scraped out the meat inside and continued to pry out the sweet meat as she talked. 'Bethyl? Can I ask you something? Do you think I should be mated?'

'Physically, you're ready for it. Emotionally, I don't know. Why?'

'Just that Polla and I were talking.'

'And?'

Kelpin became coy, which was unusual for her. 'And Polla says I should go with Magrab.'

'Magrab? Are you sure?'

'She says he's lonely, he likes me, and that he's the one I should go with.'

'And what do you think about that?'

'Well, I do like Magrab . . .'

'But not in that way. Am I right?'

Kelpin nodded miserably.

'Kelpin, is there someone else you would rather mate with? Go on. You can tell me.'

'Arlon.' There, it was out.

Bethyl was quiet for a moment. 'Arlon. Well, Kelpin, since you asked me I'll be honest with you. You don't know him really do you? I mean, how long has he been here? Nine months? He's not completely fit again yet either. He may decide to go back to his village. Then where would you be?'

She hung her head. 'He says he never wants to go back. He likes it here. I nursed him, he trusted me; he wouldn't do anything to hurt me.'

'Would you like me to speak to Arlon?'

Kelpin pursed her lips and narrowed her eyes, thinking.

Bethyl went on, 'I can bring the matter up without telling him you've spoken to me.'

Another silence. Then Kelpin said. 'Yes please, Bethyl,' and went to her for a hug.

Bethyl sat and thought after she'd gone. Kelpin had lost her own mother, found Fanna and lost her too. Scummo meant everything to her, but he was busy with Grantis, who was almost ready to give birth, waddling round like a skinny rabbit with a bulging stomach. Bethyl reflected that she herself, who had no children, was the one most closely in the mother role for Kelpin now. She had reacted badly to the three men and the threat of rape. Her wound was healed, but the indignity and humiliation were raw and painful. *Pull yourself together*, she told herself. The men had not followed her leadership – what on earth had induced Scummo to shoot Arlon in the back? Everything went wrong from that point on. But here was Kelpin asking for her advice. She must take more of a part in decisions now and not leave it to Jankin to sort out.

During that night, Bethyl was summoned from her sleep by Scummo. Grantis had given birth to a baby girl, who seemed to be healthy, but Grantis was losing blood and Scummo was very frightened. Kelpin appeared, white-faced, in the doorway and was sent away. Scummo and Bethyl cleaned and comforted Grantis. Investigating with her newly washed hands, Bethyl knew it was useless.

Grantis died from blood loss early in the morning and Scummo was heartbroken. Only Kelpin remembered the baby, who was bundled up and sleeping at her side. While Scummo and Bethyl tended to the body, Kelpin lifted up the bundle carefully and held it to her. A small screwed-up face looked at her, eyes gluey with mucus, mouth working to find something to suckle. Kelpin took the baby girl to Anga and Darfi's quarters. Without a word, Anga took the baby from her and put her to her breast. The infant immediately began to suckle, as Anga's other children came to look at the new arrival. The toddler was jealous and tried to push the baby out of Anga's arms.

'Just as well I haven't quite stopped feeding him,' said Anga, putting her free arm around the little boy. 'Poor Grantis. How's Scummo coping?'

'He's devastated. He was looking forwards to this baby. Now he's forgotten he's got one. Will it be all right?'

'Leave her with me and tell Scummo to come and see me when he's recovered a bit.'

Scummo tried to be interested in his daughter, but his heart wasn't in it. Anga, when she wasn't feeding the baby, was busy with her other children and looking after the animals and the vegetable garden.

Kelpin became concerned. 'We haven't even given her a proper name yet,' she objected. She wrapped the baby girl in a sling on her back and took her with her everywhere, feeding her on goat's milk and caring for her tenderly. Kelpin decided that as Scummo was not going to give her a name, she would have to do this, and a name was chosen: Chancy.

Kelpin had been so concerned with looking after Chancy that all thoughts of Arlon went from her head, but he noted with interest her concern for the baby, her capable brave actions, and was impressed again. Bethyl's words to him had stayed with him, and when the time was right, he would make his move. He appeared more and more often at Kelpin's side, taking the baby from her without fuss when she cried and Kelpin needed a rest. When she was six weeks old, it was Arlon, not Scummo, that Chancy smiled at with her very first smile. Kelpin, seeing it, felt heartbroken for Scummo and this tiny daughter he might never really know. She approached Scummo several times, but he was depressed and uninterested. Finally, she got angry.

'You looked after me when I was little! Why can't you do that for your own daughter? She didn't ask to be born!'

Scummo's conscience was tweaked. 'I'll come and see her.'

'When?'

He sighed. 'This afternoon. Does Anga still feed her?'

'Sometimes. I give her goat's milk in between.'

There was silence between them for a while, then Scummo said, 'Who does she look like?'

Kelpin felt a surge of hope. He had never asked about her before; maybe this interest would grow.

'You'll have to see for yourself. She's like both of you. She's your daughter, Scummo.'

They left it there.

***

As time passed, Chancy grew strong and Scummo watched her with increasing confidence and hope. He began to recover from the loss of Grantis and took more of a role in the affairs of the village.

They heard nothing from the village of Brasto for several months following Magrab's return. When a messenger finally arrived from the other village, she was unarmed and in need of food and shelter. The messenger was a young woman Magrab knew well. Since she posed no threat, the villagers of Erasil treated her with respect. Since Magrab had left, the leadership contest had become even more bitter. Duels were fought and the attention of the villagers was focused on backing one side or the other. The everyday work around the village, mostly done by women and children old enough to help, was being neglected, though the women did their best to see that the essential tasks for their survival were carried out. The messenger, Delys, had finally had enough of the infighting and squabbling and decided to follow in the steps of her friend Magrab and come to Erasil, to ask for help and advice. She had other, more serious news, and was just about to impart it when she saw Arlon.

'What's he doing here?' she demanded. They told her of the attack by the three men. 'And where are the other two?' she wanted to know. 'I hope you killed them. That Hargin was evil.'

The villagers looked at one another and said nothing.

'All you need to know,' said Bethyl finally, 'is that they were here once and now they've gone.' There was little doubt that Delys knew the truth. 'You should know, Delys, that we are a peaceful people. Unless attacked, we will not fight with others. There are too few of us survivors to do that. Instead, we try to cooperate and make sure everyone has a role to play in the survival of all of us. It's not always easy, but mostly we manage it.' She shot a look at Scummo, who looked away.

Beggis joined in. 'Welcome to our village, Delys. If you intend to stay here you'll have to work hard, take responsibility for what happens and be prepared to put your opinions forwards. We're all equals here. Bethyl and Jankin are our elected leaders, but we make decisions between us. We rely on them to advise us and see that no one's voice goes unheard.'

'That's not how it is in Brasto. Sounds good to me. Can I stay?'

And so, bit by bit, the village of Erasil became a village of peace, where disputes were settled quickly in front of all the members at the meetings, and where the skills and craftsmanship of its inhabitants and their recognition of the need to cooperate were the highly prized attributes for which it came to be known. More people from Brasto came to visit, and the villagers from Erasil returned the visits, taking with them gifts of poultry, goats or cloth. More coracles were made, more fish and eel traps made and used, more skills acquired. For a time, there was peace, equality and prosperity for all the people.

Only in the quarry bottom, where two skeletons were revealed one summer when the water level dropped, was there any reminder of what might happen if the urge to gain power and possessions gained the upper hand again.

Author's Note

The idea for this novel came after reading some research by Martin Seligman on 'learned helplessness,' when dogs were held in electrified cages, given food and shelter but no freedom, and got a light shock when they touched the cage side. After several weeks the experimenters took the tops off the cages. Most of the dogs stayed where they were, knowing they would get fed and sheltered, but a few saw an opportunity, jumping out of the cages and running away, abandoning safety for freedom. This is the story of two people who decide to leave the inhuman City and risk freedom, but this time the dogs are in charge.

Photograph: Jorge Vásquez-Rivera

MARY V. WILLIAMS is a novelist and
poet now living in Shropshire.

Mary has had various alternative careers as bank clerk,
housemother, market trader, foster parent, teacher and mental
health worker, in various locations and failed at several of them.
Eventually she obtained an MA in Creative Writing and was then
commissioned to write two self-help books for Sheldon. She has
also published five novels, short stories and poetry. She lives with
her husband and youngest son in an inconvenient cottage in
Shropshire with a well under the floor and tries to stop the
garden from getting into the house. Attracted to the odd and
unusual, and often asking the question: 'What if?' she likes to
think her writing steps away from the everyday and becomes
something different. Her fiction is published under her writing
name
M. Valentine Williams and The Marsh People is her fifth novel.

Website: www.valentinewilliams.co.uk
Email: valentinewilliams4@gmail.co.uk